He was so strung out with hot curiosity, he broke first.

He bridged the final gap between them with a kiss that healed yet burned like wildfire at the same time. Haste, heat, fury, excitement and a pinch of doubt roared through him in a heady tangle he couldn't begin to sort out. Then she kissed him back and that wild rush of feelings melted into just her, just them.

"Closer," he urged, until they shifted together so the back wall of the summerhouse stopped them. He braced against it to keep her from the cold hardness and they were locked together now as if they might dissolve walls and pillars and damp December with their own version of summer heat and never mind hard angles, chilly marble and the ever-more-ferocious storm outside.

Author Note

Welcome to *The Winterley Scandal*. Eve Winterley first appeared in *The Viscount's Frozen Heart*, the first book of my A Year of Scandal quartet, and even then I knew she would need a book of her own one day.

Five years on from that fateful year of scandal, Eve has been "out" for three years. She is determined not to let her notorious mother's reputation taint her, but then she meets the son of Pamela Winterley's last lover and must choose between keeping her spotless reputation and risking everything with this gruff, battle-scarred young man she shouldn't fall in love with but somehow can't forget.

I do hope you enjoy Eve and Colm's story, whether you have read any of the other Winterley stories or not, and thank you for being such wonderful and loyal readers.

Elizabeth Beacon

The Winterley Scandal

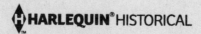

Recycling programs
for this product may
not exist in your area.

ISBN-13: 978-0-373-30749-4

The Winterley Scandal

Copyright © 2016 by Elizabeth Beacon

Printed in U.S.A.

www.Harlequin.com

Elizabeth Beacon has a passion for history and storytelling and, with the English West Country on her doorstep, never lacks a glorious setting for her books. Elizabeth tried horticulture and higher education as a mature student, then briefly taught English and worked in an office before finally turning her daydreams about dashing, piratical heroes and their stubborn and independent heroines into her dream job: writing Regency romances for Harlequin.

Books by Elizabeth Beacon

Harlequin Historical

A Year of Scandal: Spin-Off

The Winterley Scandal

A Year of Scandal

The Viscount's Frozen Heart
The Marquis's Awakening
Lord Laughraine's Summer Promise
Redemption of the Rake

The Seabourne Trilogy

The Duchess Hunt
The Scarred Earl
The Black Sheep's Return

Stand-Alone Novels

An Innocent Courtesan
Housemaid Heiress
Captain Langthorne's Proposal
The Rake of Hollowhurst Castle
A Most Unladylike Adventure
Candlelit Christmas Kisses
"Governess Under the Mistletoe"

Visit the Author Profile page at Harlequin.com.

Chapter One

It's so hot tonight I am only wearing my new rubies as I write. The stones are glorious, but the settings—oh, my diary—so old fashioned I could scream. Still, only the diamonds to coax out of Lord Chris now—and how his brother the Duke of Linaire will gobble with rage when he sees me wear them.

No, I shall wear every last one of Lady Chris's jewels, ancient settings and all, the day I get hold of the lot. The Duke of Linaire wants them for his fat mistress, whatever he says about them belonging to his nephew. He doesn't even like the boy—and how dare he threaten to have me whipped at the cart tail because his little brother loves me to distraction?

Chris's plain wife is dead and the jewels her vulgar father showered on her never looked half so well on her anyway. The truth is the Duke hates Chris for being young and handsome and having

*me. After marrying that plain heiress the old Duke
insisted one of his sons wed when Lord Horace
ran off to the Colonies with that odd female who
paints, rather than shackle himself to a nabob's
daughter.*

*Chris deserves some fun. He endured that low-
born creature in his bed for so long it must be
bliss to share it with me—and his son can't wear
the jewels, can he? So what use are diamonds of
the first water to the horrid brat?*

Colm Hancourt carefully put down the expensive notebook lest he throw it across the room and let out the
breath he hadn't known he was holding in an uneven
gasp. As the horrid brat in question, he could argue for
a hundred better uses for a fortune in gold and jewels
than decorating a vain and adulterous *demi-rep* with
them all. The fortune she had been busy spending had
been his as well—or it would have been if his father
hadn't stolen it before Colm was old enough to argue.
Whatever Lord Christopher Hancourt had done with his
son's fortune, inherited from Colm's fabulously wealthy
maternal grandfather Sir Joseph Lambury, those jewels
should be in the bank, waiting for Colm to take a wife.
So here was proof, if he needed it, they were long gone.
Colm's maternal grandfather might have left his entire
fortune to his only grandson, but that hadn't stopped
Lord Chris from spending it all before Colm was old
enough to go to school.

He bit back a curse as the shock of that betrayal hit
anew. All the wishing and cursing in the world wouldn't

make his lost fortune reappear and he should know; he'd tried every one when he was younger and seething with fury about the hand life and his father had dealt him. Rage and hurt fought to rule him even now, after eight years of soldiering and learning self-control at the charity school his eldest uncle sent him to before that. So how could he *not* curse his father for putting this heartless woman ahead of his children? That was the real question he had to answer if he was ever going to be content with what little he had left.

One thing he did know was that he should never have agreed to come here to Derneley House and meet the past head on like this. Pamela had grown up here, under the so-called care of her sister and brother-in-law, and reminders of the wretched female were everywhere. Portraits of the infamous Pamela seemed to jeer at him from far too many walls and it almost felt as if he might catch her and his besotted father up to something disgraceful if he turned round fast enough at times, although they had both been dead these fifteen years and more.

Still, he did owe the only one of his father's brothers prepared to own up to him quite a lot. The current Duke of Linaire was so sheepish about asking him to come here that he couldn't even claim he was bullied into it. No, he played down his revulsion at the idea of living in this house for however short a time he would be needed and had come here of his own free will, so he must endure this stupid suspicion that the woman who ruined his life was busy laughing at him from her front-row seat in hell.

He'd had to slot back into his old familiar disguise to live here for as long as this took as well. The Duke of Linaire's librarian had been dismissed for selling one of the finest volumes in the Linaire Library to a rival collector and expecting the new Duke not to notice. As Uncle Horace would never find a man he could trust to do this task in such a hurry, here he was, Uncle Horace's long-lost nephew, doing his best to do a good job with the neglected Derneley Library where he'd spent the last eight years with only one book at a time to his name, to be read and passed round other readers who liked to lose themselves in a book when life was almost unendurable on campaign. So he couldn't even be himself now that he was back in London after all these years. Lord Chris's son would never be welcome under this roof while Lady Derneley lived under it as well. She still raged about what she called the murder of her little sister to anyone who would listen and Lord Chris Hancourt *had* driven so recklessly along an Alpine road at twilight that the coach missed a bend and he and Pamela hurtled to their deaths. So here he was, Colin Carter again—just as he'd been in the army. He wanted to push aside the thought that he might have died under that name at Waterloo, if not for his sister Nell and the new Duke, but somehow it haunted him.

Nell had coaxed, or bullied, Uncle Horace into taking her to Brussels when everyone else was fleeing it as battle roared only a few miles away. Revulsion at what his little sister must have seen ate away at Colm every time he thought of Nell viewing the hell of slaughter and corruption the day after Waterloo. She had scoured the battlefield until she found him, dazed and half-conscious from loss of blood, and somehow got him back to Brussels to be nursed at the new Duke of Linaire's expense. When he was pronounced likely to live, Nell raced back to England and her position as governess to four orphaned girls. Colm's hands tightened into fists; his sister had to rescue him rather than the other way about and he so wanted to protect *her*; give her back the life she was born to. In his daydreams she was fulfilled and happy with a man who would love and cosset her as she deserved for the rest of her life. A reminiscent grin spoilt his frown as he reminded himself this *was* Nell he was thinking about. She wouldn't thank him for such a husband, even if it meant escaping her life as a governess. He might as well forget the fantasy of giving Nell a Season so the world could see what a wonderful woman she was. She would chafe at the controls society put on marriageable young ladies and ask for her old job back.

So where was he? Ah, yes, Uncle Horace—the second eldest of his father's three older brothers and the only one Colm liked and might even learn to love one day. Uncle Maurice, the next Hancourt in line after Horace, hated Colm for being his father's son and he'd hated Lord Chris even more for succeeding with Pamela when he failed. Maurice ought to be grateful to have escaped her clutches, but Colm knew he would never forgive that slight to his reputation as a devil with the ladies. Colm frowned and decided he could well do without his Uncle Maruice's approval, but Pamela probably chose the younger brother because he'd wed an heiress. Whispers of the fabulous Lambury Jewels locked away in a bank vault would have seemed too delicious to resist as well.

Drat, he was thinking about the wretched female again and how she had seduced and nagged and wheedled that part of his inheritance out of Lord Chris. So where had he been before Pamela interrupted his thoughts? Ah, yes, Uncle Horace—he was a much more pleasant member of the family to think about. As soon as Colm was declared likely to live, the doctors insisted Colm convalesce before he settled into his new life, and neither the Duke nor the Duchess of Linaire would listen when he insisted he was fit to work. They even packed him off to the seaside to recover, so how could he turn his back on the only other members of his family willing to own up to him?

Uncle Horace had only come back to England when he'd inherited the dukedom last year. He probably didn't realise how huge the scandal had been when his youngest brother had run off with Pamela Verdoyne and then died with her on their way to a party she'd insisted on attending whatever the weather. Uncle Horace had been cut off for refusing to marry the heiress Colm's father had wed instead by then. Sensible Uncle Horace, Colm thought wryly, and almost wished his father had run off with a woman he could love instead of meekly marrying that unlucky girl as well.

No—he was brought up short by the thought of the woman his father had loved so deeply and unwisely after Colm's mother died—he decided Sophia Lambury was a far better parent to own up to than the current

Viscount Farenze's first wife. His mother might have been the pawn her father sold for a title and a convenient wife Lord Chris didn't love, but at least she wasn't a lovely, heartless harpy.

He shot the portrait of Pamela Verdoyne-Winterley hanging over the fireplace a hostile glare. She had been ripe and lush and beautiful, he conceded, but the mocking sensuality in her sleepy blue eyes said how aware she was of her power over fools like Lord Christopher Hancourt and how she revelled in enslaving lovers until they satisfied her every whim, whatever it cost them and theirs.

He compared her image to his shadowy memories of his mother and, yes, he definitely preferred having gentle, plain Sophia as his dam. So how *would* it feel to have Pamela's blood running in his veins? Appalling, he decided, feeling sorry for the girl with that burden on her young shoulders. He didn't know her, but for some reason he'd waited in the shadows to catch a glimpse of Lady Derneley's niece tonight with the other servants. Miss Winterley had looked self-contained and almost too conscious of her mother's sins, or was he being fanciful? Dark-haired and not quite beautiful, she looked very different from her notorious mother. He had to try not to snarl at the near-naked portrait of Pamela whenever he was in this room, but now he examined it for signs that her daughter had inherited her bold sensuality. Miss Winterley had her nose and slender build perhaps, but her eyes, the shape of her face and her height were all very different. Pamela's daughter looked as if she, too, could be haunted by her mother's sins a decade and a half after they had ended so abruptly on that Alpine pass.

So at least he didn't have to fear a feral beast might lie under his own skin as Miss Winterley looked as if she did in her worst nightmares. Lord Chris was a fool who had loved a noble doxy beyond reason, though, and Colm hoped and prayed he would never love madly and without limits like his father. So they were equal in some ways. He sat back to brood on fate and their very different destinies and concluded that was all they had in common.

Miss Winterley was doted on by her family; Colm barely acknowledged by his. Now Uncle Horace was Duke of Linaire he had a roof over his head and a job, but Uncle Maurice was next in line; he would turn Colm out the day he succeeded to the title. Colm liked his new relative very well, but if anything happened to the current Duke he would have to support himself on one good leg and nothing much a year. So if Uncle Horace wanted him to list and pack the entire library to make sure Derneley wasn't selling off the best volumes to dealers behind his back, Colm would stay here and do it and Mr Carter could live on for another week or two.

Miss Winterley's presence in this house tonight, when he was sure she didn't want to be here, was still something of a mystery. He wondered how Lady Derneley managed it, when the distrust between Pamela's sister and the Winterleys, once Pamela openly gave up on her marriage, never seemed to have been bridged by either family. Luckily the maids hired for the evening whispered and why shouldn't another servant listen to gossip? Colm thought with a wry smile at his own expense. Apparently Lady Derneley had put it about that this party was to be held in her niece's honour, as a peace offering in a war where she would hear not a word said against her late sister, and the Winterleys had, not surprisingly, not a good word to say in her favour so they said nothing at all. The Winterleys had to attend or let the world know they were openly at odds with Miss Winterley's relatives. Since it was Viscount Farenze's mission in life to keep scandal at bay whenever he could, he would be furious to be forced into a corner, but his wife and daughter would even endure an evening at Derneley House to keep the peace.

That was the how of it all, so what about the why? Lady Derneley was a widgeon and all the brass and cunning in the family must have gone to her little sister, but was there a deeper reason behind her husband's scheme to get his wife's niece here tonight? Colm shuddered at the idea, but Miss Winterley had a strong protector in Viscount Farenze and he had powerful friends. Derneley wouldn't risk all that power and influence turning against him, would he? Unless he was going to flee to the Continent to avoid his debts and thought the Winterley interest didn't reach that far. No, it was too much of a risk, so Colm had imagined a furtive air about the man nobody else saw as he greeted his 'long-lost niece' as if he might cry like a stage villain over her at any moment.

Anyway, what better way was there for the Derneleys to fool their creditors a family reconciliation had taken place? The Winterleys were rich and powerful and it might work, and there were no bailiffs in the hall or toughs in the kitchens tonight. He shivered at the idea of anyone being imprisoned for debt and resolved not to long for the wife and family he might have had if things were different. Derneley's ruin was all his own work, though; Colm had nothing in common with that noble idiot. Even he knew selling the Derneley Library to the new Duke of Linaire wouldn't keep Derneley solvent long, but the man didn't seem worried. Colm wondered how the guests would feel if the bailiffs turned up for dinner, dancing and a nice little gossip with the nobs. Delighted, he suspected; they had come here to be entertained after all.

Colm eyed the beautifully bound book Pamela confided in and refused to be sorry it was probably the closest she ever got to a friend. She had hidden her diaries behind a row of sermons and he wondered that they hadn't burnt holes in the worthy volumes. The library was being taken apart and shipped to Linaire House book by book, so they would have been discovered sooner or later and Colm was suddenly very glad he was the one taking it apart, not some poor clerk happy to sell such deliciously scandalous diaries to the highest bidder. Some of the lower branches of the publishing world would love to get their hands on such 'work'. But what on earth was he going to do with them? Burning seemed a fine idea with that prospect in his head, but he wanted to find out more about his father. Lord Chris died when Colm was eight, but he'd left his children before then.

Stuffing the expensively bound books into a portmanteau and limping off into the night was a tempting idea, but his work wasn't finished and the tale that would do the rounds if he was caught creeping out of the house with Pamela's diaries would enliven the radical press for years to come. Someone might recognise his name and if Captain Carter of the Rifles was smoked out as Lord Chris's son how the *ton* would sneer at a duke's grandson forced to serve in a regiment famous for dash and daring, but officered largely by tradesmen's sons and great gruff soldiers promoted on merit.

'Oh, no, my dear, the fellow's totally unsuited to polite company even without those unsightly infirmities. Not a penny to bless himself with and even a cit's daughter wouldn't risk marrying Lord Chris's son since he's likely to spend her fortune on a doxy like his father.'

It was uncomfortable enough to imagine, what if he had to listen to real asides and furtive titters when he was openly his uncle's nephew? He'd end up calling some fool out and he didn't want to flee justice, or shoot some idiot in a duel. Nell would be furious and the thought of his lion-hearted sister made him smile. If she were here, she would bid him get on with his life and forget the past. Well, he couldn't quite manage that yet, but he would put most of Pamela's diaries back and hope nobody chanced on them before he could think what to do with them. Then, if he could only forget his sister had to work for her bread because of the selfish adulteress who had bled their father dry, he might be able to enjoy the novelty of not being shot at on a regular basis and be himself for the first time in eight years.

Colm cursed the day Lord Chris set eyes on Pamela

as he limped towards the steep little stair to the upper
shelves of the library to replace the rest of her diaries
and the Derneleys' guests enjoyed the remnants of their
host's once-fabled wealth only a few rooms away.

Eve Winterley still couldn't work out how her stepmama talked her into attending this wretched party.
She wished clever Lady Chloe Winterley, Viscountess
Farenze, hadn't right now. First there was Aunt Derneley's delusion they doted on each other to endure, then
Lord Derneley trod so clumsily on her skirt in passing as she curtsied to her dance partner that she had
to hastily leave the room. If not for that the appalling
old man who waylaid her on her way to find a maid to
help mend it she could have left this horrible house by
now... Ugh, no, she didn't want to think about him yet,
but how she wished she had invented a headache to keep
her at home tonight.

She didn't care if the gossips gloated over the split
between the Derneleys and the Winterleys. Her mother
had willed her to die in the attic of this place once upon
a time, so little wonder she couldn't wait to go home
even before... No, she wasn't going to think about that
awful old wineskin until she was safe. She wasn't sure
she could endure the thought of him and what he might
have done even then. Papa always said the best thing
her mother did was reject her and usually Eve agreed,
but tonight a small part of her wanted to throw something fragile because Pamela did her best to starve Eve
to death in the attics here instead of being any sort of
mother to her newborn babe.

Pamela didn't matter. Dear Bran was brought here to nurse Eve and then Papa rescued them both. Eve grew up knowing she was loved as surely as the sea beat on the rocks below her father's northern stronghold. Then Papa married Lady Chloe Thessaly when Eve was sixteen and what a relief to love and be loved by such a remarkable woman, she reminded herself, and supposed she would have to forgive Chloe her part in this wretched evening after all.

A nasty little voice at the back of her head whispered she couldn't escape the past in this down-at-heel mansion the Derneleys were clinging on to somehow. *What if the gossips and naysayers are right when they whisper, 'Like mother, like daughter,' behind my back?* her inner critic goaded. *What if one day I meet a man who wakes up the greedy whore in me and she makes me need ever more wild and wicked things from him and the rest of his sex as Pamela did?*

No, never, she denied it as her headache beat in her ears and she scuttled down the next half-lit corridor in the hope of sanctuary. She was a Winterley—everyone said how closely she followed her father in colouring, build and character. Even after three years out in society not a whiff of real scandal tainted her name, despite all the rakes and fortune hunters who tried to blast it so she would have to marry them or accept a lover. Still those whispers circulated without proof to back them up and malicious eyes watched for signs she was like Pamela. Anyone who mattered knew her and not the creature gossip said she was, but ageing rakes like Sir Steven Scrumble still thought they could force her into an unlit room and make her agree to marry him because she must be like her mother, or so he'd mumbled as he did his best to make sure she was the next Lady Scrumble. She shuddered at the memory of his wet mouth and invading hands and wiped a hand across her lips to try to rub out the feel and taste of him. Hadn't she just promised herself not to revisit that horror?

If she collapsed into a weeping heap everyone would know she had something to cry about and she hadn't got her flounce mended either, so she had to hold it out of the way not to trip over it and now she was lost. The wicked old fortune hunter fell into an agonised heap when she'd kneed him sharply in the privates, though, so she doubted he'd be on her tail. Uncle James was a most satisfactory mentor for a young lady who didn't want to be landed with a husband she hated. If that tactic failed, there were more to fall back on so thank heavens she belonged to a powerful clan; if she was poor and alone her mother's wild life and blasted reputation would have ruined her years ago.

Her first real suitor came so close to doing it she shuddered at the thought of her youthful stupidity. How had she ever thought herself so in love with a fool? Papa and Chloe had warned her he wasn't the man she thought. It wasn't until she told him she wouldn't elope that the gloss and excitement of having her first grown-up lover melted. He wanted her *because* she was her mother's daughter, not despite it. Memory of the hot, greedy need in his eyes as he tore her gown and got ready to rape her made her feel sick even now. That was when Uncle James intervened and, as that boy hadn't shown his true colours since, maybe his punishment worked.

Fighting the memory of that night and all the times since when even a quiet and outwardly respectable man would look at her with the memory of her mother in his hot eyes, she looked for somewhere to ply the needle and hank of thread snatched from the deserted ladies' withdrawing room. Opening a promising door warily, she checked for fat and lazy fortune hunters, then slipped inside. There was an air of peace in the old-fashioned book room; a very small fire and one branch of candles cast mellow shadows. Her uncle by marriage would never come in here for a quick read; he was probably allergic to printers' ink. She moved the candle and sat on a stiff and old-fashioned sofa by the fire to whip quick, impatient stitches into her torn flounce, glad to be alone for a few precious moments. Shifting the material round so she could reach the tear, she made herself sew more neatly, so it would look as if a maid mended it for her and that was where she had been all along.

There, that was the tear darned. Once she had the strip of fine French braid tacked neatly in place she would be respectable again. It was still trailing like a tail behind her when a suspicion this wasn't such a wonderful place to hide crept up on her. One of Uncle James's rules was assess all escape routes when you entered a strange room. She froze in her seat, needle in mid-air and every sense alert now it was too late. Another faint movement made her look round and see there was a gallery to this faded room she should have noted of earlier.

Someone was coming down a hidden stair so slowly and quietly a superstitious shiver ran down her back.

Too late to avoid whoever it was now, she wasn't about to run back to the ballroom with her braid trailing behind her, so she grasped the needle like a weapon and hoped it might work. Lord Derneley's cronies were too soft and idle to fit into the narrow confines of the ladder-like stair she could see now her eyes were used to the dim light, so this was a less substantial person. Halting steps met the marble floor at last and she squinted against the candlelight and deep shadows it cast to see whom she must defend herself against this time.

Chapter Two

'What the devil are you doing here?' a gruff male voice rumbled as Eve froze, staring at the stiffly held figure and telling herself he wasn't made of shadows.

He took a step forward and stared nearly as rudely back. He looked both old and young at the same time and she wondered how such a shabby gentleman could seem so arrogant it was as if he owned the room and not Lord Derneley's creditors. His overlong hair was neither brown nor gold but a mixture of both and his nose had been broken once upon a time. There was an air of contained power about him that didn't fit his modest shirt points and a very ordinary dark coat and breeches. He shouldn't be in the least attractive to a lady like her and yet he was. Now he turned his head as if to listen for more intruders into his domain and the candlelight struck his face full on. She could see a still raw scar high on his forehead that made her gasp, then wondered how much damage his tawny pelt hid and if that explained why he let it grow. Something wary and proud

in his unusual eyes stopped her answering his question
with a casual put down from lady to upper servant. Even
from several feet away and by weak candlelight those
eyes looked dark and light at the same time. He came
a little closer to peer down at her as if she was an exhibit in a museum and she gazed up and saw his irises
were brown, but his pupils were rayed with flares of
light gold that made them look paler.

Here was a man who kept his hopes and dreams
hidden, but when their gazes met something sparked
between them that she didn't understand. It felt as if
he was important to her somehow, but he couldn't be
so, could he? Looked at coolly he was a young clerk in
shabby day clothes and had nothing in common with
the Honourable Miss Winterley. Still she felt an eager
leap of the heart she had heard about but never expe-
rienced before; the dawn of something huge she never
believed in until now. It threatened to turn her world
upside down as they gazed at each other as if under a
spell. Which was just plain nonsense, wasn't it? There
might be enough mysteries in this stranger's striking
eyes to intrigue a flock of unwary young ladies, but
she was Eve Winterley and he was an upper servant by
dress, if not his arrogant manner as he silently dared
her to set him down as nobody.

'You took the words out of my mouth,' she informed
him huskily, doing her best to act the composed society
lady in the face of his impudence.

'Her ladyship's ball is that way, Miss Winterley,' he
said and Eve felt that tingle of warmth she'd been trying
to fight turn to ice. The coldness in his voice made her

shiver and something like disapproval iced his gaze as he dwelt on her exposed ankles and calf, then he looked away as if she offended him.

'You have the advantage of me, sir,' she said stiffly.

'Carter, ma'am,' he said unenthusiastically.

'And now I know?'

'The Duke of Linaire engaged me to sort the Derneley Library and have it packed up and sent to Linaire House or the bookbinders.'

'Well, it's a fine collection and Lord Derneley is desperate,' she said, then wondered what demon had got hold of her tongue tonight.

'His father was a notable scholar,' the man said as if every word must be paid for and he was unwilling to waste them on the likes of her.

'Maybe his son is a changeling then,' she said, her temper prickling. She refused to tell polite lies after the evening she'd endured so far and this man's hostility seemed to be coming towards her in waves now he'd taken a good long look at Miss Evelina Winterley and decided he didn't like her one little bit.

'Lord Derneley is my host,' he reproved her, as if she had no idea it was rude to make comments about one when you were under his roof.

'And therefore above criticism? I shall employ you to sit in my father's library and whisper my grace, talent and general omnipotence in my ear when I feel less than pleased with myself and the world.'

'I shall be very ill occupied then,' he said unwarily— so that was what he thought of her, was it? 'I beg your pardon, I'm sure dozens of fashionable gentlemen queue up to praise your elegance, beauty and cleverness, Miss Winterley,' he added patronisingly, as if that should make her feel better.

'Since we seem to be jumping to conclusions about each other so freely tonight, you must be a cynic and a Jacobin, Carter. Why else would you take against a lady you don't know, unless you hold a grudge against my family, of course?' she demanded, suddenly very tired of being Pamela Winterley's daughter. Tonight was bad enough without a stranger sniping at her as if she must deserve it.

Colm tried to rein in his temper, but the sight of her looking as if she had only just left the arms of her lover made him deaf to the voice of reason. *Apologise, then bow politely and leave her to her sewing, you blundering idiot*, it whispered, but this was a very different Eve Winterley from the one he saw enter Derneley's hall tonight. Then she was pale and composed; a dark-haired version of the Ice Queen, so cool and distant she could have been made of bronze and cold painted. Now she was ruffled and flushed and he still wanted to touch her, not to find out if she was real this time, but to carry on the work of the lucky devil she must have been kissing in the long-disused conservatory at the end of this corridor.

He sounded like a jealous lover and how could that be when he didn't even know her? He still wanted to be the one who tousled all that cool perfection, though. If he had sent her racing along dusty passage ways to find the least-used part of this rambling old place and set herself to rights after their amorous encounter, now that would be *much* more acceptable. Even the thought of being the one whose kisses set her delightful breasts rising and falling with every fast and shallow breath made him hard. Exploring even the edges of passion with her warm and willing in his arms wasn't to be thought of. *No, it really, really wasn't*, he argued with his inner savage.

Colm felt the gnawing of bitter envy as he let himself sneer ever so slightly at the difference between her public face and private morals. Miss Winterley was set fair to follow her disgraceful dam after all. He recalled Pamela's shocking declaration that she was writing her diary wearing nothing but rubies and that did nothing to help his wild fantasies about seeing her daughter in a similar state of nature.

'How can I feel anything about your family when I don't know them?' he asked as coolly as he could while he tried to shackle his inner sensualist.

'I don't know; how can you?'

'Obviously I cannot.'

'Yet you have your shallow prejudices about me and mine and seem to think it quite acceptable to show them off. For a mere librarian you are very daring, Mr Carter,' she said with a pointed stare at the scar on his forehead he usually felt so defensive about.

'Librarians do not spring fully formed from the head of Zeus like the goddess Athene, Miss Winterley.'

'Waterloo?' she demanded rudely and he supposed he'd asked for it by leaping to conclusions about her as well.

He nodded, still unable to talk about that terrible day. Not even Nell knew the terror he had felt, the dreadful urge to turn his back on his men and this hell of powder and shot and pounding artillery all around him and walk off into the woods to find peace. Now that his emotions seemed too close to the surface he was afraid he might let her see things he didn't want any other human being to know about. She was his enemy; Winterleys and Hancourts had hated one another since his father ran off with her mother. It was probably his duty to think the worst of her, but as his lust and temper cooled he took a second look and wondered if he misjudged her.

'I can see how a library might offer peace and quiet after that,' she added as if she understood a bit too much. 'Will this be enough for you after a life of action?'

'I don't know, Miss Winterley. No doubt I shall find out when these books are safely housed in my employer's various houses.'

'And rescued from the neglect of nearly half a century,' she agreed rather absently, as if her real thoughts were elsewhere.

'Indeed,' he said, sounding stuffy even to his own ears. 'I wonder they are not in worse condition.'

'Fascinating as you find this topic, Mr Carter, I need to get back to the ballroom before people notice I have been away too long. Kindly turn your back, or go away, so I can finish sewing this braid back in place and go.'

'I still have work to do tonight,' he said, wishing he had pushed the open volume of Pamela's diary he had kept out to read under something else, so there was no risk she might spot it if she wandered closer to the library table to see what he had been doing. 'Here, let me move the candle so you can see better and be gone all the sooner,' he offered ungraciously and moved it before she could argue. Then he meekly turned his back as ordered and hoped that was distraction enough from her mother's appalling scribbles.

'You are almost as eager to see the back of me as I am to go,' she said, her voice muffled because she was paying close attention to her gown.

Colm was tempted to use the old mirror nearby to sneak another look at her fine legs and ankles as he fantasised about the thread pulling up her hem as she worked on the most awkward part of the braid once again. The unresolved question of who did that damage plagued him and he could still hear her move, feel her presence in this shadowed and oddly intimate room and long to be someone else.

'You can't marry a librarian if we are caught here in such a compromising position,' he explained gruffly.

'Even if you are a hero?'

Wouldn't it be fine if they truly felt easy enough to laugh together? They never would if she knew who he really was. After tonight they could go back to different worlds. Except he thought Uncle Horace and his Duchess had plans that might make those worlds collide. Heaven forbid, he thought. He hated the idea of who he really was frosting Miss Winterley's eyes when they met as polite strangers.

'I am nobody's hero, Miss Winterley,' he said dourly. 'They usually end up dead and not maimed like me.'

'If that scar was on the back of the head I suppose I might believe you got it running away,' she said as the faint sound of her needle penetrating the heavy satin of her gown reached his over-sensitised hearing and he held his breath against the quiet catch of her breathing and what it was doing to his dratted body.

'Maybe I walked backwards from the guns?' he said wryly and she chuckled. The warm sound of it brought back all the temptations he had been fighting since she walked into the room and he saw her all flustered and compelling from his perch at the top of the spiral stairs, before she even knew he existed.

'And maybe a bullet bounced off somewhere else and hit you in the leg, but somehow I doubt it.'

'I could have been devilishly unlucky.'

'You could.'

'Are you done yet?' he asked sharply, because it felt dangerous to argue, then almost laugh with her.

'Eager to be rid of me?'

'Eager to keep my job, Miss Winterley. That will not happen if we are found alone here with the door shut.'

'Yet the new Duke seems such a reasonable sort of man,' she said as if he could be explained away with a careless smile and a shrug that said of course we were not up to anything untoward, how could a viscount's daughter and a librarian be anything but strangers?

'Your papa doesn't look so where you are concerned.'

'True, but he's not here and now I'm set to rights he won't need to be.'

'Kindly hurry away then and make sure of that, if you please. Can I turn round, by the way?'

'Yes, I am quite neat and unmarred again,' she said and he frowned as he turned and met her challenging gaze. 'I cannot say it has been a pleasure meeting you, Mr Carter.'

'Good evening, Miss Winterley,' he said curtly and wished she would go away and leave him in peace.

'Good evening, Mr Car…' she began, then faltered as the sound of hurrying feet sounded outside. 'Where can I hide?' she demanded urgently.

He darted a look at the alcove set aside for a clerk to catalogue new finds in the days when Lord Derneley's father collected rare volumes from anywhere he could. Even that dark corner couldn't conceal a young woman in pale and rustling silk. She gave him an impatient look and darted towards the narrow wooden stair he had climbed down so carefully only minutes ago. She scrambled to get out of sight and was lost to his view, if not to his senses, just in time not to be seen when the door opened and Lord Derneley sauntered in.

'Thought you could have helped Lady Derneley with the wallflowers, Carter,' he said distractedly, looking round as if this half-empty room was a surprise to him.

The thought of Miss Winterley standing so near and still made Colm tense as a drum. He breathed more shallowly for fear she might make a noise and be found and what on earth would they do then? An offer of marriage from him would hardly quiet the scandal. Yet there was something furtive in Derneley's pale eyes that said he knew she had flown somewhere to set her appearance to rights and he intended to find her. That suspicion he had earlier that the man was up to something devious as far as his wife's niece was concerned returned in spades. He felt a fierce need to protect her from whatever moneymaking scheme the rogue had thought up at Miss Winterley's expense.

'It seemed best that I not embarrass the young ladies, your lordship,' he said and when the man looked baffled Colm pointed at his damaged leg.

'Oh, aye, quite right. Forgot you're a dot-and-carry one and can't dance. Make the poor little things a laughing stock if you tried, I suppose.' The man's glassy gaze lingered on the scar high on Colm's forehead, then flicked away as if he was being delicate about mentioning yet another reason he could not show his face in public.

'Quite,' Colm managed flatly, willing the girl hidden so precariously nearby not to move even a finger while this noble rat was in the room to hear her and force her to do whatever he had in mind.

'I'll tell her ladyship that's why you're hiding yourself away then, shall I?'

'Thank you, my lord,' Colm made himself say as humbly as a clerk should when invited to join the nobility at play, even if it was only to dance with wallflowers.

'Ah, there you are, Derneley,' Viscount Farenze said from the doorway.

Colm knew who he was because he was standing by his daughter's side earlier, looking formidable and aloof and ready to challenge any man who put a finger on his eldest child against her will. Colm marvelled at Lord Derneley's stupidity for thinking he would get away with whatever he was up to without being flayed alive.

His fury sharpened as he wondered if Derneley had been forcing his attentions on a girl he shouldn't even think of touching, but no, he looked too sleek and fashionable to have done anything so repellent. No doubt it would take hours to redress, so that was one horror he could discount. Which left his first thought when he saw Miss Winterley so disarrayed and seductive looking; she had a lover and Derneley knew. And wasn't that a guilty secret she and her father would pay handsomely to keep that way?

Lord Farenze eyed Colm coolly before he took a quick scan of the room from the doorway, then stepped inside. Colm thought of Miss Winterley a few heartbeats away from disaster again and he didn't want her to be found out, lover or no. A sneeze or a snatched breath could give her away and then where would they be?

'Came to find Carter here,' the master of the house said uneasily under his one-time brother-in-law's stern gaze. He even managed to make it sound logical for the host to seek the humblest gentleman here in the midst of his own evening party.

Colm called on all his experience of hiding his feelings not to glare at the man. If it wasn't Miss Winterley who was a hair's breadth from disaster, he might be stifling laughter instead of a savage growl as the man let his gaze shift past half-empty book stacks and sharpen on the deepest shadows as if he was looking for her. There was something damned odd going on; he hadn't been imagining things earlier. Colm couldn't help wondering what Miss Winterley was thinking, standing in semi-darkness and wondering what Derneley was up to as well.

'I'm weary of cards and gossip and my wife is deep in conversation with Lady Mantaigne, Derneley. I might as well keep Linaire's librarian company for you, as you have a great many other matters to attend to tonight. You know how I dote on books and a good host can't absent himself from his own party for long, can he?' Lord Farenze said so genially Colm shivered. The man's good humour had so much steel in it he was surprised Lord Derneley wasn't shaking in his boots.

'Always knew you were an odd fellow, Farenze, but I suppose you're right. Best get back to m'wife's party before anyone notices,' Derneley agreed airily.

'I'll join you as soon as I've picked this learned young man's brains,' Lord Farenze replied and Colm eyed him uneasily as Lord Derneley finally ran out of reasons to stay in his own library and left with one last frustrated look round the room, as if he might spot Miss Winterley climbing a half-dismantled book stack, presumably desperate for a good read.

Chapter Three

'Hold still,' Lord Farenze murmured, as if he could see through all that finely carved wood and a wall to his daughter's hiding place. Colm held his breath as Lord Derneley's steps faded rather slowly down the marble-floored corridor and Lord Farenze finally shut the door on him. 'It's safe to come out now, Eve,' he said softly.

'How did you know I was here, Papa?' she said and did so as if nothing much had happened.

Colm took a second look to be sure she wasn't on the brink of hysteria. No, Miss Winterley's blue-green eyes even had the hint of a smile in them now. If not for the way her fingers fisted into her palm on the side her father couldn't see, he might think her calm as a millpond.

'The same way I did at hide and seek when you were a child; you are in the place that makes the most sense,' her father said.

'Oh, I see,' she said and Colm wondered why she still looked so white and strained now her father was here to make all right if another lord came in and caught them having a bookish discussion instead of dancing.

'I wish you both goodnight, my lord, Miss Winterley,' he said stiffly, feeling he was the invisible upper servant everyone thought and it hurt his pride somehow now he'd finally met Miss Winterley face to face.

'First promise not to tell anyone I was alone here with you tonight.'

'I am not a braggart, Miss Winterley,' he argued before he could think straight. Colm saw Lord Farenze's eyes harden and found it difficult to meet the steely distrust in the man's level gaze, but he did.

'If any scandal is whispered about my daughter, the person who spread it is likely to regret he was ever born,' the Viscount threatened so quietly it was far more potent than if he'd shouted and shaken his fists.

'Don't, Papa,' Miss Winterley said with a weary wave of her hand that touched Colm far more than feminine hysterics ever could. 'I think we can trust him.'

'I don't trust any man with your safety and peace of mind tonight.'

'Please give him your word as a gentleman not to reveal I was here alone with you, Mr Carter, or we'll be here all night,' she said with a pleading look Colm couldn't resist, however little he'd wanted to be part of this scene.

'I promise not to whisper scandal about Miss Winterley, my lord.'

'You seem to be a man of words, Carter.' The man gestured at the chaos of packed books and the stacks waiting to say Colm might not be beyond writing scandal even if he didn't speak of it.

'I wouldn't write anything that damaged a young lady's reputation either.'

'I am suitably grateful,' Miss Winterley interrupted their silent battle with rather magnificent irony.

'And I have nobody much to write it to if I did,' he told her as if that ought to make this better. He doubted it did from the chilly look she gave him. 'I don't know what you're talking about anyway.'

Lord Farenze looked hard at him. 'Derneley is up to something and the servants will gossip, so you had better add a promise to tell me what they have to say about us to that gallant oath, Carter. Then I might trust you to leave my daughter's reputation alone and let you leave this room in one piece.'

'Very well, my lord. I vow to report faithfully what the servants are saying or not saying over breakfast. I hope that will be all?'

'Not quite, I am also unreasonable enough to expect you to come to Farenze House tomorrow and tell me about it in person. Do not put anything in writing.'

'I have work to do, my lord, but I dare say his Grace will spare me from it for an hour or so to take some air, if I ask him nicely,' Colm said not quite humbly enough to be truly Mr Carter, who only wanted his bed and an end to this ridiculous situation.

'Oh, come on, Papa. Leave the poor man be. Don't forget someone I wish I had never set eyes on could be back in the ballroom by now and busily spreading rumours,' Miss Winterley said with a pained look in the direction of the ballroom that said her ruin might be going on even as they dallied.

'Even Derneley isn't that stupid and I bloodied the nose of that someone else you are talking about. I doubt he'll say anything for a while, let alone admit he was bested by a slip of a girl he thought to force himself on, then knocked out by her very irate father,' Lord Farenze added matter of factly.

Colm went very still as he realised why Miss Winterley had really come in here to repair her gown. What a fool he was not to see the difference between a young woman dishevelled by her amorous beau and one attacked by a raddled old rake. His own convalescence in Brighton had given him the inside track on all the society gossip his breathless landlady gathered from friends who let out rooms or their houses for the Season. So he sorted through the guests he'd seen arrive tonight and came up with the ideal candidate. Sir Steven Scrumble was on the lookout for a wife with enough blue blood and powerful connections to drag him back to the heart of polite society. The man would pay generously for such a bride and Derneley must have sold him a perfect chance to rape Miss Winterley and force an April-and-December marriage on her. The very idea made his flesh crawl, so goodness knew what it did to hers. Scrumble was very rich, so selling a convenient accident to her gown and a neatly empty sewing room wouldn't trouble Derneley's conscience. He clearly didn't have one. Then, with his ill-gotten gains and the money he got from the Duke for his father's books, Derneley might have made it across the Channel and disappeared. Colm thought Derneley's creditors would soon learn Lord Farenze wouldn't lift a finger to save his one-time brother-in-law and they would fore-close. Serve the vicious sot right, Colm decided as the Viscount frowned as if he wished him a thousand miles away, then did his best to reassure his daughter.

'I made it clear you won't be marrying him if the whole world is baying for you to do so; I'll kill him first,' he told her.

'I'm not dashing round the world evading justice even for you, Papa, and Chloe has had quite enough of living in shadows. What if he tells everyone anyway?'

'And admit he was bested by a defenceless young lady? The man's not that much of a fool.' Lord Farenze went on with a sideways look at Colm that told him not to be one either, 'Even in his cups he'll remember what I threatened to do to him if he didn't keep a still tongue in his head.'

Colm wanted to find the cur and add his fourpen-nyworth to the mix. He could hardly threaten to have the bastard drummed out of the clerks' guild though, could he? Their inequality of power and rank would forbid the man fighting if Colm challenged him to meet at dawn, swords or pistols at the ready. Reminded how little he and Miss Winterley had in common, he used a trick he'd learnt in his youth and retreated into his thoughts until he was calm again. He went back to the table, realised Miss Winterley had put the candle back in the ideal place to highlight what he'd been reading before he got distracted and tried to slide Pamela's jour-nal under a sheaf of ancient letters.

'Wait,' Lord Farenze said sharply, catching that fur-tive movement as if he was the one who'd spent eight years sharpening his senses in the Rifles and not Colm. 'What have you got there?' he asked and came closer for a better look. 'I've seen a notebook like that before and that looks like my late wife's scrawl. Let me see.'

'My employer paid a fair price for any item in this room he chose to take away, my lord,' Colm protested half-heartedly.

'And it pains me to see such a fine collection neglected, but if that's truly a volume of my late wife's scribbles then it isn't Derneley's to sell. As her husband I lay claim to it.'

'Papa—' Miss Winterley touched her father's arm '—surely all her scandals are already out in the open by now? We really must go.'

'I'll not have them reawakened in the yellow press and we shall say you wanted to look at the portrait of your mother you knew Derneley had hidden away somewhere in this house. We can explain our absence to your stepmother when we return to the ballroom and the gossips will nod and whisper she has a great deal to bear, but I'm not leaving this room until you explain what you have there, Carter, and if there's aught else I should know about in this musty old collection.'

'I really couldn't say, my lord. I only found the first Lady Farenze's diaries hidden behind a shelf of sermons this afternoon.'

'You have to admire her cheek, don't you?' he said to his daughter and Colm saw the man behind the stern mask before he sent Colm another challenging stare. 'How much have you read?' he asked menacingly, as if it was an intrusion he found hard to forgive.

'Only this last one,' he said, refusing to stand here like a schoolboy sent for punishment and say nothing in his own defence. 'I certainly won't tell her secrets to anyone else,' he promised easily enough.

He had more reasons not to want them known than the Farenze family, and reading Pamela's words really hadn't got him any closer to his father. A woman that self-obsessed was hardly likely to waste pages describing her lover, was she? He would do better to put her and her entire family behind him forever the day he left this place and handing them over might help him do it. The sneaky thought that Pamela's daughter was more difficult to forget nagged at him, but he did his best to ignore it.

'Will you hand over anything else you happen upon before your work here is done?' Miss Winterley asked as if she had caught her father's distrust of him.

'Anything that concerns you, yes,' he said with a weary sigh.

'Good, now we must leave the lad in peace, Eve,' his lordship urged his daughter when she would have argued. 'He can rehash this argument with me in the morning, but you're right, it's high time we returned to the ballroom.'

'We can hardly carry a stack of my late mother's diaries with us. Will you bring them to Farenze House for us, Mr Carter? I would be most grateful.'

Since she didn't wheedle or make any attempt to charm him into doing her bidding, Colm saw no reason to object and delay their departure. 'I suppose it's easy enough for me to carry books in and out of here, so, yes, I'll bring them when I call on your father tomorrow. Now please, will you both go? I don't want to be caught up in the affairs of the great and the good any more than you want me to be.'

'Thank you,' she said and they were back to humble clerk and lady again.

'Goodbye, miss, my lord,' he said with a bow that would do a butler credit.

'Goodbye, Carter,' she replied with a dignified nod and took her father's offered arm to be escorted back to civilisation.

He watched them go and wondered. How would it feel to stroll back into that ballroom with them, sauntering confidently at their side as an equal in birth and fortune? For a moment he thought wistfully of all he once had and didn't regret it as much as he thought. The polite world looked bright and glittering and sophisticated from the outside, but he didn't think it gave the Miss Winterleys of this world much joy. He had grown accustomed to a life where worth and courage counted for more than birth and fortune. When you were all hungry and cold and miserable, on the retreat through harsh country already ravished by French troops, birth and privilege didn't count for much.

As for knowing young ladies like Miss Winterley outside the charmed circle of the *ton*, that was clearly impossible. He put the very idea behind him, limped back up those stairs one last time and packed the eight volumes he had found into a handy little box, stowed it under his arm and was glad neither Winterley was waiting below to see him descend on his clerkly behind as he needed one hand and his good leg to get him down again without disaster. Confound his weak leg and the suspicions Lord Farenze had put into his head about his fellow servants. They were probably too busy to search for such scandalous gems in the library their master had sold off tonight, but Colm turned the key in the lock and pocketed it when he left the library all the same.

'So are you going to let me read my mother's journals, Papa?' Eve asked her father as soon as they were safely out of earshot.

'Certainly not.'

'You do know you can't protect me from her sins for ever, don't you?'

'Yes, but please don't expect me not to try. Even when we're both old and grey, I shall still be your father and convinced it's my role to keep my daughter safe.'

'Nobody could guard me as carefully as you have done, Papa, but I am an adult now in the eyes of the law.'

'I know that too well,' he admitted with a frown that spoke volumes of his concern for her peace and future happiness.

Eve had to live with her mother's many scandals hanging over her, but the world must deal with her as she was, not as they expected from her mother's wild ride through life. 'I do love you, Papa, and Chloe and Verity and the boys, but I need to live my own life.'

'Your stepmother has told me time and again not to follow you about like a mastiff and glare at any young idiot who notices you are a woman. Don't ever fool yourself, I like watching you hurt yourself on briars that aren't of your setting though, my Eve.'

'If I am to live any sort of life I must find my own way through them, though.'

'I suppose so, but not right now. It's high time we got back to indifferent wine and weak lemonade and rescued your stepmother since not even she and Polly Mantaigne could keep the curious at bay for the amount of time we have been gone. The poor girl will have talked herself into a headache again by now.'

'You are a fine and remembering sort of husband; I do love you, Papa.'

'Don't try to wheedle your way round me with soft words, minx; I'm still not letting you read Pamela's selfish outpourings.'

'Spoilsport,' Eve pronounced him and took a look at herself in one of the long mirrors placed at strategic points even along this dimly lit and seldom-visited corridor. She looked remarkably unscathed. 'Aunt Derneley is the vainest woman I have ever encountered,' she said after she twitched a frill back into place and brushed a piece of lint from her skirt.

'Only because you didn't know your mother,' Lord Farenze said as he removed a cobweb from his daughter's dark hair. They re-entered the ballroom to run up against a clever scold from Chloe for avoiding their social obligations and a frown of concern for the headache Eve didn't know she had until now.

Chapter Four

'What's he like then, Eve?' Miss Verity Revereux demanded the next morning as she bounced on to Eve's bed before staring wistfully at herself in the mirror across the room and wondering out loud if she was developing a spot.

'What was who like? And it seems unlikely since you were blessed by far too many good fairies at your birth and never had a single blemish I know of,' Eve said.

Then she remembered what a grim situation her honorary sister was born into. Her mother died as she gulped in her first lungful of air and poor Chloe was left with a newborn to care for at the tender age of seventeen as her twin sister died in childbirth. Eve groped about for a rapid change of subject and hit on the least welcome one to hand. 'Whomever can you mean anyway?'

'The man you met last night from the dreamy look on your face.'

Eve frowned and did her best to avoid the apparently guileless blue eyes Verity had inherited from her father. Neither Captain Revereux nor his beloved daughter were the innocents they appeared, so Eve hardened her heart against the plea in her best friend's eyes and turned to her lady's maid instead.

'You were right, Bran, this colour looks better on me this morning,' she said with her head on one side as she studied the choice of morning gowns on offer. 'I'm not sure which sash to wear,' she added, hoping to divert Verity with fripperies. She ought to know better, she supposed. Verity might look like an angel sent to humble lesser beings with her golden beauty, but looks could be deceptive. When her father was at sea they were all inclined to spoil her and Eve wished the gallant captain would hurry home and check his beloved child's wilder starts before they got her into real trouble.

'I can stay here all day if I have to, Eve dear,' Verity told her. 'Miss Stainforth has agreed to go and see a dentist at last, so I have all the time in the world to plague you until she is feeling better.' Verity lounged back on the bed to prove it. 'I loved it at school, but I'm so glad Papa insisted on hiring Miss Stainforth to teach me instead. Now I can be with you and Aunt Chloe and Uncle Luke all the time when he has to be out of the country and you can't lie to me at a distance. I can't see why you treat me like some artless child who must be kept in ignorance of the important things in life, Cousin dear. I preferred you before you made your curtsy to society and became so *terribly* worldly wise.'

'No doubt your governess left you plenty to do, Miss Verity, and you ought to be doing it right now,' Bran said sternly.

'She was in so much pain she forgot and why should I have my head stuffed with more facts and figures that I shall be expected to forget the moment I set foot in my first ballroom?'

'Our sex makes up half the world, Verity, and if we were all wilfully ignorant it would fall apart. You should be worrying about the poor lady's pain and suffering, not gloating over your freedom like some horrid schoolboy let off his lessons,' Eve tried to scold. Verity looked unimpressed and went on sorting Eve's sashes.

'Lady Chloe will find you something useful to do since your poor governess was in too much pain to bother, young lady,' Bran added with a look at Eve that said her disturbed night was showing on her face.

'No, don't bother her at this hour of the morning,' Eve intervened. Chloe was in the early stages of pregnancy yet again and if this one went like the last two, her stepmother would not be ready to deal with her wayward niece for another hour or two yet. 'You can take a stroll with me to Green Park among the nursemaids and governesses. I need some fresh air and you will be working too hard this afternoon and poor Miss Stainforth won't be well enough to accompany you out anyway.'

'Sourpuss, but I'm not put off that easily. You didn't answer my question, Eve Winterley. Are you quite sure you didn't meet the man of your dreams last night?' Verity asked, being of an age when fairy tales weren't quite impossible and beckoning womanhood whispered how wonderful if they happened to her.

'I never had those sorts of dreams, but, no, I did not,'

Eve said firmly, pushing a mental picture of the gruff, wounded and annoyingly unforgettable Mr Carter out of her mind. 'If Betty comes with us to the park, will you stay and make some of your peppermint tea for Lady Chloe, Bran?' she asked once Verity was fully occupied with finding her pelisse and muff, then dragging her favourite maid away from her duties as well as the second footman. Verity loved a romance and as Eve refused to live one for her, she must have decided to promote that one instead.

'Of course I will. You have a good heart under those stubborn ways, haven't you, my chick?'

Eve eyed her own reflection in the mirror and saw an almost perfect lady of fashion staring back at her. She almost expected a magical image of Mr Carter to peer into the glass behind her and smile mockingly, so she turned away with a sigh. Hadn't she had just told Verity she didn't have daydreams and here was the least comfortable hero she had ever encountered intruding into them?

'I'm too old to be anyone's chick now,' she replied to Bran's question lightly enough before she left the room.

'You'll never be too old for that, my love,' Bran whispered as she watched the almost sisters join up on the wide landing, then go downstairs for their walk. 'And perhaps I've good reason to worry about the dark circles under your eyes and stubborn set to your chin this morning.'

'Ah, now don't remind me, I'm determined to recall your name for myself, sir. There now, I knew it would come to me if I thought about it hard enough. You're Mr Carter, are you not? I dare say you have been calling on my father?' Miss Winterley's pleasing contralto voice asked Colm as if they had met at some fashionable soirée.

Damnation, Colm thought darkly; he thought he was safe out here, trying to get some air into his lungs before making his way back to Derneley House. Lord Farenze's daughter wasn't as indolent as most of her kind and fate wasn't on his side this morning either.

'Good morning, Miss Winterley,' he managed dourly.

'It is, isn't it?' she replied brightly, as if his failure to sneak past her unnoticed made it a lot better for some reason.

'We should not linger together in public or private, ma'am,' he told her in an undertone he hoped he'd pitched too low to carry to the ears of a nearby knot of overgrown schoolgirls giggling over something best known to themselves.

'We should not linger anywhere, then? You are very unsociable, Mr Carter, and the title *ma'am* is reserved for ladies with considerably more years in their dish than I have.'

'Forgive my ignorance, Miss Winterley. It's as well I have no inclination for high society and it has none for me,' he said with an odd pang at his exile from the polite world that felt nothing like the burning resentment he had once struggled with.

A Mr Carter had to shape his life around his work, so Colm tried hard not to meet Miss Winterley's challenging gaze with one of his own and wondered how it would feel to have the wealth and status his father took for granted back right now. Perhaps then he could meet her gaze for gaze and it wouldn't matter that his father once ran off with her mother. With all that noble blood and nabob wealth at his back Colm Hancourt might have challenged Miss Winterley back and…

No, there was no and…for them and there never would be. Even when he was under his uncle's roof and being himself again he wouldn't have much more than a rifle and a tiny annuity. Mr Hancourt worked for his uncle and most of his salary would go on being the Duke of Linaire's nephew. He must have better clothes and a sturdy horse and anything else could go into a small dowry for his sister. He and Miss Winterley would still not meet as equals and she would probably hate him for who he was when she found out. So he hoped she would tire of such a stiff-necked block and dismiss him before he said something disastrous.

'You go off into a world of your own at the drop of a hat, don't you, Mr Carter? That could get you into all sorts of trouble at Derneley House,' she warned lightly.

'I beg your pardon, Miss Winterley,' he said. 'I'll go about my business and leave you to enjoy the sunshine.'

'Please don't go,' she protested impulsively. 'My cousin has met some old school friends and is catching up on all she's missed since they last met.'

The three of them were standing a few yards away, so absorbed in excited conversation they might as well be the only people in the park. 'I thought your cousins were still in the nursery,' Colm said, revealing he knew more about her family than he wanted to admit.

'Uncle James's various chicks are, but Verity is my stepmama's niece. I'm surprised you haven't heard the story yet; it caused a sensation five years ago when my father married Lady Chloe Thessaly and the truth had to come out.'

'I have spent the last eight years in the army. The sayings and doings of the great and the good passed us by for most of that time.'

'I suppose you had more important things to think about than gossip and scandal, but you must have been little more than a boy when you took up your commission to have been in the army for so long, Mr Carter.'

'A compliment, Miss Winterley?'

'An observation,' she said with a slight flush on her high cheekbones that told him she thought it might have been as well.

'I was sixteen,' he said, his eldest uncle's brusque dismissal of his hopes and dreams of being a writer and scholar one day like his determinedly absent Uncle Horace sharp in his voice. He heard the gruff sound of it, shrugged rather helplessly and met her gaze with a rueful smile. 'I thought myself the devil of a fellow in my smart green uniform,' he admitted and suddenly wished he'd known her back then.

He'd felt so alone under his boyish swagger the day he entered Shorncliffe Camp and began the transformation from scared boy to scarred Rifleman. Mr Carter came into being in a regiment where officers won their rank largely by merit and gallantry in battle. Colm wanted a plain name to go with his dashing uniform mainly because he wanted to fit in and the Hancourts

wanted nothing to do with him and Nell. Eight years
on he must be Carter for a little longer, but at least nobody was trying to kill him.

'Were you a Rifleman, then?' she asked and he supposed he must have looked bewildered. 'Since you wore
a green uniform it seems a strong possibility,' she added
logically.

'Aye,' he said, 'some folk call us the Grasshoppers
because of it.'

'To survive eight years as a Rifleman you must be
brave as well as fortunate, whatever they called you,'
Eve managed to reply lightly enough.

Instinct warned her not to let him know how she
pitied a boy who began his dangerous career so young.
What if he was born rich and well connected instead?
Would she have met a rather dazzling young gentleman
in an expensive drawing room when she came out and
fallen for his easy charm? Or would she have thought
him as shallow and unformed as the other young men
who paid court to her with an air of fashionable boredom she didn't find in the least bit flattering? She could
have found the way his thick honey-brown hair curled
despite his efforts to tame it fascinating. His gold-
flecked eyes might have danced with merriment and
lured a discerning young lady into falling in love and
his scarred forehead would be unmarred. As for that
lame leg—that would be as long and strong and lithe as
the rest of him. That charmed and charming man would
laugh and smile with her, then grow serious long enough
to look deep into her eyes with his soul alive and clear
in his own. And then he would kiss her.

Her breath caught in heady anticipation in the much less magical here and now and she almost gave her thoughts away by moving a little closer to him and behaving like a besotted ninny. A dreamer deep inside her whispered it would be almost unbearably glorious, whichever version of him did the kissing, but that might be Pamela's daughter speaking and Eve didn't want to listen to her. Carter certainly didn't adore her and he was the Duke of Linaire's clerk and librarian, for goodness' sake.

'I was just lucky, I suppose,' he said with a self-deprecating shrug as if nothing else could account for it.

Eve shivered at the thought of a stray bullet or sabre slash that might have ended his life and refused to think of the number he must have survived right now. 'I doubt any officer could survive long on luck in a regiment like yours,' she challenged.

'You would be surprised and at least I had enough of it to know when it ran out. This summer I was at the end of it and sold out as soon as I recovered enough to sign my name after Waterloo.'

'You seem determined to make light of your experiences.'

'A limping man stands little chance of surviving a forced march or fighting retreat, but let's not speak of such horrors on a day like today. Didn't you promise me a fine story about your cousin by marriage and your stepmama just now?'

'Did I?' Drat the man, having a conversation with him was like trying to hold a slippery trout wet from the river. Last night he seemed almost too dashing to be an upper servant, today he carried his shallow dark hat as if itching to have it back on his head and go before someone caught him speaking to a lady. 'It's no secret now, so you might as well hear it from me. Lady Chloe and Verity's mama were twins, Mr Carter. At much the same age as you joined the army, Lady Daphne Thessaly wed a young naval lieutenant to avoid an arranged marriage. Her father was furious at being robbed of what he saw as his right to sell his daughter to a rich old man so he had her husband pressed, then left his twin daughters to birth her baby in such dire conditions it's a miracle Verity and her aunt survived, but Lady Daphne died in childbed. Lady Chloe spent the next decade acting as Verity's mother and became a housekeeper, then my father spent most of it trying not to be in love with her.'

'And when he couldn't resist any longer they told each other their secrets and seized the day?'

'I don't recall it being that simple, but the end result is they are very happily wed and Verity lives with us when her father is at sea,' she said and wondered why she hadn't let him go in the first place. It was that bland mask of the onlooker on life that did it, she supposed. For some reason she itched to rip it off and show the world a real man stood here, despite the repressive black garb and his fiercely guarded aloofness. Now she waited for his stiff farewell and told herself to let him go this time.

'Would my sister had had an aunt like your stepmother to love and protect her when I was sent off to school by our uncle,' he said instead and why was she this glad he hadn't mumbled a hasty farewell and limped away?

'What happened to her?' she said with all the horror stories of girls sent out as apprentices by their cruel relatives in her mind as she saw him frown.

'Oh, nothing very awful, she was put in the care of a governess until she was old enough to go to school and our family could forget us. My wicked uncle still found her useful as a stick to beat me with; if I ran away from school or tried to argue with the career he had in mind, my sister would be apprenticed to a milliner. I'm sure you know what happens to most girls bound to that trade, Miss Winterley. Even at eight years old I knew I must be a pattern card to save her from such a fate.'

'How cruel,' she exclaimed and felt furious with his appalling relative when he shrugged.

'It's the way of the world, my father annoyed two of his brothers so much they would have loved to have nothing to do with his children, but the scandal would have deafened them if they let us go into the poorhouse.'

'What did your mother's relatives have to say for themselves?'

'She was an only child and her parents died before her. If she had any relatives I don't know of it,' he said as if he wished he'd never told her so much in the first place.

'I am astonished her friends and neighbours let your uncle treat you both so, then,' she said although Mr Carter didn't want her to feel anything for him or his.

'They would shake their heads and mutter it was terrible we were left destitute, then whisper about bad blood and decide we were best forgotten,' he told her with some passion in his voice at last. 'Poverty stalked my sister's childhood and she is always a hair's breadth away from it even now, Miss Winterley. One wicked thought in an employer's head; a wrong word or unwitting action can get a governess dismissed without references. I can't endure the thought of such a life grinding her down as the years go on, so it is up to me to find a way out of such an existence for her, before it drives the youth and laughter out of her completely.'

Eve only had to see the purpose burning in his fiery gaze to know she was right about the hidden depths he tried to keep to himself. He wasn't the flat character he tried to be; he couldn't be if he pretended he was until doomsday.

'Your uncles are as guilty as your father of not making sure she is provided for. You will need very broad shoulders if you intend to take the sins of your entire family on them, Mr Carter.'

'You are very direct this morning, Miss Winterley.'

She shrugged. 'For direct I shall read rude, but I have no patience with pretend ignorance, sir, and if you had moved in polite society for the last three years you would not have any either. Your sister might count herself lucky not to be watched like a prize heifer by every idiot on the marriage mart if she knew how it felt.'

'Are they all idiots, then?'

'Not all, but no sensible man will hold an interesting conversation with a marriageable young lady for long unless he is in serious need of a wife.'

'So there is some merit in being ineligible after all,

then?' he joked and Eve felt a tug of temptation to make him do it again.

He was so unaware of how handsome he was when he forgot to guard his tongue that he could steal an unwary female's heart before she knew she was in danger. Lucky she wasn't unwary then, wasn't it?

'Why come to London for the Little Season then, since you dislike it so much?' he asked as if truly interested.

'The House is sitting and Papa hates coming on his own. My parents worry about me if I don't come with them and there's Verity's future to think of as well. If I refuse to take my part in this pantomime the *ton* plays out twice a year she will be an oddity by association. That would be so unfair when we're not related except through Papa and Chloe's marriage and a common link with my little half-brothers.'

'So you only dress and dance and behave like a fashionable young lady who is enjoying herself for the benefit of others?' he said with a sceptical glance at her fashionable pelisse and high-crowned bonnet that said he thought her vain and not very self-aware.

Chapter Five

Miss Winterley looked as if she might agree she was that saintly for a moment just to spite him, then mischief danced in her eyes and an irresistible smile tugged at her temptingly curved mouth. Colm had to struggle with a terrible urge to kiss her breathless, silenced and deliciously responsive—in the middle of Green Park for goodness' sake. What business had such a controlled and confident lady turning into an enchanting mix of funny, wise and daring when she smiled?

'I love my finery and attending the opera and theatres and real concerts that are not put on by supposedly musical ladies to show off their airs as much as their talents. I should not see my family and friends anywhere near as often as I do if we could not meet up in town either. My Uncle James has grown so fond of country life I sometimes wonder how Aunt Rowena manages to drag him here as often as she does though, but I can put up with the Lady Derneleys and Mr Carters of this world in order to keep in contact with the friends and relatives who truly matter to me.'

Thanks to his Brighton landlady even Colm knew of James Winterley's transformation from idle London rake to country squire and father of a ready-made family. Then there was the Winterleys' close connection to the Marquis of Mantaigne and his mixed bag of a family by marriage—oh, and Sir Gideon Laughraine and his lady. Here was the truth of things: Miss Winterley was at the heart of a group of impressive and powerful aristocrats and he was only even a secretary thanks to his Uncle Horace's bad conscience.

'Then I hope you enjoy your latest visit, Miss Winterley,' he said with a stiff bow and half raised his humble and unfashionable hat.

'Thank you, Mr Carter,' she replied with an ironic lift of her fine dark brows and a regal nod. 'How very kind of you to wish me well.'

'Good day, Miss Winterley,' he said repressively and got ready to limp back to his books and papers and packing crates.

'And a very good day to you too, sir,' he heard her reply lightly by way of dismissal from a lady to the upper servant he really was nowadays.

The thought of how much clear water lay between him and Miss Winterley mocked him all the way back to Derneley House and made him limp more heavily than usual for some strange reason. 'Even a lunatic wouldn't be fool enough to yearn for that particular moon, Colm Hancourt,' he murmured under his breath as he went.

He was fairly sure he was still sane, but that was about all he had to offer any woman deluded enough to want him. He was scarred and limping and about as

penniless as a man could be without actually living in
the gutter. Before he met Miss Winterley he had still
been able to convince himself he only wanted his lost
fortune back for Nell's sake. Now he had a sneaking
suspicion he'd lied. Was there any hope Miss Winterley
might ever look on him as a possible lover if he wasn't
who he was? Of course not. The idea was ridiculous
and he must put it from his mind right now.

So that left him with his sister Nell still to save from
a life of genteel poverty or a rich man's bed and no wedding ring. The very thought of either fate for his bright,
brave sister horrified him enough to make him put aside
air dreams and concentrate on her future instead. There
was one elusive possibility he'd been turning over in
his mind since he read the last entry in Pamela's diary
last night. He shrugged off the idea it had been wrong
to read them before he passed them over to their rightful owner as ordered. He had as much right to know
the wretched female's thoughts during the time she was
with his father as anyone still alive. The woman was
annoyingly evasive about the Lambury Jewels after that
crow about the rubies, at least until the end of her diary
when she must have left for that last wild adventure
with her lover. Before she went she railed at her lover's
refusal to hand over the last of his wife's jewellery: the
magnificent diamond set Joseph Lambury had made up
for his daughter after Colm was born. So when his father left England with his *inamorata* they should have
been in the bank vault his uncle had sworn was bare as
a pauper's pocket when Colm plucked up the courage
to ask before he left for the army.

A slender thread of hope dangled in front of Colm's eyes as he speculated how much the diamond set might be worth. He vaguely recalled seeing his mother wear them when she was dressed up for a ball grand enough to warrant such splendour. There had been a tiara and a magnificent tumble of diamonds round her neck that sparkled fascinatingly in the candlelight when she came to bid him goodnight. Heavy bracelets weighed down her slender wrists and they laughed together as he playfully moved her hands so they would make rainbows from her rings even with the nursery night lights. A coachman shouted at a carter and their loud exchange of insults jolted Colm out of the past and into a very different world. For a moment he had been back there with her, sharing a careless moment of loving intimacy with his mother and remembering so much about her he thought he'd forgotten.

He felt almost sorry he had that memory to cherish when Nell was too young to remember much more about their mother than a vague impression of pale hair and warm arms. They had talked about their parents one night this summer in Brussels, when the pain of his wounds kept him awake and she insisted on waking with him. It taught him a lot, that time when even he wasn't quite sure if he was going to live or die. The most important thing he had found out was he and his sister still shared a strong bond, despite all the efforts two of their uncles and aunts made to keep them apart. All those years of pretending the Hancourt-Winterley scandal died with their brother and not even the last

Duke and their Uncle Maurice could make Colm and Nell strangers to one another.

Which brought him back to the diamonds; the last Duke of Linaire must have had them broken up and sold, he supposed. Colm thought about the hard-eyed man who informed him his father was dead as if he ought to be glad. That man was capable of it, but could he have got away with it? That was less certain and whispers of what he'd done would have haunted the cold-hearted devil to his grave. Nothing Colm had heard since he came back to England said any of those whispers existed. The diamonds might still be hiding somewhere, waiting to be found and claimed by him. A beat of wild hope thundered in his heart as he thought what that would mean for Nell's future happiness. A real dowry, a secure home and perhaps living under the same roof as her brother for a while before she wed a man who deserved her, if such a paragon existed. Colm almost smiled, then changed his mind as he realised how unlikely his latest daydream sounded. If he could find diamonds nobody had seen for fifteen years; if he could prove they were his; if he could sell them for the fortune needed to buy a modest home and a farm to support it; if Nell would leave her noble orphans and join him there...

So many ifs made a fantasy, but if there was some trace of his mother's diamonds, Uncle Horace might help him find them. Colm knew his uncle and aunt felt they had let his little brother's children down by staying away when their father died. Now they were back in England the duchy wasn't the rich inheritance it was before the last Duke and Colm's grandfather spent money like water. The current Duke couldn't afford to dower his niece and establish his nephew as the gentleman his birth argued, because Uncle Maurice would be watching his future inheritance like a hawk. The new Duchess was unlikely to produce a child after a quarter of a century of marriage, so Lord Maurice would insist on an allowance as his brother's heir before Lord Chris's children got a penny of Hancourt money beyond the twenty pounds a year already settled on them by the last Duke. Those diamonds might be a false hope, Colm mused as he made his way down the back steps of Derneley house, but sometimes it was better to have one of those than none at all.

The work of getting the Derneley Collection listed and packed up ready for its new home, so he could get out of this house, felt more urgent today. As Colm went about it he couldn't stop thinking of his latest meeting with Miss Winterley. He didn't number many fine ladies among his acquaintance, but something told him she was an unusual one. This morning she seemed as relaxed as if he was a fashionable gentleman in Hyde Park at the fashionable hour, instead of an almost servant in Green Park at some unlikely hour of the morning for a lady who had been at a party late into the night. He let his hands slow for a moment as he thought of her in the clear light of a fine autumn morning. Her skin was flawless, he recalled, and she was still young enough for a late night and early morning not to be written under her eyes. Her bonnet was modest by the standards of the current fashion for vast pokes that hid the wearer from view if there was any danger of shadows. So now he knew that her eyes truly were a rare shade of blue-green and could haunt a man to his grave if he wasn't careful. Add a slender but womanly figure and the smile that made her unique and he had best think about diamonds again and forget Miss Winterley as best he could.

Anything more than a stiff acquaintance between that lady and Mr Carter was clearly impossible, so he thought about that passage he had copied out last night in his room and with the door safely shut behind him. He took out the paper he kept in his jacket pocket lest some servant find it and scanned Pamela's words for anything that passed him by last night. He was bone weary at the time and his head so full of Eve Winterley and her icy father he couldn't think straight. There might be a stray word he'd missed the sense of as he wrote it down. The last page of her diary seemed to sum the woman up perfectly.

Knowing the full power of my own beauty at last and feeling men lust for me so deeply they can't fight it is wonderful, but jewels never fade. I don't intend to be deprived of a single stone, and they will never make me feel less than beautiful, however old I get.

So had written the woman who would never get much older than she had been when she'd made that last entry in the diary.

Colm's mouth twisted in distaste as he re-read her self-centred ramblings, but he felt a spark of regret for a vivid life cut short all the same. He was sorry Lord Farenze would have to read his late wife's words and wonder what made her as she was. Colm had no idea how it felt to walk in the Viscount's expensive shoes, but he didn't envy him the memory of a wife no one man could satisfy. Her words told him enough about Pamela to know she would have left Colm's father for another lover, however deeply Lord Chris adored her. Colm was almost glad Lord Chris hadn't lived to watch the woman who cost him so dearly walk away without a backward look.

Emotions he didn't want to imagine underlay the dark fascination of a duke's youngest son and the runaway wife of a very young peer. If he let himself dwell on such wild passions he might feel an echo of them for some unsuspecting female. A picture of Miss Winterley looking horrified as he poured out his insatiable desire for her made him flinch, then smile at the next image of her speechless with shocked surprise that he could feel anything at all, let alone that. She was so unlike her dam, Colm felt guilty for misjudging her last night and uneasy about the thunder of passionate need in his own veins as he watched her ghost into his temporary lair breathless and far too desirable for her own good before they had even spoken to each other.

Eve had given her father time to read all Pamela's letters and diaries before confronting him the day after she met Mr Carter in Green Park. It must make painful reading for him and she doubted her mother's self-centred outpourings shone much light on what had made her long for a succession of ever wilder lovers.

'You really won't let me read a word of my mother's papers, will you?' Eve challenged as she followed him into his study after breakfast.

'I wish I could burn the lot right now, so there would be no risk of you or anyone else ever reading a word of her selfish drivel,' her father said with a preoccupied frown at the locked drawer of his desk where she guessed the diaries were sitting like a row of fat little grenades that could be so destructive in the wrong hands she shuddered at the thought of it.

'Then why don't you?' she asked with a nod at the fire burning steadily in the grate on this fine but chilly morning.

'Because it isn't right to deprive that boy of a chance,' he murmured as if he was fighting the urge to do it anyway.

'What boy? Oh, you mean Lord Christopher Hancourt's son, I suppose. I thought he was dead; nobody has heard of him for years and his family never talk about him or the little girl I remember someone mentioning once.'

'Their father spent the lad's rightful inheritance on your mother and I can't believe that fool was besotted enough to simply hand over all those jewels to her. She knew the Lambury Jewels weren't even his to give, but she seduced and sulked as only she knew how until she got them out of him. There isn't a single word of remorse about the boy and his sister in the books and papers Carter handed over.'

'It would be beneath him to hold back a single letter of hers once he made you that promise,' Eve argued against Mr Carter holding something over them. Her father's acute gaze focused on her as if he was trying to read her thoughts and feelings about a man she didn't even like. Of course she didn't feel anything for the stiff-necked idiot, how could she? She still felt the need to affirm his honesty for some reason. 'He wouldn't keep anything that didn't belong to him,' she added.

'That's what I'm afraid of,' her father murmured so low she wondered if she was mistaken. 'Nothing Pamela did should shame you, love,' he said out loud and with such sadness and concern in his eyes Eve felt guilty about reminding him of those dark days in both their lives, not that she could remember them.

'Nor you, Papa,' she said. 'She did enough damage when she was alive. Please don't agonise over her sins now she's dead. The memory of them kept you and darling Chloe apart for years, so don't fret about things she never felt a second's worth of unease about now.'

'Yet if I burn these books I might deprive that boy of the better life and we Winterleys have done enough damage in that quarter already. If there's any chance those jewels she writes about so gleefully can be found and I destroy a clue to where they are, then I shall be the one in need of a few scruples and not Pamela.'

'We must find the man Lord Chris's son must be by now and help him as best we can then. If that's what it takes to make you forget all the evil Lord Chris and Pamela did between them, we have no choice.'

'Any gossip now sleeping safely might wake up

and bite you if he or his sister come forward, love,' he warned with a brooding look Eve couldn't quite read.

'Don't you think I'm strong enough to ignore such poisonous gossip by now?'

'Sometimes I wonder if you're not too strong, Eve. If I had only worked my way past Pamela and caught your stepmother ten years before I did, you and Verity would have had easier childhoods. I was a fool not to seize the day and your stepmother a lot sooner than I did.'

'Well, there's no denying Chloe is perfect for you in every way my mother never was, but Verity and I did very well with one of you each for the ten years you two spent apart. We do even better now you're together and happy, instead of apart and secretly miserable, but there's no need to mourn what we didn't have because you were stubborn as a rock, Papa. We were both very much loved and cared for even before you and Chloe let yourselves be happy together.'

'I'm glad you know we love you, but are you sure you're prepared for the old gossip to be stirred up if I find Hancourt and help him search for any remnants of his inheritance that might be lying around unattended?'

Eve had had to prove over and over again how unlike her mother she was when she made her debut in society. The idea of facing that ordeal again was daunting and made her pause for a moment. No, peace wasn't worth having if it came from playing the coward, she decided. She would have to be more cautious than ever about dark corridors and deserted ladies' withdrawing rooms, but the sneaky thought that meeting an intriguing and gruff young gentleman at the end of her last adventure made it almost worthwhile was nonsensical, wasn't it?

'Even the whisper of a lost fortune could do that anyway, but I don't see how we can stand in his way, if he's still alive, of course.'

'And I suspect he is,' her father muttered with that odd look on his face again and Eve was tempted to stamp her feet and demand he tell her everything he was keeping back. She was a young lady now and not a harum-scarum miss, so she could not and she knew that look of old. He wouldn't even tell Chloe what was in his thoughts until he was ready and a show of temper certainly wouldn't help.

'Your Mr Carter might be in the Duke of Linaire's confidence, Eve. You could always ask him to find out what happened to Lord Christopher's children next time you meet him in Green Park.'

'How did you know about that?'

'Luckily Verity doesn't know it was meant to be a secret.'

'But it wasn't. I met the man there by pure chance. I suppose he was taking the air on his way back from delivering my mother's papers to you.'

'And yet you spoke with him at length in the sight of all those nursemaids and governesses. Don't deny it, Eve; I had the tale from more than one source.'

'I didn't think you listened to gossip, Papa.'

'I do when it concerns my daughter. Have a care, my Eve. Carter might be a wounded hero of however many battles of Wellington's he is old enough to have fought in, but he clearly hasn't a feather to fly with. He wouldn't be sorting dusty old books for Linaire at Derneley House if he had.'

'I never took you for a snob, Papa, and I only met the man two days ago. I am hardly likely to fall in love with such a rude and stiff-necked idiot anyway, even if I had known him since we were in our nurseries.'

'It doesn't take long to do that,' he warned her ruefully. 'Love can come without an invitation and when we're least expecting it. Be careful it doesn't creep up on you in the worst possible circumstances and bludgeon you over the head like it did your unwary papa.'

'It won't. I don't intend to succumb to passion. If I wed at all it will be to a gentleman I have learnt to know and respect after months, if not years, of friendship.'

'What of mutual attraction and downright lust? I know you're my daughter and I should be glad you are going to be so sensible about picking a husband, but I don't want you to miss out the crucial parts of a happy marriage.'

'Not many fathers encourage their daughters to become besotted with a gentleman they have not even met.'

'How do you know that if you only intend to wed a not-very-exciting friend? And I only want you to form a passion for the man if he is right for you.'

'Logic will tell me that, I have no need for the sort of insane urges that ruled my mother's life.'

'No, but you should think a little more about your own before you marry a block, love.'

'If I was really looking for one of those, Mr Carter would fill the bill very nicely.'

'Believe that and you'll believe anything,' her father said darkly and Eve wished she'd picked a better example than the Duke of Linaire's whatever he was: secretary, librarian, man of business? Possibly only the Duke and Mr Carter knew the answer to that question.

She remembered how it felt to have Mr Carter's gold-brown eyes focus intently on her when he forgot his false humility. No, he wasn't a wooden soldier at all. Papa was quite right; there was a sharply intelligent and sensitive man under that quiet exterior and she would do well to remember it if they ever met again, which seemed very unlikely as he was the Duke of Linaire's clerk and not part of the *ton*.

'My one-day marriage and Mr Carter aside, what do you mean to do about the Hancourts, Papa?'

'When I track them down, I shall make sure they know all I do. I don't know if that will help much, since I don't properly understand it myself.'

'What does she say, then, Papa? You can't hint at something that might be a clue, then refuse to tell me any more lest you offend my delicate sensibilities.'

Eventually he handed her a list he had copied out, and censored, from entries in Pamela's diaries where she gloated over the fabulous jewels she had coaxed out of her lover one by one. Eve could hardly believe any woman could lust after cold gemstones so ruthlessly and it left her with an unpleasant taste in her mouth, despite all her assurances to her father that Pamela had done her worst as far as her daughter was concerned.

Chapter Six

As she tried to go about her day as normal Eve was annoyed with herself for constantly drifting off into a reverie. She hoped her father wasn't right to be uneasy about Mr Carter. No, of course he wasn't. She was immune to love and passion; if she wasn't she would have let it carry her away long ago. An unwanted image of Mr Carter waiting to lead his men into battle flitted into Eve's mind all the same. He would exude confidence even if he was terrified and look unforgivably handsome in his Rifleman green uniform while he was about it. A silken voice whispered in her ear that was how a real man should look and never mind the marks of battle the great idiot thought wiped out any manly beauty he had—Mr Carter was more a man than the weak-willed and self-indulgent aristocrats he was supposedly inferior to.

Take Lord Christopher Hancourt, since he was in her thoughts as well today. That weak and overindulged man had never faced a moment of real hardship or dan-

ger until the very last seconds of his life, but Carter had
defied both for nearly every day of the last eight years.
How irritating if her father was right and he really had
intrigued her too much for comfort. The one man she
could never marry was the only one to make her think
twice during this tedious time she had to spend away
from her real life at Darkmere or Farenze Lodge near
Bath.

Anyway, she had learnt long ago not to trust a man's
passion for a willing woman the hard way, hadn't she?
Her first real suitor seemed so earnest and naïve and in
love she somehow fooled herself she loved him back.
She doubted that spotty youth sat comfortably for a
month after Papa and Uncle James thrashed him like
a sniffling schoolboy, but she learnt a hard lesson that
night. Her mother's wicked reputation would descend
on her if she wasn't very careful indeed and she had
been ever since. Too careful, perhaps, given how she
was having to struggle to get not very humble and de-
cidedly awkward Mr Carter out of her mind now.

It was probably the silly, rebellious part of it that once
believed a boy's lust was love whispering that Mr Carter
was uniquely formed to understand her. He could see
past the gloss Winterley money and prestige added to
her unremarkable looks. He seemed to know about the
true heart she'd learnt to keep so safe, even she had almost forgotten she had one. He might do any and all of
that, but it wouldn't do either of them any good. They
were as divided from each other as the Ganges was
from the Thames, or the icy poles at opposite ends of

the earth. Made of the same substance, but thousands of miles apart in every way that really mattered.

Colm thought he would hear no more of the Winterley family, but it was only a few days after their last encounter that Miss Winterley confounded him all over again. He turned over the brief note an urchin had delivered to Derneley House before he ran off. No, the hastily scrawled words really were as brief and uninformative as he'd thought they were the first time.

> *Please come as fast as you can. I am waiting with a hackney at the corner of the mews. Do not tell anyone you are meeting me and try not to be seen.*
> *E.W.*

One of the more innocent letters Colm's father had sent to her mother years ago had fallen out of the sealed note to prove this wasn't a hoax. It was ten o'clock on a dark autumn night, for heaven's sake; even meeting him at this hour of the night would mean certain ruin if they were discovered. He shrugged into his dull coat and reached for his shabby hat, even as he told himself he was a fool to think of going anywhere with her. He still slipped into the garden through a side door and locked it after himself in the hope nobody would even notice he had gone.

'Hurry,' her low and deliberately gruff voice ordered as soon as he crept out of the garden gate. He saw a hackney doing its best to pretend it wasn't there and finally had to believe this was really happening.

'What the devil...?' he began only to have her reach out and tug him into the carriage as if there wasn't a moment to spare.

'Take us to the place we agreed inside ten minutes and I'll pay you twice the price,' she ordered the hackney driver as coolly as if she kidnapped limping clerks every night of the week.

The coach shot forward so fast Colm was surprised they didn't tumble out. There wasn't even time to gasp out another question before they were clattering over cobbled streets as if their lives depended on it and she wouldn't be able to hear him. Exclusive parts of Mayfair flashed past until they reached Oxford Street, crossed it at a reckless pace, then finally slowed as they neared Cavendish Square and stopped just short of it.

'Shush!' she whispered as Colm climbed down and stood on the cobbles, feeling like a mooncalf as he tried to make sense of the world and she handed two guineas to the jarvey, then grabbed Colm's arm as if she owned him.

As soon as the shabby little carriage was out of sight he stood stock still, so she had to let him go, fall over, or cling to him like a limpet. Luckily she did the latter, but gave an irritated click of her tongue, as if all this was his fault and he decided he'd had enough.

'Explain,' he demanded abruptly.

'Aren't you supposed to be a man of action and not words?' she muttered, as if she was having severe doubts about bringing him along after all.

'Not any more,' he replied gruffly.

'Imagine you still are and simply use the brains officers in your regiment are supposed to possess, although I see little sign of them right now.'

'Never mind trading insults with me; I'm not going a step further unless you give me a very good reason to do so.'

'My cousin has been reckless and silly and I must get her away from here before it's too late to remedy. You are here to help me do so—now *will* you hurry?'

'Your parents are responsible for her, they ought to know what she's been up to and make sure she never does it again.'

'Believe me, she won't. Now move, you great ox, before it's too late.'

Cavendish Square, now why did that ring a bell? Colm let himself be prodded into motion while he reviewed a half-heard conversation between Derneley and his lady about their evening.

'Lady Warlington's masquerade,' he murmured as it all fell into place.

'That will turn into a drunken romp long before midnight. Lady Warlington's brothers will see to it if nobody else does,' Derneley had joked. His wife agreed and put it with the slender pile of invitations they still received now they were so widely known to be drowning in River Tick.

'Exactly,' Miss Winterley said now, as if that explained everything.

'Why would Miss Revereux be anywhere near such an event, especially seeing that she isn't even out?'

'Because an empty-headed youth begged her to meet

him there and it probably seems like a huge adventure to her,' she muttered.

'Who is this idiot?'

'Verity is only fifteen and Lady Warlington's youngest brother is startlingly handsome, so I suppose it's understandable she sighs over the silly boy and imagines herself in love with him. He should never have dared her to meet him tonight, though. If she's at this wretched party dressed as I suspect she must be from the items missing from the dressing up box, she won't have a shred of reputation left to lose if we don't find her before anyone else does, for he won't care about ruining such a young girl's prospects. I suspect he would find it horribly amusing.'

Fuming at the very idea some lout might casually wreck such a young girl's future before she was old enough to be out of the schoolroom, Colm let Miss Winterley bundle him towards the back of Lord Warlington's town house and they waited for a chance to slip inside without being noticed. At last a door opened to let in cold night air and Colm finally saw the way Miss Winterley was dressed and he knew why she needed him with her and nobody else. Who but Mr Carter could Miss Winterley rely on to pass through the servants' hall at this time of night with little more than a raised eyebrow if they were caught?

She made a fine serving wench, he admitted numbly, as the fact he had been on hand at the right time and dressed more shabbily than any other male of her acquaintance stung more sharply than it should. Any doubts he had about her clever cover failing them when they got to the public rooms faded when she scooped up a discarded mask as if she was diligently tidying the chaos, then unearthed a domino from behind a classical statue. Thrusting both at him as if he ought to know what to do next without being told, she went to forage for her own disguise whilst he gathered his wits enough to meekly put them on. *Who am I supposed to be this time?* he silently asked his reflection in a nearby mirror. *A somebody pretending to be a nobody*, the false image mocked back at him. He looked almost like the man he could have been—a rich idler who thought it amusing to ape a clerk when he had never done a decent day's work in his life.

A loud bellow sounded along the corridor he had seen Miss Winterley disappear into just now and it was echoed by another drunken sot who sounded far too castaway to move very fast. He should have remembered what happened to the confounded female when she wandered about once-grand houses on her own. Cursing himself for being so glum about Miss Winterley's uses for him tonight, he had let her go by herself. Colm was halfway along it, and bad leg be damned, when she came dashing towards him as if the hounds of hell were on her tail.

'Hide me,' she gasped as heavy treads sounded behind her.

There wasn't a niche big enough to hold a classical statue or a handy cupboard, so he tugged her into his arms and put his body between her and whoever was trying to chase her down this time. He pushed her against the nearest marble column as if they had been aiming for the right place to dally with each other ever since they stumbled out of the ballroom frantic for one another only moments ago.

'Not like tha—' she was saying even as he kissed her passionately.

She struggled fiercely for a moment, then gave in with a huge sigh, went gloriously responsive and kissed him back as if she had been starving for this since the night they met as well. For a moment he let himself dream she wanted him as urgently as he did her. Her mouth first softened, then seemed to ask for impossible answers under his. *Are you my special he?* she might as well be asking as she explored his mouth with an edge of wonder under the inexperience. *Could you be the lover I have dreamt of since I was woman enough to ache for him?*

Yes, yes, to all of it. To every question you could ever ask of that man, yes, the true Colm under all his careful defences whispered back. He forgot where they were and what the world would say if it knew who he was and simply kissed her and let his senses drown in blissful unreason.

'Tally-ho,' the less drunken of the two voices bellowed almost in his ear.

Colm cursed reality and tried to think straight when all he really wanted to do was go on kissing Eve Winterley and feeling something beyond his wildest dreams for this dear enemy of his. He raised his head as if bitterly offended and impatient of any interruption of that soul-stealing kiss and it wasn't any effort at all to glare at the swaying idiot as if he hated him.

'I saw the pretty little vixen first,' the buffoon had the audacity to say, as if Colm would apologise and politely step aside then leave him to do his worst. 'Don't think we've met, I'm Louburn, y'know?'

'I don't think we have either, but my wife avoids drunken fools whenever she can and I am not about to introduce you to her,' he said and felt Eve shaking with nerves in his arms as he cursed the nearest buffoon virulently under his breath.

'You claim you're my sister's guests, yet you're married to a servant girl? That don't sound right to me,' the second drunk managed, and now Eve had two of Lady Warlington's notorious brothers on her tail. A flutter of panic joined the butterflies Mr Carter had set spinning about inside her with that heart-stopping kiss. If she was desperately unlucky one of these fools would be sober enough to realise who she really was and that she wasn't married to anyone, especially not to Mr Carter, usually to be found in the latest Duke of Linaire's library.

'Even cast away you should be able to recall you're doing your best to spoil your sister's masquerade and not in some dockside tavern, Louburn,' Carter told the elder Louburn brother so brusquely she wondered why she'd ever have thought him too withdrawn and mild-mannered to be an effective officer.

'We ain't met before, have we?' the slightly less drunken brother asked blearily.

'Let's just say your reputation goes before you and leave it at that, shall we?' her brave cavalier said icily and Eve wondered how the menace under that weary comment could pass these idiots by when it made her tremble and it wasn't even directed at her.

'Wife or not, she ain't wearing a mask, is she?' the more eager Mr Louburn asked, as if his stinking reputation was something to be proud of and he wanted a woman right now, so one ought to be instantly available—willing or not. The more she thought about Verity wandering unprotected about such a house on such a night the more anxious Eve was to find her and get them all out of here before tonight went even more disastrously wrong.

'No, and that's because we were looking for privacy and you interrupted us. Why would my lady need a mask when I know every inch of her and can recognise her even in the dark? Not that I need explain myself to a sot like you.'

Even Eve believed in the outraged aristocrat Mr Carter was pretending to be at the moment. He had put aside the would-be humble and workaday Mr Carter and spoken with such authority it almost seemed rude *not* to believe every word he said. She shivered at the thought that here was the true man under his mild disguise and decided it was a good idea to go along with him and pretend she was his modest wife, caught in not very modest circumstances. She buried her head against his shoulder for good measure and to stop the wretches from taking a second look at her and realising where they'd seen her before.

'Come on, Bart, there's far better sport to be had elsewhere without having to mill him down to get to it and I'm thirsty,' the less amorous brother said with fading interest in anything but his next drink.

'Two of us, don't you see? We can easily take him on between us, Rolly. Nobody'll be any the wiser if we throw him outside, then I can tup his wife in peace and they won't tell anyone, will they? Scandal as much on them as us, see?' he said, tapping his finger where he thought his nose ought to be.

Eve felt the tightly wound tension in Colm's surprisingly powerful body at that despicable threat to treat them both as if they'd been put on this earth to meet a lusty drunkard's convenience. The pent-up violence crackled in the air all around them now. Suddenly this farce had threatened to turn very dark and she didn't want Mr Carter to get hurt, any more than she wanted to be violated herself.

'And there are only two of you?' Carter drawled with such terrible confidence she wanted to cry out a warning that they were notorious brawlers and he must find a safer way to stop this threat to their safety and sanity. 'Hide your face,' he whispered to her as he pushed her behind him, then turned on his latest adversaries with such calmness her hands did as they were told before her mind could argue. She peeped at what happened next through shaking fingers and for a moment was quite sure her eyes were deceiving her.

It was over too fast for her to have time to pile into the mêlée and never mind Carter's high-handed efforts to keep her out of it. She would have kicked and bitten and clawed against the casual brutality of these two so-called gentlemen, except they were dealt with so swiftly and efficiently she had no time to form her hands into claws and spring into action. A sporting man might call it as pretty a display as he ever saw outside a boxing ring, she decided in dazed shock. Perfectly flush hits to the jaw one after the other and there was nothing left for either of them to do but stare down at a heap of unconscious Louburn brothers, until Carter shook out his protesting hands in brief agony and gave her a harassed glare. While she was still struggling to come to terms with his might and such an unexpected skill he dragged first one Louburn, then the other back into the ruin they had made of a once-elegant room and locked the door on them, then pocketed the key with an exasperated sigh.

'Well, I told you not to look,' he said gruffly as he straightened his domino and handed her one he must have found in that rogues' den the Louburns had made of their brother-in-law's home, along with a far prettier mask than the one that hid most of Carter's thoughts from her right now and made his eyes look even more intriguing when he stared down at her as if he wanted to read all the confused thoughts and feelings scurrying about in her reeling head. Not that she could afford to be intrigued by the man, she reminded herself hastily, as she numbly put on her new disguise and wondered what disaster they should expect next.

'I wasn't… Well, no, that's not quite right, I'm not…'

You were not what, Eve? her inner critic mocked. *Not shocked, not awed and feeling a little bit breathless at the power and deadly purpose of the true man under Mr Carter's pretend humility? Not secretly long-*

*ing for him to repeat that kiss with interest added on to
say thank you for saving you from the worst of his kind
and that you did rather like it the first time?*

'Never mind what you are or are not right now. How
the deuce are we going to find your little sister or cousin
or whatever it is you two call one another in this bear
garden?'

'Oh, yes, Verity,' she murmured, still so off balance
from that kiss and his heroics afterwards she had almost forgotten why they were here in the first place.
'She has no idea aping Caro Lamb in breeches could
get her into far more trouble than if she came dressed
as an opera dancer,' she blurted out Verity's disgraceful disguise and heard him groan even above the din
of excited chatter and laughter and the orchestra desperately trying to be heard above it all in the ballroom
at the end of this side corridor.

'Oh, good, now we only need to find the next riot and
suppress it, then lock up the rest of the Louburn family
and get out of here without being recognised, then we
should all be able to go home and sleep serenely as if we
never left our beds in the first place,' he said with such
irony and an angry glare that seen through the filter of
his dark mask looked almost fearsome, except he was
also looking rather deliciously mysterious, flighty Eve
pointed out helpfully. 'The girl is obviously not fit to be
let out without a keeper,' he growled and she sighed to
oblige that silly version of herself and wondered if he
might be persuaded to visit a more sedate masquerade
with her if she asked him very nicely.

Ridiculous idea, her sterner inner self pointed out,

and she tried hard to concentrate on what he'd said instead of feeling prickles of something that must be forbidden slide down her spine at the sound of his voice so gruff and dark and the stern glint of his eyes through that mask. She shivered, although for some reason she was incredibly warm, and even that didn't seem to put all these wicked ideas out of her mind and certainly did nothing for her rebellious body.

'She is only fifteen,' she said as if that ought to explain everything and she struggled with the fact her grip on this misadventure seemed to have slipped and she was following him like a meek little acolyte behind a high priest, or a besotted girl after the man she thought was the love her life.

If not for Verity, she would be quite content to drift among the elegant chaos of this rather wild party and feel deliciously daring yet utterly safe in the company of a tall, dark and compelling man of mystery. Mr Carter always wore a disguise, she decided; she doubted he ever let the world see the real man, even if he could afford clothes the dandies of the *ton* wouldn't shudder to be seen standing next to. Yes, if not for Verity she would be quite happy to stay until too close to midnight and run the tempting risk of being caught in the least desirable company the Honourable Miss Winterley could find herself in if she tried.

She hardly recognised the cool and controlled Eve Winterley she had made herself become when she realised how eagerly the *ton* was waiting for her to turn into her mother. The female clutching Carter's strong hand as if he was her rock and only chance of safety in

a sea full of storms was a stranger. So much for not re-
lying on a man to make her feel strong; for never looking for all the things her mother spent her life longing
for. Eve still didn't want a man's unconditional surrender, or constant proof he worshipped her like some
pagan goddess. The very idea made her shudder with
revulsion, but a mutual surrender to something more
than the coolly logical marriage she had thought she
wanted seemed so very desirable right now it felt sin-
ful. At least she understood that raw state of wanting a
little better after his heady kiss and the shock of seeing
Carter the fighting man emerge from the shadows. Another mask, she decided as the music and wild laughter
got even louder. How many disguises could one man
wear and not lose his true self?

Chapter Seven

'Eve...' The desperate whisper came before someone noticed she and Carter were standing on the fringes of this wild party and came to find out who was hiding under their ingenious disguises.

If they weren't careful they'd be seen by too many curious eyes under the glow of what looked like a thousand candles in the noisy ballroom ahead of them and someone might recognise her. Eve could just see the curtains of an alcove off the corridor they were almost at the end of and thanked heavens they had not had to brave the full glare of the crowd ahead to search for her almost cousin.

'Verity?' she whispered sharply. 'What the deuce are you doing here?' she asked, hoping the boy who carelessly drew a fifteen-year-old girl into this rowdy chaos didn't come to find out if she had turned up for an assignation she was far too young to understand.

'I was looking for a way out,' Verity said, looking very pale and deeply shocked by what she had seen so far, as well as a bit woebegone.

Perhaps this latest escapade had overwhelmed even her high spirits and it would make her think twice about trying to run before she was ready to walk in so-called polite society. Eve couldn't think it very polite, or even glamorous after this circus herself, so maybe letting Verity see the dark side of it all wasn't such a bad idea, if they could only get her out of here relatively un-scathed and with her reputation intact, despite Rufus Louburn's worst efforts.

'At least you have done one sensible thing tonight, then,' Eve whispered sharply, not inclined to be dis-armed after what she and Mr Carter had already been through on this little madam's behalf.

'Leave her be for now, you can scold her once we have all got safely away,' Carter cautioned softly. 'And let's hope we don't have to go back the way we came. Those two drunken idiots could be awake and howling for revenge on us by now,' he murmured in her ear. She stifled a giggle as he managed to make a joke of what could have been a vicious struggle for more than she wanted to think about right now.

'Ah, I thought so. I knew there had to be more than one back stairway down to the vast basement there must be under the house,' he whispered as a jib door Eve hadn't even thought to look out for opened under his probing fingers and showed her once again that he was a lot more composed than she was after that earth-shaking kiss. It had seemed about to make her world anew for a wild moment and perhaps it was only one on a long list of such sweet encounters for him. Didn't soldiers have a sweetheart in every town they passed through? The contrast between dashing Mr Carter of the 95th Rifles and the shabby clerk she'd met that night at Derneley House made her wonder if there might be other versions of this complex man for her to discover, if she dared to look.

At least the narrow stair he'd found was lit by the occasional ensconced candle, she saw with a shudder. The bareness and gloom behind the narrow door made her feel as if the walls might press in on her, but this was what maids endured every day of their lives so their employers could enjoy the privacy and luxury of nigh invisible service. If she and Verity had been born to poverty they might be the ones labouring every hour God sent at this very moment; enduring the insecurity and danger that went with being young and female in such a household. Instead they were stumbling down the bare wooden stairs in Mr Carter's wake and Eve couldn't let her fear show with Verity between them and her fragile young shoulders shaking so hard she was clearly on the verge of hysteria.

'Oh, Eve, thank God you came.' Verity launched herself at Eve once they reached the bottom of the cramped stairway and it opened into a grim little stairwell with gloomy corridors stretching four different ways. A storm of frightened tears threatened until Carter bowed as if Verity was a lot more grown up than she appeared right now and bade her a smooth, 'Good evening, Miss Revereux.'

'You're Eve's Mr Carter, aren't you? I remember you from the park.'

'Maybe I am then, but we really must get out of here

before midnight when everyone is obliged to take their masks off, you know? If we meet any servants on our way, we shall have to pretend to be a very scandalous trio indeed. You and your cousin are going to be my pretty ladybirds for the night. Do you think you can act such a wild part? I know it's a lot to ask after all you witnessed tonight, but I really don't want to be dragged back into that ballroom and made to unmask, do you?'

'No,' Verity said with such a fervent shake of her head Eve wondered once again exactly what she *had* seen tonight.

'Very well, you only need endure this pretence for a few more minutes and then we'll have you out of here and back at Farenze House as if you were fast asleep all the time,' he said with a grin Eve caught herself being fiercely jealous of.

She wondered at herself again when he draped an arm round each of their shoulders and hugged her so close every inch of her skin felt man-warmed and prickly and responsive to him and him alone. Heaven forbid Verity felt even a hint of the sizzling excitement that was running through her like wildfire. At least that notion sobered her sharply enough to seem cool when he looked down at her with one raised eyebrow, as if to say, *Needs must when the devil drives, so don't blame me.*

'Is my scar visible?' he asked prosaically and she gave an almost wifely sigh and raised both her own brows at his unexpected vanity. 'I don't want us to stand out in any way but the obvious,' he whispered as if he had read her mind and couldn't believe she thought him so shallow.

'Set me free,' she demanded and reached up to ruffle his unruly hair until it curled as far as Mr Carter had left her length enough to work with. As she pushed and pulled it to hide the mark of his ordeal at Waterloo her hand shook as the reality of how close he'd come to death hit home and made her eyes water at the thought of never being able to know him at all. Reminding herself she couldn't afford to fall in love with this mystery of a man, she stood back and eyed her handiwork critically. His hair had felt as intriguing as she thought it might the first night they met. Soft and at the same time full of life and she still wasn't quite sure if it was more gold or brown in the dim light, any more than his eyes could decide between the same colours as they watched her with a question in them that had nothing to do with how unmemorable she had managed to make him.

'That's better,' Verity said in a whisper that barely wobbled at all, so at least she was beginning to recover some of her usual spirit.

'And don't push it out of your eyes when you're not thinking and ruin my handiwork, will you?' Eve chided him. And how had she let herself notice that he did exactly that when he was distracted? They had not met enough times for her to need two hands to count them on and she was picking up on his habits as if he was her lifetime study. This silliness really would have to stop. 'And you had best lean some of your weight on me and do your best not to limp as well,' she added briskly.

'I suppose I must,' he said ruefully. 'Now if you will both loosen your laces and ruffle your own hair and try to look a lot more undone than you are right now, ladies,

I think we will be able to get on with this private masquerade of ours *and* have you both safely back home before the clocks strike midnight.'

Two hours could drag by on broken wheels or be so full of incidents it was almost impossible to believe so little time had passed since she set out, Eve mused. Verity even seemed to be enjoying the joke now. She unbuttoned her velvet jacket and undid the laces of her shirt so it would gape open to prove she really wasn't the uninformed youth her breeches argued. If this charade reignited her step-cousin's adventurous nature, Eve supposed she had to be glad, even if she didn't want Verity thinking such folly should ever be repeated. She would just have to find a way to calm her down when they got home, lest Verity wake half the household with overwrought high spirits. Eve felt cool air on the exposed upper slopes of her own bosom as she did as Carter asked as well. Very adult emotions shivered through her when his gaze followed the soft stuff of her borrowed gown as it fell open, then he lingered hungrily on the last remaining slice of ribbon that left her shift straining on the edge of decency between her breasts, as if he badly wanted to undo it and explore even more of her than he already had.

'That will have to do,' she told him severely, because she badly wanted him to as well and that was wrong in so many ways she could hardly count them.

'At least that much temptation should distract any healthy males we happen to meet on our travels,' he said as if that was all that mattered, and he was right, wasn't he?

Luckily most of the servants were still upstairs waiting on the company and the kitchen maids too busy in the scullery to see aught but steam and a mountain of dirty dishes and pots and pans. Which only left a chef sitting at the smaller table in the kitchen and trying not to fall asleep in the remnants of one of his own creations and a pastry cook to be shocked by the quality sneaking out through their domain with a few flustered giggles from the so-called ladies and a bad-dog smirk from a happy-looking gentleman who was stealing away from this wild party with a woman under each arm.

'Lucky dog,' the chef said with a regretful sigh and a jaded look at the bridling cook, as if to say some men had all the luck tonight and he wasn't one of them.

'Devils the lot of them and just look at that brazen hussy flaunting her legs and everything else she has like some doxy in the Haymarket,' the cook said in disgust. 'All of them no better than they should be and yet they calls themselves quality, disgusting is what I say they are.'

Verity giggled delightedly and Eve gave Carter an angry nudge to let him know he would have to put more of his weight on her shoulders if he was to pass as a run-of-the-mill rake and not a limping one. 'La, but he's even more drunk than I thought he was,' she hissed at Verity in a stage whisper, hoping any sign of a stagger in his step would seem to be from too much alcohol and not war.

'Let's hurry up then, before he finds another bottle and climbs into it for the night,' her devious little relative by marriage replied in the affected tones of a lady intent on being very unladylike indeed and daring the world to stop her.

Eve managed a false titter and even wiggled her hips so provocatively the chef ought to remember her walk and not Carter's, if anyone asked him to describe such a disgraceful trio, should the Louburn brothers escape and start baying for Carter's blood.

'You win,' he murmured so softly only she could hear him and he finally let some of his weight fall on her shoulder until they were safely across the vast kitchen and out of the open door, into the dark coldness of the night and up stone steps into the street that served the back of these tall town houses.

'Hush,' he ordered them both when Verity would have said something gleeful about their lucky escape and danced about in triumph, 'you're not safe home yet. Take off that mask now and button yourself up again before you catch your death, there's a good girl.'

Eve could sense Verity's mouth firming sulkily at being called a good girl after such a grown-up adventure, but if anyone deserved to be treated like a naughty schoolgirl tonight it was she. 'Or shall we call you a crass idiot for what you did tonight if you prefer not to be called so?' she whispered severely in Verity's ear.

'I'm so sorry, Eve, really I am,' the contrary, exasperating and disarming girl said humbly.

'There will be plenty of time for all that later,' Carter told them both impatiently.

Eve felt his fingers searching for the strings of her mask because she hadn't hurried to do as she was bid fast enough. *This has to stop*, she told herself, as her breath caught at the heady sensation of his fingers winnowing through her disordered curls. A foolish little shiver slid down her neck when he brushed against her vulnerable-feeling nape and the whole of her body wanted to respond to him as if he was her lover now. A longing she had never wanted to feel until she met him shook her right down to her toes. She told herself it was a sigh of relief that she let out when he found the strings of her mask, undid it and put the silly, frivolous thing in his pocket before she could grab it as a keepsake of a night she ought to want to start forgetting even before it was properly over.

'That's better, this time we are going to be a respectable, middling sort of couple with a very sulky young gentleman in our charge. As long as you keep that cap on and don't speak above a whisper we may get away with it in the dark, Miss Verity,' he said softly as he pushed the odd stray wisp of golden hair under the velvet jockey cap Verity had at least had enough sense to wear when she set out on this shocking scrape tonight.

Carter offered Eve his arm as if they were about to take a stroll in the park and what could she do but take it like the obedient wife she was supposed to be right now? Control of their latest misadventure had slipped inexorably from her fingers the moment they got into Warlington House and she supposed he had got them this far without disaster, so she might as well go along with officer Carter for a little longer. They crept round the most shadowy edge of the square and were soon out of it and back in the wider world again. Eve allowed herself a moment to imagine how it would feel to be creeping through the darkness without him and terror whispered in her ear. Luckily he was here, though, and she could wait to review imagined terrors when they were safely at home and in their beds. Right now it was still quite early by *ton* standards, so now and again a fashionable town carriage would rattle past on the way to a different party or to clubs and less public assignations. It wasn't as busy as it would be in the spring, but Mayfair was still lively on a chilly October night.

Eve was glad she could walk in Carter's shadow as they passed tall town houses where entertainments were being held tonight, or a smart coach swept past on the way to somewhere else. How could she feel so safe and oddly interested in how the night felt when she wasn't part of that busy round of doing nothing much in grand style? Because Carter was here, she let herself know. His muscular arm was warm under her fingers and his body so close it felt as though he was her security and such a sure strength—why would she let him go at the end of this reckless adventure? *You know why*, common sense and her mother's blasted reputation whispered in her ear and how ardently she wished they would go away right now.

'Is there some way you can get back inside without being found out?' Carter murmured when they finally reached Farenze House and all seemed serene, so at least neither she nor Verity had been missed.

'Yes,' Eve whispered. 'Goodnight and thank you, Mr Carter.'

'Hasn't he got a given name?' Verity asked a bit too loudly.

'Hush, Verity, and don't be nosy. Remember what you did tonight before you say another word to those of us who were forced to lie and risk far too much to rescue you from your stupidity.'

'I was going to say then we are deeply in your debt, whoever you are, sir,' Verity managed with almost grown-up dignity.

'Please don't mention it and I mean that in every sense, by the way. It will be best if we pretend we can't really remember one another if we ever happen to meet again, Miss Revereux. Now I must bid you both goodnight and try to smuggle myself back into Derneley House unseen, before Mr Carter scandalises the whole neighbourhood by being caught out here with two young ladies so late at night.'

A brief touch of Eve's hand as if he was bidding goodnight to a nodding acquaintance and Mr Carter strode off into the darkness as if they had imagined him. He might be gone from their sight, but Eve knew somehow that he stopped to watch them creep inside the house and make sure they were finally safe. He was simply that sort of man, she admitted to herself as she rushed Verity up the stairs so she could light a candle and show it at the window just long enough for him to know they were safe home and had not been caught.

'Go to bed, Verity, you will answer to me in the morning and you're lucky I didn't call Papa and Chloe back from their dinner with the Laughraines. I only decided not to do so because I won't have Chloe upset by your idiocy at the moment and risk harming the baby.'

'I thought you weren't going to ring a peal over my head until tomorrow,' Verity said sulkily.

'Then you'd best hurry to get into bed before I change my mind, and before you do kindly hide that disgraceful disguise you stole before Bran finds it and raises the roof,' Eve ordered wearily, sinking down on to her own feather bed and wondering if she had it in her to undress, let alone brush her curls into good order, then hide the best gown she must somehow get back to the head housemaid's room in good order tomorrow, before the girl realised her box had been tampered with and it was gone.

'He is very handsome,' Verity said with a sneaky look, as she pulled off her cap and let her golden mane tumble down over her shoulders. Then she even had the cheek to sit and brush it with Eve's hairbrush as if this was a night much like any other. 'Lend me a nightdress and I will go,' she responded to Eve's unspoken demand to be left in peace.

'Why should I?' Eve demanded grumpily. It seemed unfair that Verity had come out of tonight's brouhaha looking like a part-time angel and Eve's whole life felt as if it had been turned upside down and she couldn't seem to get it right again.

'Because I don't want to be caught wandering the corridors at night in these very comfortable breeches and a gentleman's shirt. I won't go away and let you dream of Mr Carter until you let me change into something less improper.'

'You should have thought of that before you stole those breeches from the attic and remember you're the one with cause to feel ashamed of herself tonight and not me, Verity Revereux.'

'True, but I didn't drag the most intriguing stranger I ever met into the midst of a potential scandal, then watch him deal with it as if I couldn't take my eyes off him either.'

'At least I didn't risk my reputation for the sake of an idiot.'

'Rufus is very silly, isn't he?' Verity said with a heavy sigh that admitted she was shocked and disappointed by her evening.

'Yes, and his looks are only on the outside, Verity, inside he is no better than his brothers.'

'He didn't even bother to wait for me. I went to so much trouble to get into that horrid house undetected, but he was dancing with a woman old enough to be his mother when I got there. Then he kissed her and they disappeared for ages and ages,' Verity said tragically, then shrugged and went back to plundering Eve's drawers until she found a nightdress warm enough to roam draughty corridors and not catch cold. 'I realised Rufus is fickle as the wind and dim as a rushlight tonight,' she added mournfully. 'And he isn't even very nice either; I really can't imagine what I ever saw in him now.'

'Good, so now you know that very handsome males are often a little stupid and spoilt with it—I suppose they have no need to try very hard.'

'Your Mr Carter isn't an idiot.'

'Nor is he my Mr Carter; only imagine the fuss if he was,' Eve managed to joke weakly.

'I suppose there would be a whisper or two, since he

obviously hasn't got much money, but the tabbies would soon find something else to talk about if you two were boringly happy with each other and your father approved,' Verity said as she striped off her breeches and hastily pulled Eve's nightdress over her head.

'Do you really think so?' Eve said. The idea of being Carter's lady tugged at her heart and reminded her how wondrous it felt to be kissed by a man who really knew what he was doing. No, it was every bit as impossible now as it was the night she first met him and every night since. 'Papa would never allow it.'

'Maybe I was a fool tonight, but my parents' story tells me that it's folly to turn away from true love whenever it comes along. I had to find out if Rufus was only perfect on the outside, Eve. You know better than anyone that you can't judge a person by the family they were born into, although in his case I suppose I should have done.'

'It's as well you don't love him then, isn't it? Now go away, Verity. You're the last person who should preach to me about love after what you got up to tonight. Thank your guardian angel that we found you before the whole world knew you were abroad in breeches and then go to bed.'

'You went straight to Mr Carter as soon as you found out I was gone though, didn't you?' Verity said and left Eve sitting staring at a closed door and wondering if such chaste solitude was what she truly wanted.

Of course it was, she informed her inner doubter bracingly. She had not met the right man yet and sooner or later *he* would turn up to make perfect sense of her life. All she had to do was wait and refuse to be side-tracked by contradictory, gruff and unsuitable heroes like Mr Carter and her life would be as close to perfect as anyone's could be in this faulty world.

Chapter Eight

It took Colm another week to pack up the Derneley Library. With a sigh of relief he bade farewell to the few staff still working at Derneley House and limped out into a foggy autumn morning. It was time to bid farewell to Mr Carter and he must learn to be a Hancourt again. Someone had to stop the Hancourt estates slipping into chaos and it might as well be him. It would give him something to do, but as Uncle Horace and Aunt Barbara were childless he'd best not get too comfortable. Lord Maurice Hancourt would dismiss his nephew the day he inherited the dukedom, so somehow Colm would have to save enough from his salary to be able to offer his sister a home if she needed one, so he hoped the current Duke would live a long and happy life.

Nell wouldn't give up her post simply because he wanted her to, so perhaps he could suggest Uncle Horace needed her to stop his houses becoming dusty old book warehouses, because Aunt Barbara wasn't going to worry about housekeeping when she had so much nature left to paint. Nell couldn't claim she wasn't needed then, but he could almost hear her argue she was needed where she was now, thank you very much. He smiled ruefully at the notion his sister was quite happy in her current post as governess to four orphaned girls and virtual mistress of Berry Brampton House. If the Earl of Barberry ever set foot in the place, a single lady with any regard for her reputation would have to leave it though; so Colm had best start saving, even if Barberry had sworn never to visit the estate his family begrudged him so deeply.

Ten minutes later Colm limped up the steps of Linaire House, still mulling over his schemes to get his sister away from her current employment. The butler looked outraged when he limped up the front steps and coldly informed him servants used the rear entrance.

'I am expected. Mr Hancourt,' he informed the man with the cold authority he'd used on soldiers who thought him too young to be obeyed, but this man was made of sterner stuff.

'So you say,' the butler said with a regal sniff and a contemptuous look at Colm's shabby garb and the battered portmanteau he was carrying himself.

'My uncle is eager to have me supervise the unpacking and arranging of the Derneley Library. I wouldn't like to be the one who delayed that project,' he said and made as if to leave, even if he had no idea where he would go.

'His Grace did say he was expecting a member of

the family,' the man said dubiously, but at least Colm was allowed inside so his tall story could be examined.

Hearing voices, the Duke of Linaire emerged from his study. A smile lit his rather homely face and he hurried forward to make Colm feel more welcome here than he ever was as a child. 'Colm, my boy, how glad I am to see you at last. D'you know the bookbinder says he can't find that exact shade of Moroccan leather to replace the damaged covers?' the Duke of Linaire asked as if his nephew was so much a part of his life he didn't need to explain him to his staff.

'Let the boy settle in before you put him to work again, Horry.' Aunt Barbara emerged from the study behind him and greeted Colm with a kiss and a quick hug that made him blink and return it with a feeling he wasn't as alone as he'd thought. 'Not that I'm not delighted to see you as well, dear. Your uncle has been longing for a sympathetic ear to pour his tale of woe into all morning and I would dearly like to get some of this mist and murk in my sketchbook before the sun breaks through. So you are doubly welcome.'

Colm cast a look at the dreary townscape outside and raised an eyebrow at the unconventional Duchess to say there was little chance of that happening quickly.

'It seems unlikely now, but I don't have much interest in old books at the best of times and I'd forgotten how unreal London looks in the fog,' she admitted with a longing glance out of the window. Colm wondered once again how two people with such different interests could be so devoted to one another. 'That's enough of our woes, have you breakfasted, my boy?' she added, although it was nearly noon.

'Some time ago, Auntie dear,' he told her with a grin and she just smiled placidly and told him not to be disrespectful to his poor old aunt. Since his late Uncle Augustus once had him beaten for just speaking in his presence, this was a vast improvement on his last stay at Linaire House already.

'Then go on up and settle yourself in before your uncle puts you to work. He forgets how ill you were this summer and will answer to me and your sister Nell if he wears you out with his wrong shades of leather and the best way to arrange his musty old books. Then there's whatever real business you must sort out for us.'

'This is real business,' Uncle Horace protested, but shot Colm a concerned look and told him unpacking the undamaged books could wait until tomorrow.

Not quite sure he wanted a day of leisure when his thoughts were still so full of Winterleys, Colm went upstairs to unpack his bag before his uncle's valet could do it for him, then went downstairs again to find his uncle and see if he had forgotten he had given him the day off yet.

'Glad you're here at last, m'boy,' the Duke of Linaire muttered vaguely.

'It's good to be back. Is all well with the books I sent on?'

'Yes, yes, you did a good job. High time someone rescued that fine collection from Derneley, but I should never have sent you there. Barbara says I should be ashamed of myself for making you keep that disguise you've worn for so long.'

'Lord Derneley didn't look directly at me once he realised I was wounded at Waterloo and have the scars to prove it. I doubt he'd recognise Carter as your nephew if we happen to meet by chance.'

'Hah! Man's a buffoon; doesn't deserve what you and the other brave lads did to keep him safe in his bed. Not that it will be his bed for much longer if the rumours are true.'

Colm doubted it was officially his right now, but he didn't want to think about that selfish peer or his empty-headed lady any more. 'He certainly doesn't know how to treat fine books. Some are nearly beyond repair.'

His Grace shook his greying head and looked pained. 'I read your lists as they came in and warned the bookbinders what to expect. Disgraceful, that's what it is and I had a good mind to drop my price to compensate for all the work that will have to be done in order to get them back to scratch.'

'I suspect your money is already spent.'

'Aye, and I shook hands on the deal; Barbara says she's coming with me if I negotiate for more than a child's primer from now on, but my word is my bond and I can't go back on it, can I?'

'No, even if your money goes the same way as the rest,' Colm replied and his uncle's one extravagance *was* dwarfed by Derneley's complete set.

'At least those fine volumes are safe now and I can't wait to see them set out in good order in their new home.

Barbara says I must wait for the plasterers and carpenters to finish before I ship any back to Linaire, though.'

When someone managed to distract the Duchess from her paints for the odd hour she was one of the most rational women Colm had come across. He didn't blame her for refusing to give up the joy and purpose of her life to run the vast houses her husband had inherited last year. If he had a wife himself, he wouldn't want her to give up her interests to devote herself to him either. Not that he could afford one, but his aunt and uncle's marriage was bigger than the usual society match and no wonder they sacrificed so much to make it happen. How wrong to visualise the wife he couldn't have as dark haired and possessed of a pair of fine green-blue eyes and the warmly irresistible smile Miss Winterley saved for best. She wouldn't have him if he had stayed the rich grandson of a duke instead of a barely solvent ex-army officer and it was high time he forgot her.

'Nearly forgot to give you this, Colm.' His uncle interrupted his thoughts, offering him a tightly sealed letter. 'Farenze's man brought it here with your real name on. Thought you wouldn't want it sent on to Derneley House.'

'No indeed, thank you,' he replied as he eyed the crisply folded letter with his lordship's seal stamped emphatically in the wax and wondered how he'd given himself away. Did he look like his father? Colm wondered, a little bit horrified by the idea and it was too long since he last saw him to know. The Derneleys hadn't seen through Mr Carter's plain old clothes to Lord Chris's son underneath so perhaps he didn't, but they would never truly look at a servant. A shrewd man like the Viscount might have seen Hancourt traits in him, but the idea felt disturbing.

'Do you mind if I read this right away, your Grace?'

'No more of that, lad. Be obliged if you'd call me Uncle Horace. When someone *your Graces* me, I still think they're talking to my father or Gus. Makes me shudder if you want the truth.'

'Me, too,' Colm admitted.

'Both tyrants, but they're dead now,' said the Sixth Duke with a furtive look round as if to make sure. 'Had the devil of a job persuading Barbara to marry me because of them and she's been the making of me. You should find yourself a fine girl with a mind of her own to make you happy after all you went through in Spain and Belgium.'

'I doubt if I could persuade her to see past my father's scandal and my empty pockets.'

'Nonsense, a lady of character will see what a fine fellow you are and never mind the rest.'

The only lady of character he wanted to know that dearly was uniquely designed not to be able to see past who he was, so Colm shook his head, then turned Lord Farenze's letter over as if that might tell him what the man had to say to Lord Chris's son without him having to open it. *Stay away from my daughter you lying rogue?* His heart sank at the idea she knew who he really was and still played the game of pretending he was Carter. Had she and Miss Revereux laughed together about his credulity after their misadventure? *Stop tor-*

turing yourself and read the confounded thing, his inner officer ordered impatiently.

'Go and read it before you wear it out, lad. Oh, and your Aunt Barbara has sent for a tailor; he's to wait on you today so he'll probably be here soon. Don't argue, my boy, Barb says she can't endure dining with a nephew dressed like a curate much more than a week. The man's to send his bill to me, so don't argue about that either. Consider it a uniform if you won't accept it as a gift to my nephew.'

'I had to pay for my uniform,' Colm objected half-heartedly.

'Then take a few decent clothes in the spirit we offer them,' his uncle said wearily. 'Dashed if I ever came across anyone as poker-backed as you are.

'Thank you then, it will be a relief not to worry about paying my tailor,' Colm said and wished it was really a joke as he wandered upstairs, past his bedchamber and the chance of meeting that tailor before he'd had chance to put Mr Hancourt back together, then up more stairs to the bare rooms where the last Duke grudgingly housed him and Nell until they were old enough for school.

It looked the same as ever; no need to make it bright and comfortable for children his uncle and aunt didn't have. Colm wondered fleetingly if he might be Duke of Linaire himself one day if Uncle Maurice's wife kept producing daughters. It wasn't a prospect he relished, even if he and Nell would have half a dozen old-fashioned homes to choose from. He liked the Duke and the Duchess and would rather have the modest house and a wife to make it a home he had dreamed of when

trying to sleep on a bare mountainside or as he and his
men were waiting for battle.

Colm went to the governess's desk and extracted a
penknife to slip under Lord Farenze's seal. He should
have known the man was too shrewd to take anyone at
face value, but what did the Viscount want? He'd best
read the letter instead of staring at it as if it might bite.
Addressed in a bold, impatient hand, it was a master-
piece of distant politeness. They had matters to discuss arising from certain documents delivered to Lord
Farenze. Since his lordship now knew who Colm was,
they probably did as well. Tempted to wait until he had
new clothes and looked a little more gentlemanly, Colm
limped up to his room and wrote out an offer to call on
his lordship tomorrow morning instead.

Chapter Nine

'Mr Carter, my lord,' the Viscount's stately butler announced Colm solemnly the next day.

'Come in, Carter, and bring burgundy, please, Oakham,' Lord Farenze said as if it was quite normal to offer his good wine to a humble clerk.

'Good morning, my lord,' Colm said quietly.

'Don't stand in the corner like a nervous sheepdog, man, take a seat,' his host ordered him impatiently.

'Thank you, my lord,' Colm said and did as he was bid.

'Should I feel rebuked by your faux humility?'

'Of course not, my lord. What right has Mr Carter to correct the manners of his elders and betters?'

'Oh, *touché*; you learnt more than you want to admit in your old employment.'

'Old employment, my lord? What work could a humble clerk do to teach him to be bold?'

'Recently healed scars and a halt in a man's step are all too common since Waterloo, so pretending the whole business was nothing to do with you attracts attention rather than deflecting it, Hancourt and you will have to resume your true identity under your uncle's roof, won't you?'

'Did my uncle give me away somehow?'

'No, your father did. You are the spit of him at the same age,' the Viscount said dourly, as if he was trying not to hold it against him.

'Barring the scars, I suppose?' Colm said, wondering how he felt about being so like his father and what conclusions this man had made about him on the strength of his outward appearance.

'Your hair is a shade darker and you're leaner and perhaps taller, but that could be due to you leading an active life before you were injured.'

'I wouldn't know whether I look like him or not; there are no portraits of my father left at Linaire House and I don't really remember what he looked like.'

That was the bare formalities out of the way, so Colm tensed, waiting for an order to stay away from the Winterleys from now on. God-send the man had not found out about Verity's misadventure or the roles he and Miss Winterley took in it on that night he was trying so hard not to remember.

'You should visit your late father's godmother,' Lord Farenze said. 'She owns a very fine portrait of him taken in his youth and it confirmed all my suspicions about you.'

'And now?' Colm challenged because he couldn't endure sitting here squirming while the man made up his mind whether to dislike him for being his father's son.

Then the ageing butler re-entered, followed by a footman with that wine and Colm had to be patient after all. He watched his glass being filled with rich wine he didn't intend to drink and bit back a sigh.

'That will be all, Oakham,' Lord Farenze said, 'close the door behind you.'

Ah, so they were about to stop dancing about, were they? Colm put his glass down virtually untouched and tried to look a lot more relaxed than he felt.

'I would rather you and my daughter had not met that night at Derneley's, or in the park the next morning, but what's done can't be undone.'

At least Miss Winterley's father didn't know about their disgraceful escapade in Cavendish Square. Colm blanked the thought of it from his mind so his lordship couldn't read it and listened for what came next.

'You have little to offer any woman, let alone my daughter, but you were alone with her for far too long before I turned up to make you respectable.'

'That's true,' Colm admitted carefully.

'Yet you stayed in that library although you knew you were the last man on earth she should be alone with like that.'

'Now there I must argue, my lord. Sir Steven Scrumble proved a worse rogue than me that night,' Colm said bitterly. Having to name that piece of filth as a brother in infamy made him feel as if he was indeed lying down with swine.

'You're splitting hairs, Hancourt. My daughter has fought against the blight of her mother's blown name all her life. If any gossip gets out about her being alone with you in a closed room at Derneley House that night, I'll rip you to shreds.'

'I have already promised to keep silent.'

Deeply offended by Lord Farenze's doubts, Colm wanted to spring to his feet and stalk out in a noble huff, but years of military discipline kept him sitting here and wasn't it true you should know your enemy? There was little doubt Lord Farenze considered him one of those since he refused to take Colm's word for the iron promise it truly was.

'I saw the way you looked at my daughter and you have wild blood in your veins, however hard you try to deny it. If you were still rich as Croesus, you'd have an uphill struggle persuading me to consent to a marriage between you and Eve. You would have to love each other to the edge of reason for me to even think about such a repellent idea. Imagining the public mockery and doubts such a marriage would arouse makes me shudder for my daughter and say that, no, even that would not be enough. Steer clear of her, Hancourt, maybe then I'll admit you're a better man than Lord Christopher Hancourt ever was.'

'I have met Miss Winterley only twice and you really think I see her as a fine opportunity to better myself? I don't recall offering her marriage on such a short acquaintance and you will just have to believe I have absolutely no intention of ever doing so in the future since you don't respect my word of honour.'

'You don't want to marry her?' his lordship asked, sounding as if he was genuinely surprised any young man in possession of his right senses wouldn't want to do so.

He was quite right, of course, but Colm had learnt the difference between wanting something and being able to have it at a very early age and he couldn't argue with the facts. Why would Miss Winterley love him anyway, even if he was fool enough to fall in love with her? He recalled for a dangerous moment how perfectly she had fitted into his arms and how ardently she responded to his kisses, but he was sitting across from her father, for goodness' sake. If the man could read his mind right now he'd challenge him to a duel, or horsewhip him out of the house.

'No, I don't and even if I did I have to admit that if my sister was being courted by a vagabond like me I'd move heaven and earth to stop him as well. I will do my best to avoid your daughter if we happen to meet by chance, Lord Farenze.'

'Oh, no, don't do that. She'd soon realise I've warned you off and insist on conversing with you as if you're the most interesting young man on earth every time you set eyes on each other from that moment on. Don't you know anything at all about contrary young ladies with too much spirit and stubbornness to meekly do as they're bid, Hancourt?'

'Not really, there are very few of them to be found on the average battlefield.'

'There were plenty in Brussels last spring.'

'Not when you had as much to do as we did and so little time to do it in, and certainly not if you are as poor and unconnected as Captain Carter.'

'You're not Captain Carter, though, are you?'

'No, but I'm not quite the Duke's nephew yet either.'

'You can't escape the bed you were born in,' Lord
Farenze said as if he was trying hard not to hold his
breeding against him, but still unconvinced he was any
better than his father at heart. He watched Colm with
his grey-green eyes suspicious and very guarded indeed
for a moment, then seemed to make up his mind to trust
him so far and not much further. 'My wife has invited
your uncle and aunt to Darkmere to view our collections and for her Grace to paint whatever she chooses,'
he admitted rather grimly. 'I couldn't rescind her invitation when I realised his Grace's nephew has been
included in my lady's hospitality, since your uncle and
aunt seem reluctant to part with you so soon after they
nearly lost you at Waterloo.'

'Oh,' Colm said, almost silenced by the novelty of actually being wanted by family for once in his life. This
certainly wasn't the moment to feel almost unmanned
by the idea and he scrambled round for an excuse to
stay away of his own accord, but his latest adversary
was too far ahead of him.

'As a public declaration of peace between Hancourts
and Winterleys it could hardly be bettered, so I expect
you to accept my wife's invitation to Darkmere, but
be very careful how you conduct yourself when you
get there.'

'Of course, Lord Farenze,' Colm said stiffly, thinking he would almost rather be back with his regiment
on a forced march.

'I am sorry to be so blunt. Eve's happiness and peace

of mind come first with me, but I am ashamed of offering hospitality with one hand and snatching it back with the other. If not for my daughter, I could like you very well and, according to a man who knows more about most people than they probably want him to, you're a brave man and a good officer.'

'I thank him for his good opinion,' Colm said, wishing he could go to Darkmere Castle as anyone but Colm Hancourt for a foolish moment.

'I'm glad we've had this talk. Now my wife can go on peace-making and you will have to endure the sharp edge of my daughter's tongue once she finds out how neatly you deceived her. I hope I can rely on you to infuriate her even more?'

'I think you can be quite certain of that, my lord,' Colm said glumly.

A week later Farenze House was closed up and the knocker had been taken off the door. Colm noted the blank unlived-in look of the place when his uncle's carriage swept past at the start of its own long journey and he rode behind as the Duke of Linaire's almost noble nephew on a horse Captain Carter could only dream of. Colm watched the ponderous coach navigate the busy streets, then gain the Great North Road with mixed feelings.

He was Colm Hancourt again for the first time in years, but he had little control over his destiny.

For the next few days he tried to forget their ultimate destination and enjoy the tour of the greatest houses and

collections in the land before they ended up at Darkmere
Castle. At first all he noted was mud and the biting cold,
then the quiet beauty of the late autumn landscape stole
his heart. He didn't suppose dire poverty felt better in
Britain than in the war-ravaged lands he'd quit with a
sigh of relief after the first, fragile peace was made and
Bonaparte went to Elba for a nice little holiday before
Waterloo. It wasn't much to boast about, but a British
pauper could aspire to more than he was born to and
stand some chance of achieving it.

This particular Briton had gone from fabulous fortune to nothing much at all, so he'd done it the other way
about, but he was privileged all the same. He was the
Duke of Linaire's nephew and dressed as a gentleman.
He had a good horse to ride, warm clothes to wear and
the luxury of sleeping in the best inns when they were
not staying in some of the finest houses in the land.
This was a chance to learn more of his own country
than a London childhood and eight years in the army
allowed until now.

He rode out on a crisp November morning a week
or so after leaving London as courier to his uncle and
aunt and wondered at the meandering route they only
seemed to decide a day at a time.

Wherever they were going he had settled into being
Mr Hancourt again, he reflected, as he got a lower bow
from the landlord of the Swan and Whistle than Mr
Carter would have done. Life was less dangerous than
it had been as a humble ensign, lieutenant, then captain
of the 95th Rifles. Colm once swore to manage without

a family who saw him as an embarrassment, but eight years of war had tempered him. He managed a self-deprecating grin at the thought of that angry resolution and hoped he was a better man than he was when he invented Mr Carter.

But for Miss Evelina Winterley he might even be content and it would be so much better if he could forget her until she was under his nose again, but somehow he couldn't. He had too much time riding ahead of the ducal carriage to think right now. While Miss Winterley should have vanished from his thoughts after her father's warnings it was impossible to forget a lady of character and grace to order. He caught himself smiling at thin air as if she was smiling right back. Just as well he was riding ahead of his uncle and aunt today and not by the side of the coach because this way neither of them could ask what he was grinning at.

He groaned quietly. This was nonsense, wasn't it? He had nothing; he wasn't quite nobody, but what sort of a gentleman lived off his wife's dowry and his uncle's charity? Not his sort, he told himself against the wild thunder in his blood that turned hot and primitive at the thought of having Miss Winterley as his wife. Her father was right and even if she wanted him right back that would fade when the sneers and whispers made her wonder what sort of a fool she was to wed the penniless son of her mother's last lover. He didn't love her; they had only met three times, for heaven's sake, so how could he? This stupid feeling that they were perfectly designed to fill the dark and empty places in each other's lives was a snare to avoid at all costs. Longing for a woman he couldn't have would drive him mad. He could stop himself wanting what he couldn't have if he worked hard enough. If he put his mind to it and perhaps wasted far too much of his meagre savings on a mistress, he could stop himself longing for impossible things and forget how urgently he wanted Miss Winterley that night at Warlington House and ever since.

Lord Farenze had made it very clear he was to arrive at Darkmere as the Duke's nephew and act as if he had no idea Miss Winterley ever met a librarian in a dusty book room, or a lowly clerk in the respectable confines of Green Park. Colm thought the man was worrying without cause. He hadn't seen any signs she even liked him in the lady's lovely turquoise gaze. The sneaky idea that if his lordship was worried about his daughter's feelings he must have good reason to be banished somehow. Yet he only had to think of their first meeting in Derneley's neglected library to become that tongue-tied idiot again and as for that confounded kiss...

Best not to think about that. What else was there? At that dangerous point the yard of tin sounded and he turned round to see a groom waving at him to stop.

'Colm, dear boy, we were supposed to turn off at the last crossroads, but you're so deep in thought we missed it. Anyone would think you were Wellington busy planning a battle,' Aunt Barbara said when he was in earshot.

He'd been thinking of Miss Winterley most of the morning then and wasn't it a good thing her father didn't know? 'I am a clod, your Grace,' he admitted with a sheepish grin. 'We could take the next turning and get back to Berry Brampton as best we can.'

'I'd sooner find somewhere Rooksby can sweep round so we can head back rather than risk being jammed down a narrow lane,' the Duke argued mildly.

'I should be paying attention,' Colm replied, feeling a fool for letting Miss Winterley get between him and his duty yet again.

Chapter Ten

'I quite thought the Duke of Linaire would be here by now,' Eve said to her father as they rode back to Darkmere in Verity's wake one day in early December. Chloe had given up riding until her latest baby was born now and Verity wanted to spend as much time as possible with her beloved aunt. Verity's life was changing and she was poised on the edge of womanhood. Eve shivered at the thought of that night at Warlington House and feelings she didn't want to think about ran through her as Carter's kiss felt so vivid on her lips it was almost as if she could still feel the warmth, strength and excitement of his touch with all her senses. Verity wasn't the only one confused by the war between mind and body as she tried to come to terms with a new reality.

'The Duke said they were to call on friends and fellow scholars on the way,' Lord Farenze replied, seeming oblivious to the battle she was waging against a heady memory. 'Are you bored with our company then, Eve?'

'No, but it will be awkward for you to meet Lord Christopher Hancourt's son under your own roof, won't it, Papa?'

'Maybe I already know him,' her father said with that closed expression she had seen a little too often lately.

'What's he like, then? Goodness knows what he's been up to so far, it seems a deep dark family secret.'

'Goodness might know, but you'll find out soon enough.'

'I wish you'd stop being so mysterious and tell me about him.'

He shot her a sceptical look, as if he'd like to get inside her head and have a good rummage about. 'I shall let you judge for yourself.'

'Why do you seem to dislike him already? You were living apart from my mother when Lord Christopher Hancourt became her lover.'

'Maybe I can't forgive his father for being such a confounded idiot then?'

'There are so many of them in the world according to you, Papa,' she said sweetly. 'What was so special about that one?'

'You think I'm a grumpy bear?' he said, neatly avoiding her question.

'I think you might be if you hadn't had the sense to marry Chloe. She usually laughs you out of your dark moods now and I'm very grateful for the improvement in your temper.'

'If my temper is so uncertain, I like to think my daughter is shrewd enough not to provoke it too often.'

Eve couldn't tell if he knew how disturbed she was

by Mr Carter. He should have faded more with every mile they travelled from London, but it was as if she had brought the fogs and gloom of the capital with her to Darkmere and him as well. Try as she might she couldn't get the wretched man out of her head.

'I did say it improved when you married Chloe, didn't I?' she teased lightly enough.

'So you did.'

'I shall risk it and ask again why you hated Lord Christopher for running off with my mother so much then.'

'It's complicated.'

'And you still think me too young to hear the full story, I suppose? To you I'll always be so; isn't it about time you realised that I need to know?'

'I'll discuss it with you after you wed and can understand the contrary passions of men and women better. The truth is I don't really want to think about your mother and her last lover at all. If Lord Christopher Hancourt ever thought she would bring him joy, I suppose I ought to pity him, though.'

'You acquit me of any stain from my mother's sins, but seem reluctant to give his son the same immunity, Papa.'

'I never said I was logical about it,' he said austerely.

Eve almost gave up on the subject to stop that bleak look silvering his eyes whenever he thought of his first unhappy marriage.

'Hancourt is more of a man than his father was, but I don't want him near you, love. I know how young men think and feel, I was one myself once upon a time.'

'I have no intention of encouraging Mr Hancourt as more than a simple acquaintance.'

'Far from simple, I suspect.'

Eve rolled her eyes at the grey sky over their heads and waited for something more worthy of her father as an excuse. 'I have no intention of falling in love with the man, or is he still a boy? He can't be very much older than I am.'

'You must judge for yourself, but I wish your stepmother had been a little less generous with her hospitality for once.'

'I'm hardly likely to fall in love with Lord Christopher Hancourt's son at first sight, so you're worrying about things that will never happen, which isn't like you.'

Her father still looked troubled as they rode along the Northern Avenue towards the more workaday side of Darkmere and the stables. 'I only ever want to do what's best for you, Eve,' he said at last.

'Anyone would think Mr Hancourt was going to ride up the drive on a knightly charger and carry me off across his saddle brow. How astonished the poor man would be if he knew we even considered him as an impassioned suitor for my hand. He's never even set eyes on me and I don't inspire that sort of romantic passion in a young man's heart, thank heavens.'

'Only because you have never met one who could wake the passion under the careful control you assume in public,' he said a little too seriously.

'Don't worry, Papa, I shall lock myself in the Sea

Tower and throw away the key if I begin to harbour even one warm feeling towards Mr Hancourt.'

And once the week or so the Duke and Duchess of Linaire were due to spend here was over, they need never see Mr Hancourt again, Eve decided as her personal groom hurried up to help her out of the saddle and Papa's attention swung back to his wife.

'I think it's sweet the way he fusses over her,' Verity objected when Eve whispered Chloe might not welcome her husband's anxiety until she had finished being unwell for the day when they met later. 'For years she had to be strong and self-sufficient for my sake and she deserves to be doted on by your papa.'

'She does and I'm so glad she dotes on him as well,' Eve said. 'Would I could love and be loved like that,' she added with a sigh. 'I'm not the sort to inspire such a grand passion in a man.'

'Nonsense,' Verity argued loyally. 'It just takes longer to win your good opinion, but I am shallow as yonder puddle and don't think true love is for me.'

Eve suspected Verity's infatuation with the youngest Louburn brother was responsible for that declaration and the accompanying grimace. It was good that Verity had realised how much danger she was in that night, but Eve didn't want her to wear a hair shirt.

'As if Chloe would let you be a careless butterfly even if you were that way inclined. Stop belittling yourself.'

'I've good reason to be wary after I nearly landed us both in the basket that last night in London. Now we're home and the world fits as it should again, I can't imagine why it mattered so much to see Rufus that night. It wasn't as if he was leaving for far-off lands or about to marry someone else; marriage is clearly the last thing on his mind.'

'I doubt he has very much on that at the best of times, but I expect your parents' love affair led you to expect something truer and deeper of first love than it can usually bear, Verity. I know your mother was barely half a year older than you are now when she fell fathoms deep in love with your father. You had a very different childhood, though, and Chloe always put your welfare first so you don't need to escape a lonely childhood and an uncaring father. Captain Revereux adores you and can never wait to get home and spend time with you. Find a decent man to fall in love with and remember your mother and father paid a terrible price for loving so passionately and so young. Even the thought of you suffering like they did makes me feel quite faint'

'Please don't turn into a hysterical female for my sake then, for I can't have been in love with Rufus Louburn to have forgotten him so quickly and I promise not to imagine myself in love with a handsome face ever again. So stop frowning and come and play with the babies; I swear little James has grown a new tooth since yesterday, so no wonder he was fretful last night.'

Would that logic and determination were strong enough to stop a woman falling in love, whispered the secret Eve, under her good sense and virtuous reputation. *Be quiet*, the everyday one ordered and hurried after Verity before the reckless creature could come up with a scathing reply.

* * *

'Fine sight, hey?' the Duke of Linaire asked as the coach stopped so they could wonder at the famous prospect of Darkmere Castle ahead.

'Indeed,' Colm replied, 'caught by the afternoon sun like that it makes me wish I could paint.'

'Would that I could as well,' the Duchess observed ruefully.

'Come now, m'dear, I never came across a lady who could hold a candle to you at watercolour.'

'I want to paint as I see, not as I can,' she objected, her gaze sharpening as the sun caressed the famous old fortress and the last rags of autumn leaves left on the noble trees planted to shelter it from the worst of the wind shone russet and gold.

'We've lost her again, m'boy,' the Duke said with an indulgent look at his wife. The Duchess collected her sketching equipment, then he jumped down to help her out of the coach. 'I shall tell Farenze you'll be along when the muse deserts you, my love,' he added as his wife's maid joined her with a resigned nod to say she would get her mistress up to the castle before daylight faded completely.

'Hmm? Yes, that would be as well,' the Duchess said absently, making rapid pencil strokes in her sketchbook to capture Darkmere with the low winter sun on it and an angry sea and sky behind.

'I hope Lady Farenze is as tolerant as she seemed in London,' the Duke said with a last proud look at his Duchess before they went on without her.

'Since she asked me to come here with you, she must be,' Colm said ruefully.

'Nonsense, lad, you have to meet them sooner or later. I suppose we'll soon find out if her ladyship's forbearance extends to my bookishness and your aunt's painting. We rely on you to do the polite, my boy; you do it so much better than we ever could.'

'Then we had best not unpack too hastily.'

'Don't be such a defeatist, lad; you and Farenze have more in common than either of you realise.'

His daughter for one, Colm thought gloomily and doubted Miss Winterley would ever be a bond between them.

Lord and Lady Farenze welcomed the two guests who turned up without a blink. The Viscount even seemed mildly amused that the Duchess of Linaire had absented herself before she could even arrive and Lady Chloe was too good humoured to take offence where none was intended.

'I have learned to love this wild and glorious place and often wish I could paint it myself,' she told them when they turned up at her door a duchess short. 'I lack both skill and talent with watercolour myself and am in awe of those with both. I should love to see your wife at work, your Grace, and promise not to be offended if she would rather not have a spectator. A true artist must be respected.'

'I am sure my wife will be delighted,' the Duke said and exchanged a wry glance with Colm at the thought of Barbara's contempt for would-be artists who only wanted to talk of their own efforts. *Polite dribbles of paint on expensive paper*, the Duchess dismissed the correct and soulless watercolours that usually caused a young lady to be thought accomplished.

'I don't suppose she will, but if I promise not to make silly observations and sit still, maybe she will rescue me from being kept indoors and coddled half to death,' Lady Farenze said with a militant look for her husband.

'You may have to clean brushes, sharpen pencils and act artist's assistant, Lady Farenze,' Colm warned, as he concluded rumour was right and the lady must be with child again. 'My aunt never intends to be a tyrant, but forgets everything but the next mix of colour and stroke of her brush once she is at work.'

Chapter Eleven

A whisper of movement on the edge of his senses and Colm saw Miss Winterley pause in the doorway of what looked like a family sitting room to glare at him. For a moment he thought she was going to rip up at him for letting her believe Mr Carter was a real man. He was a real man, Colm decided, in a hot daze at the sight of her so passionately angry he wondered candles didn't light spontaneously in their sconces all around her. Very real, he discovered, as all the enchantment he'd been trying to argue himself out of for so many miles flooded back. He wanted to step forward and greet her very personally, ask if she'd thought of him as constantly as he did about her and please excuse all his deceptions. They were not alone, though, and she didn't look in any mood to listen even if they were.

'Good day, your Grace, welcome to Darkmere,' she said with genuine warmth. She let it drain away when she turned her unique blue-green eyes on Colm. 'I suppose you must be Mr Hancourt. How do you do, sir?'

she said, so icily indifferent that the hand he hadn't even known he was holding out to her fell to his side.

This was the guarded and coldly aloof young woman he had spied from a distance that first night at Derneley House and he wondered if he would ever crack the ice he could almost see forming in the air between them again. Unlikely—she didn't hate him that night and she certainly looked as if she did now. She might sound cold and look it, but the fury in her eyes was hot and hasty—if there was a vat of boiling oil handy he'd be very warm indeed right now.

'Miss Winterley,' he returned with an elegant bow he didn't know he had in him. Something tender and tentative shrivelled under that Ice Queen stare and he was her parents' guest after all, even if her father had put stern limits on his hospitality back in London.

'I hope you had a comfortable journey, your Grace?' she asked his uncle with a sweet smile.

Colm had to admire her acting, even if the fierce guard she put on her fury made him wonder if he would ever know the real Eve Winterley. Why did he want to? She was Pamela's daughter and that divided them efficiently as a wall. He had to control his unfortunate sense of the ridiculous as he imagined Miss Winterley building it herself, setting stones and hurrying the masons along lest the barbarian invader come back. It wasn't funny being her enemy, though, and he saw hurt as well as fury in her turquoise gaze. Nothing could have sobered him more surely, not even Lord Farenze's hard gaze reminding him of that promise he had made to keep infuriating Miss Winterley. Right now she looked as if she would like him to leave before he'd hardly got over the threshold, so at least his host should be happy.

'Very comfortable, thank you, my dear,' his uncle said genially.

'I'm so glad the Duchess has found something worth painting already,' she went on greeting his uncle as if Colm didn't exist. 'After seeing some of her paintings when I was in London I thought she would enjoy our magnificent scenery.'

Colm wondered if he was invisible and decided Miss Winterley had even better ways of humbling an errant gentleman than that icy glare she treated him to just now. Why had he ever worried about her among the less scrupulous rakes of the *ton*? She could wither the worst of them with a pointed stare and that air of charmed ignorance that he even existed as she chatted about the landscape.

'You must be a fine diplomat to have persuaded my wife to let you see her work when you were last in London, Miss Winterley,' Uncle Horace said absently and Colm followed his gaze to the open door of the library and wondered if he might wander off to inspect it much as his wife vanished into the castle grounds. Serve the infernal woman right if she was left stranded by his bookish uncle before she could trot out her next platitude, he decided disagreeably.

'My father will tell you I rarely give up until I get what I want, your Grace, but I hope you will ignore him,' Miss Winterley joked with a fond look at her father and no sign that the Duke and Duchess were unwelcome, so it was probably only him she wished a hundred miles away.

'Can't do that, m'dear. Your father might not let me have the run of his library if I'm rude to him,' the Duke said with the wry smile that made him endearing, despite his limitations as a duke and guest who hated being lionised.

'So, how does it feel to be yourself again, Mr Hancourt?' Miss Winterley's coolly ironic murmur came as they followed her parents and guest of honour upstairs to the rooms the Duke and Duchess had been allotted, before Uncle Horace could plunge into my lord's library.

'Very odd, Miss Winterley,' he answered honestly. 'I was Carter so long I almost forgot about myself.'

Her sidelong glare told him he'd better not think that was an excuse for deceiving her. 'Why did you invent him in the first place?' she asked distantly.

'Grandsons of dukes don't serve in the 95th Rifles, Miss Winterley. I would have been out of place.'

'And the scandal would follow you?' she challenged as if he was a coward to hide behind that alias so long.

'Yes, of course. You know as well as I do that it goes everywhere with me,' he said bleakly.

'Which is why you clung to Mr Carter after the war was over and he could be safely pensioned off, I suppose?'

She sounded so indifferent they might have been discussing a stranger. Colm hoped the Viscount was listening and approving of the void that now gaped between his least wanted guest and the daughter of the house. Or did he know how much of a challenge that icy façade of hers was to a red-blooded male? Colm was torn between a longing to drag her into the nearest empty room and kiss her until she forgot all about Carter and his sins and everything else and this thorn in his pride that argued he should limp back downstairs and ride away from a place where a man of his birth would never be truly welcome.

'Not entirely. My uncle wanted me to bring his new purchases safe back from Derneley House and I could hardly go there as my true self, could I?'

'I doubt it would have been very comfortable, considering who you really are, but Lord Derneley is hardly in a position to argue with your uncle, is he?'

It would have been damned *un*comfortable to live under that particular roof as himself, Colm reflected, but he couldn't argue with the daughter of the house when he was only supposed to have met her minutes ago. So he gritted his teeth and supposed it was another way for her to punish him for being who he was.

'The view from here is reckoned to be one of the finest in the Borders,' she pointed out helpfully as he paused on the half-landing to rest his knee before limping up the rest. She knew he was struggling and had given him a chance to pause even though she still looked furious with him. It seemed that Miss Winterley was an enemy in a million and how he wanted to be disarmed by her, but he didn't think she would accept if he threw his rifle at her feet and her father might even shoot him with it.

'Don't pity me, Miss Winterley,' he made himself say brusquely instead.

'I don't,' she said with her chin raised haughtily and her eyes on the admittedly wonderful view up the Darke Valley from the wide range of leaded windows.

Uncle Horace was being gently but firmly shepherded up the next half of the wide staircase and into a fine suite of rooms allocated to the ducal couple by his hostess. Colm hoped he could retreat to his own room soon and lick his wounds, then he might be able to reassemble the Duke of Linaire's nephew in good time for dinner. Even furious with him and chilly as a Northumbrian snow storm, Miss Winterley made him feel as if she showed up in full vivid colour and her father's castle and all its inhabitants were somehow at a distance from them both. Which would never do, he reminded himself, and tried to pay more attention to his host and hostess as they caught up with them.

'Most comfortable,' the Duke said, looking a little awed by the elegant splendour made ready for him, as if someone might denounce him as a fraud at any moment and send him to an attic nobody else was using. 'I do hope Colm isn't too far away, my lady? My wife thinks the lad's leg bothers him more than he will admit, so we'd rather not have him run up and down the stairs of one of those fine towers of yours, Farenze, if you don't mind? I dare say there's enough room in this splendid suite to lodge him in here as well if you're cramped for space.'

For a moment Lady Farenze looked startled at the idea she might not have enough room here to barrack an army. 'You are our honoured guests, your Grace. Mr Hancourt has been allotted the Silver Room just along the corridor,' she said with the poise of a natural hostess and years as housekeeper in a noble household.

'I am grateful for it, my lady,' Colm said sincerely and caught a sharp glance from his host, as if his words had an edge he didn't intend.

He silently cursed his father for running off with another man's wife—whatever the state of their marriage at the time—and putting this perpetual barrier between him and the Winterley family. It looked as high as the castle walls at the moment and he felt too weary and battered to try to scale it again right now.

'Mr Hancourt is such a dashing gentleman,' Eve's friend Alice Clempson remarked after dinner the following evening.

'He is well enough, I suppose,' Eve said warily.

She hadn't forgiven him for deceiving her so completely yet and their neighbours were finding her relations with Lord Christopher Hancourt's son so fascinating she could scream. Still, she must try and forget about him. As the granddaughter of an iron founder, Alice wasn't considered good *ton* by some of those neighbours. Eve wondered if it might be a good idea to borrow the air of weary sophistication Alice assumed as a defence against their critical gaze right now. Then they could both sit here and ignore the stares of the curious together, as if they had no idea they were being watched.

'If his father was even half as handsome and romantic looking as the son is I can't blame your mama for finding him so irresistible,' Alice said with what sounded suspiciously like a besotted sigh.

'You mustn't say such things to me, Allie,' Eve was shocked into saying.

'Miss Mendaville-Rouste is making enough noise to drown a cathedral choir. Someone should tell her mother the girl can't play two right notes in succession.'

'Well, you still can't say them, even if nobody else can hear you for that infernal thundering on Chloe's poor pianoforte. I hope we don't have to have it restrung or whatever it is they do to pianos.'

'You really aren't musical, are you, Eve, dear?'

'No, but neither is Miss Mendaville-Rouste.'

At least they were talking about the wretched girl now and not Mr Hancourt, Eve thought with a sigh that was lost under the racket the determined pianist was making. How could her usually clever and tactful friend say such things about a man Eve was doing her best to take no notice of? She managed to ignore him for most of the day without actually being rude and came down tonight determined to show the world she was *not* like her dam. It was easy to resist being charmed by Lord Chris's son *and* to seem deaf to the gossip his presence was stirring up in the area. She did very well throughout dinner and tea in the drawing room afterwards, despite one or two impudent comments from the sillier young ladies and some who were old enough to know better.

'*All this must be such a strain for you, dear Miss Winterley...*'

'*What a true gentleman your dear papa is to make*

*such a public display of peace between your family and
Mr Hancourt's after what happened, my dear.'*

Worst of all was: *'I think it's such a very romantic
tale; those two headlong lovers galloping off into the
night to meet their deaths in eternal togetherness.'* This
from one poetically inclined young woman Eve was
tempted to slap. She managed a sickly smile instead and
handed the silly creature a second cup of tea, whether
she wanted one or not. A hasty visit to the ladies' withdrawing room in a little while would serve the senti-
mental idiot right and might teach her to think twice
before she spouted such nonsense next time.

'We could still be overheard,' she cautioned under
cover of the Haydn sonata Miss Mendaville-Rouste had
gone on mangling even now the gentlemen were back
in the room.

'I doubt anyone can hear themselves think with that
row going on, let alone listen to us. Nobody can stop
the silly girl when she's got the bit between her teeth,'
Alice said with a glare at the pianoforte where the well-
bred and talentless Miss Mendaville-Rouste was thundering on with steely determination.

Eve shot a furtive glance at Colm Hancourt and wondered how long she could ignore his manly presence
without offending the Duke and Duchess. One thing
was certain: she could never watch him as openly as
Alice was when Eve gave her a disapproving glare.

'He has a limp,' she pointed out half-heartedly.

As if that would blind any rational female to his
hawkishly masculine features, unruly tawny hair and
supple height. As for his gold-on-brown velvet eyes...

She shivered and caught herself on a reminiscent sigh. No, meeting his wary gaze full on was not to be thought of right now. Mr Hancourt could lure her into a world Eve Winterley couldn't afford to explore and as for a repeat of that kiss…it wasn't delight she felt as she recalled the warm shivers running all over her sensitised skin that night when he kissed her as if he meant it and looked at her afterwards with a brief, intimate smile in his eyes before glaring at the Louburn brothers as if he'd like to run them through for just looking at her the wrong way. She only shivered now because she was afraid she was more like her mother than she wanted to be, of course.

'And who knows what wounds Mr Hancourt might have that we cannot see,' she added almost to herself. Was she trying to convince herself or Alice that she had better taste than to admire or even—heaven forbid— lust after the son of her mother's last lover? And this Hancourt male was a proven liar as well.

'Whatever they might be, that slight halt in his step doesn't trouble me. It makes him look dashing and then there's that scar, that turns him from the usual sort of fit and healthy gentleman into something of a pirate, don't you think?' Alice went on blithely. 'A very handsome and well-behaved pirate, of course.'

Eve only just stopped herself glaring at her friend because she could enjoy the luxury of eyeing Mr Hancourt without a flurry of excited comments from her fellow guests sweeping round the room like an autumn gale. Alice could size up the lying toad as a potential husband and decide she liked him well enough and never mind his scars, his limp or his lack of a fortune, and his imitation of an almost humble clerk Alice didn't even know about. It was true, though; Alice and Mr Hancourt might suit each other very well. Oh, dear, she could have eaten too much of the fish course at dinner because there was that sharp sick feeling deep inside her again that must not be because her friend and the Duke of Linaire's deceitful nephew could have been made for one another.

'I doubt he'd enjoy being likened to one of those, however civilised,' she said tightly.

If Alice did decide he would make her a suitably gentlemanly husband and Mr Hancourt agreed, Eve sincerely hoped they would move a long way from here, so she wouldn't have to watch them be deliriously happy together. She felt horribly unworthy of her clever, generous friend as she struggled with a sneaky idea Mr Hancourt could have changed her own life in so many ways, if he wasn't Lord Chris's son. And a liar and deceiver, and a cold fish who walked away from a woman after kissing her until she didn't know if it was night or day. Give her a few more minutes and she was sure she would be able to produce a dozen more reasons why he was as far from her ideal lover as it was possible for a man to be. And if he had wanted to be that lover he would have come to her after that kiss and admitted who he was, wouldn't he? The fact he had not proved he was an adventurer and a liar and had probably left a trail of broken-hearted women stretching all the way back to Portugal behind him when he moved through Europe on the Duke of Wellington's coat-tails.

'It seems to me you aristocrats suffer from the circumstances of your birth every bit as much as we parvenus at times,' Alice said with more insight into Eve's contrary feelings in her steady blue eyes than Eve wanted to see. 'Mr Hancourt is as hemmed in by who his father was as Papa is by his father being the village blacksmith before he made his fortune as an iron master. Your polite world isn't so different from the one we humbler beings have to find a way through, is it?'

'No, not that different at all,' Eve admitted and ordered herself not to watch Mr Hancourt pretend he was deaf as he sat beside the Duke and Duchess of Linaire. He was dressed in immaculate evening garb and looked very worthy of the honour as all three of them took pride of place as guests of honour. Which only proved how deceptive appearances could be.

'Mama and Papa would like me to marry a true gentleman. Mr Hancourt would fill that bill nicely, don't you think?' Alice speculated with a nod at the dratted man as if Eve might not have noticed him sitting there bold as brass and twice as handsome.

'He doesn't have a fortune of his own,' Eve whispered back.

'I don't think that would be an obstacle, do you?' Alice asked with a wry smile and of course the Clempsons had more money than they knew what to do with and one child to spend it on.

'He is a proud and aloof man,' Eve said unwarily.

Alice raised an eyebrow and shot a significant glance at Colm, who was now busy coaxing the very shy young woman he had partnered at dinner to converse with him.

He was trying to include her in the circle of not quite fledged young ladies and gentlemen who usually ignored her as too quiet to say boo to a goose. How dare he add kindness to all the other reasons Eve had to regret the old scandal that stood between them? Never mind the scandal, he'd told her he was someone he was not and he let her think they might be friends if they were born a little more equally. And they had been born that way, after all. The difference was she had stayed in her privileged place and he had been deprived of his by Lord Christopher and her mother. She recalled the vast fortune Lord Chris and Pamela ran through before they died and felt guilt slide under her shield of righteous fury at the wretch who had deceived her so easily in London. Was part of it because a sneaky voice in the back of her mind argued he would have told her who he was if he wanted to be more than Mr Carter ever could be to her? It seemed shallow to be glad that if they should ever, by the slenderest and most unlikely chance, happen to love each other they might marry if they could only get past his silly pride. What an unthinkable idea, what madness had come over her? She didn't want to marry him and if he felt even a spark of love for her he was very good at hiding it. He sat there like the prize exhibit at the fair and all the silly chits in the area sighed over his scar and limp and mysterious past and little Miss Browne was probably fathoms deep in love with him now he'd been so gently encouraging. Eve and Mr Hancourt were as far apart as ever and she was glad, of course she was.

'He doesn't look high in the instep or particularly

chilling to me, Eve,' her so-called friend said as she shot
him a glance that seemed far too warm and approving
to Eve. 'Indeed, Mr Hancourt seems quite genial and
looks very intelligent so I expect he will make some
lucky female an excellent husband.'

'I doubt he'd live easily on his wife's fortune,' Eve
said almost under her breath. It wasn't a warning to
Alice as much as a reminder to herself not to see him
as a suitor. Not that he'd shown much sign of wanting
to spend five minutes talking to her since he arrived
here with his aunt and uncle, let alone finding the time
and effort to offer her marriage. The fact she would
have frozen him into an ice sculpture if she could, then
walked away as if he might contaminate her if he had
tried to speak to her privately was neither here nor there.

'Love might reconcile him to being poorer than his
wife in the end, don't you think?' Alice said as if she
was far more of a romantic than Eve thought.

'I try not to,' Eve replied with a stern look to say this
topic was worn out.

'One day you will fall fathoms deep in love with a
fine mind and a handsome face and throw your bonnet over the windmill, despite all your resolutions to
be coldly logical about the whole business of marriage,
Evelina Winterley. Don't you shake your head at me and
frown as if I've suggested you might get scurvy. Nobody is immune to loving and needing another human
being almost as dearly as their next breath. Your parents certainly are not and neither, I am thankful to say,
are mine.'

'You wish to make a love match, then? Nobody

would think so from the way you just assessed Mr Hancourt's assets as a potential husband.'

'I am open to the possibility of falling in love with a man of his looks, bearing and proven ability as a leader of men, that's all. Given my position in life and his as the only grandson of a duke so far, I would be a fool not to be. That doesn't mean I intend to fall in love with him, but at least *I* can see him as he really is. Perhaps those of us who lack my objectivity should think twice about their prejudices?'

'I really don't know why I ever thought I liked you,' Eve said with a huff of annoyance and she was glad a temporary lull in the poor, mauled sonata for dramatic purposes meant neither of them dare say much until it began again.

Chapter Twelve

For a while Eve simply sat and simmered and did her best to ignore her mischief-making friend. Alice was saying what most females in the room were thinking. Mr Hancourt *was* handsome, clever and well born. He had no fortune, of course, and had been forced by his circumstances to take paid employment as his uncle's secretary and whatever else it was he did. Still, he was nobly born and respectably occupied and if the world found out what he'd been doing for the last eight years he would be lionised. Eve sighed under the cover of the final crashing chords of Miss Mendaville-Rouste's musical disaster and decided life was far too complicated.

'That was quite delightful, Miss Mendaville-Rouste, but you must be quite worn out,' Eve's stepmother stood up and announced firmly. 'I shall call for more tea to revive you and I'm sure your mama will insist you rest after your labours.'

Mrs Mendaville-Rouste was perhaps more sensitive, or less tone-deaf, than she appeared when her daughter took over the pianoforte with such verve and so little talent. She nodded and beckoned her eldest daughter to sit by her proud mama. Eve watched the charade with cynical eyes and concluded Mrs Mendaville-Rouste knew the Viscountess Farenze had more power and status among the *beau monde* than she could dream of, despite her much-trumpeted blue blood and Mr Mendaville-Rouste's ancient name and equally ancient manor house. Less powerful families than her own must think twice before inviting Mrs Mendaville-Rouste and her eldest daughter to any entertainment that could include music, however amiable Mr Mendaville-Rouste and his son might be. Eve speculated on an upcoming outbreak of broken instruments, or the woodworm, afflicting genteel houses in the area, until some worthy and deaf gentleman carried off Miss Mendaville-Rouste to his distant hearth and kept her there until she got over the notion she could play anything more complex than a penny whistle.

'Your stepmother is a wonderful woman, Miss Winterley,' Colm Hancourt observed softly from behind her and made Eve jump, then look round furtively to see if anyone else had heard him.

Where was Alice when she needed her? Watching smugly from across the room as she deftly helped Chloe with the re-introduced tea things and handed out cups with such grace and deftness it was almost a weapon in her battle with the local dowagers. Her friend wasn't taken in by a handsome face after all, then, Eve concluded, as she nodded helplessly when Mr Hancourt indicated the empty chair next to hers and raised his eyebrows in silent question. The dowagers soon lost interest in her supposedly impudent friend and shifted in their seats to watch or listen to whatever Eve and Mr Hancourt might have to say to each other instead.

'True,' she managed to say calmly enough although her heartbeat had speeded up ridiculously for some odd reason, 'and never more so than when she selflessly rescued us all from our headaches.'

'That's not all she rescued us from. My aunt was within seconds of marching up to the pianoforte and slamming the lid on the wretched girl's fingers if it was the only way to stop her. She has a true artist's love of the beautiful and that was nothing of the kind.'

'I suppose we ought to make allowances,' Eve said half-heartedly, since her ears still felt persecuted and now her breathing was oddly congested as well.

Impossible to blame Miss Mandeville-Rouste for that when the cause was sitting right next to her. She shot Alice another sidelong glare to demand rescue, but the scheming wretch pretended not to notice.

'I really cannot imagine why,' he argued.

What had they been talking about? Oh, yes, making allowances for the Mandeville-Rouste girl. What a good thing one of them had a firm grasp on reality.

'Miss Mandeville-Rouste is doing nobody any good and putting off every available suitor for miles around, unless I miss my guess. But how frustrating it is for some of your guests that we were not put in the centre of the room instead of my aunt and uncle. We could be so much more easily overheard and commented on like figures in a masque,' he drawled with a politely blank look of enquiry at the middle-aged lady who was trying so hard to listen to their every word that she was nearly falling off her chair.

Eve suspected it was his cold stare that made the woman blush and move further away rather than any sense of shame. He probably had no idea how effective that chilly glare could be and she shivered at the memory of it sending ice down her own backbone that first night at Derneley House.

'Since you have buried Mr Carter on some foreign battlefield, our neighbours must be wondering what you have been doing with yourself all these years,' she murmured and encountered a lazy warning in his brown and gold eyes not to give him away that made Alice's words echo in her still-aching head.

He truly was a brave and intriguing gentleman, wasn't he? And a lot more dangerous than she had let herself realise at their first two meetings. She looked for the limping and oddly dazed-looking clerk she encountered in Lord Derneley's library in this assured and elegant gentleman. Mr Carter had disappeared and she wondered why she regretted him. Mr Hancourt had a confidence Carter lacked, for all his daring deeds on the battlefield. This version of the man wore his new clothes with quiet elegance and looked as if he might have got his scar and limp during an illicit duel over a lady's reputation.

'Thank you for the warning, Miss Winterley. My uncle has perfected a look of blank incomprehension I am doing my best to copy. It serves him very well in the face of awkward or impertinent questions,' he told her with an almost smile that must have their would-be audience perching on the edge of their seats again.

'My friend Miss Clempson would say he can do that because he's a duke and you might get away with it as the grandson of one,' she managed to reply. Alice might have blushed if she was here instead of across the room, pretending not to see Eve's silent pleas for rescue, but she refused to feel guilty about using her so-called friend as a decoy.

'Miss Clempson is obviously as perceptive as she is lovely, I must cultivate her acquaintance.'

'Please don't,' Eve said impulsively. 'Miss Clempson is more easily hurt than she would have the world think. She has to walk a fine line in local society, given her supposedly humble birth.'

'Almost as fine a one as you and I do, Miss Winterley?'

'And only we know how thin that is, Mr Hancourt.'

'I do have the benefit of being a male, don't forget,' he pointed out as if she could when the fact of him next to her seemed burned into her senses.

How could she not remember he was acutely masculine from the tip of her toes to the last hair piled up on her head? She felt a flush of heat unthinkably deep inside her and threatening to overwhelm her in public, and that was exactly the sort of giveaway she couldn't afford.

'As such, my reputation can endure more strain than a lady's under the same circumstances,' he added, as if she might not have noticed she was about to blush and stammer while he stayed perfectly cool and collected.

'You have your father's example in front of you to argue with that idea, Mr Hancourt, just as spiteful reminders of my mother's sins will check me if I forget to be proper for more than a moment,' she said stiffly.

'I doubt you ever do that,' he said dourly and he didn't mean it as a compliment.

'I did at that horrible masquerade,' she admitted to her fan.

'That wasn't unwariness, it was love for a girl you think of as your little sister,' he said in a low intimate tone that set her nerves jangling.

She didn't want him to admire her for protecting those she loved. She didn't want him to understand her either. Even as a friend Colm Hancourt would be dangerous, but they could never be anything as simple as friends.

'I should never have left Lady Derneley's ballroom alone that first night, despite the rip in my gown, and I ought to have seen how restless Verity was before that horrid masquerade,' she said all the same. 'I'm used to the idea I must take more care than any other female I know to keep my good name, but in the future I shall guard Verity's as well.'

Why was she telling him this when she had been so determined to ignore him once she knew who he really was?

'My sister suffers much the same way, although her circumstances are very different.'

'Is she Miss Carter?' she asked, certain Miss Hancourt had endured far worse than she had without a protective family to shield her.

'She chose another name and don't ask me to give her away when she has a living to earn, Miss Winterley.'

'You don't trust me, do you, sir? Why would I harm a lady I have never met, particularly when we share in a scandal that's none of our doing?'

'You won't deliberately cause mischief, but what you don't know you can't give away by accident.'

'How kind of you to trust me so far and no further.'

'War has not made me kind,' he said bleakly.

'I doubt it changed you very radically. It seems to me a man is kind or unkind by nature and war brings out what was in him all along.'

'So you think me one of the unkind ones?'

Reluctant to let him know about her real thoughts and feelings towards Mr Carter-Hancourt, she eyed him cynically. A hint of hurt in his eyes made her sorry she'd baited him like that because she was still angry with him for deceiving her. He was a sensitive and lonely man under his various masks. For a dangerous moment she wanted to take his hand and offer her warmth and some of the human contact he'd lacked for so long. Quite impossible with their eager audience, of course, and he might pull away even if she forgot them and that would be one humiliation too many.

'I suspect being one of the kind ones made you hate what you had to do at times.'

'You're right,' he said, the memory of those things bleak in that changeable gaze of his.

How had she not let herself notice his deepest thoughts were reflected in his eyes before now? Maybe they hadn't been; perhaps he had never let her see them before. 'Then I'm glad the war is over and you came home.'

'So am I, now,' he said with such warmth in his eyes she really ought to avoid them from now on.

'Yes, your uncle and aunt are very pleased to have you with them, are they not? And all our local beauties are lining up to sigh over your piratical looks and mysterious past. If that has been repeated at every stop on your journey here you must be very glad not to be with the army now, sir,' she teased, when she had been sure they would always be worse than strangers now the truth was out.

Who would have thought Miss Winterley could joke with Mr Hancourt with half the neighbourhood looking on and her hurt at being deceived still raw? She looked around where those neighbours were, still wishing they could hear every word.

'I expect their doting relatives are lining up horse-whips to use on me right now, since I'm so ineligible,' he said ruefully.

'That would make you more irresistible to them,' she said lightly and she heard him groan at the idea of a pursuing pack of eager young ladies.

How dare he be so different from most young gentlemen she met? He didn't seem the least bit flattered that he looked like a hero to most of the young ladies he came across. It would help her forget Mr Carter's gruff strength and his kiss if only Colm Hancourt was an idler or even a deliberate charmer. He really was no help at all, she decided, and it was high time they parted as well. Stay together much longer and gossip would go round the area like wildfire, so she made herself rise to her feet and dipped a curtsy to the graceful bow he'd acquired with his new clothes.

'And here comes my darling stepmama. I trust Miss Mendaville-Rouste is recovered from her exertions on our behalf, Mama Chloe?'

'I think so, dear,' Chloe said with an insincere smile at the nearest listeners. 'I doubt the rest of us will get over them for at least a week,' she added in a hushed whisper for their ears alone.

Eve concluded her stepmother liked and trusted Mr Hancourt more than she wanted her to, since she had let him hear her private thoughts. Luckily he went to speak to Alice and looked more at ease with her than the giggling misses waiting to flirt with a duke's handsome nephew. They were soon drawn into a knot of young ladies and gentlemen noisily playing parlour games and Eve noted how much better Alice fitted in than usual. He really was kind and she hoped it was only kindness that made him insist Alice was included in every pleasure on offer. The idea of her friend wed to a man with so much pride and so little money made her fear for Alice's future happiness. She was concerned about her friend's welfare and Colm Hancourt would hate to depend on his wife. Even if Eve was rash enough to want him herself that would lie between them like a castle full of stumbling blocks and Alice's fortune dwarfed her own marriage portion.

'I like your Mr Hancourt, Eve,' Chloe announced happily and jolted Eve out of her troubled thoughts.

Eve met Chloe's violet gaze and frowned, then shook

her head to discourage her from saying such things. Chloe let her gaze linger speculatively on Mr Hancourt's half-tamed golden-brown locks currently so close to Alice's beautifully dressed blonde head and Alice did look comfortable at his side. A true friend would forget her own tumultuous emotions and be glad of a chance her friend could be happy with him. Not sure she was that saintly, Eve did her duty as daughter of the house for the rest of the evening without once telling the ladies probing for juicy gossip to go hang, but the effort made her headache thunder more fiercely than ever.

At last parents began to signal their offspring it was time to go home and Eve told herself off for being so glad the young women she had grown up with were carried off to rest. They would have to make do with their usual supply of young gentlemen when Mr Hancourt left the area and she felt a nasty little dip in her stomach at that reminder he would be gone in a few days. She frowned as one of those very young gentlemen bowed and managed to seem even less tempting than usual.

'G-goodnight, Miss W-Winterley,' the boy stammered, then almost ran after his parents with whatever he meant to ask unsaid.

'I feel honoured to have won a mere frown now I've seen your gorgon's glower, Miss Winterley,' the cause of her ill manners muttered as the last of the guests left and she realised she hadn't made her escape fast enough.

'Goodnight, Mr Hancourt,' she said severely.

'You could try to sound as if you mean it, ma'am.'

Ma'am? How dare he make her sound like an antidote? 'I wish you every second of slumber you deserve,' she said so carefully he should know he would not have many then.

'We will have to talk some time,' he warned, 'unless you have changed your mind about putting the past behind us?'

'Did I say I wanted to do that? And I'm not a gorgon.'

'I said you had a frown that would do credit to one, not that you resemble one in any other way, Miss Winterley,' he assured her solemnly.

'Our opinions of each other are irrelevant.'

'Which is probably as well, don't you think?' he asked with a weary smile.

'I do my best not to at this hour of the day,' she replied with an air of boredom that was a lie since being with him seemed to revitalise her. She would be counting the hours until a lazy dawn if she wasn't careful.

'Then you should seek your bed and rest,' he said, mock concern and something a lot more dangerous in his eyes and why had she ever thought him kind?

'If only my father's guests would do so I could,' she said grumpily. Being rude betrayed the fact he disturbed her so much her temper was constantly on edge and she had been determined to be coolly indifferent to him tonight. The bittersweet memory of one brief, disturbing kiss, snatched to add to their disguise as husband and wife, brought weak tears to her eyes for a disastrous moment, but she shook her head and refused to let them fall.

'May I hand you your candle then, Miss Winterley?'

he asked with a graceful flick of his long-fingered hand towards the patient footman waiting to hand them out and go to bed.

'Of course. My father and Bramble will be in as soon as the last of our guests are safely on their way home, Hastings, so you may go to bed at long last.'

'Thank you, Miss Eve. I can't say it won't be welcome tonight.'

'I'm sure it will, so please do as Lady Chloe said and leave the rest until morning,' Eve said, then went upstairs as fast as she could without extinguishing her candle, a rather mocking 'Goodnight' echoing in her ears from Mr Hancourt.

Chapter Thirteen

'Please sit down, Hancourt,' Lord Farenze said the next morning with a wave at the chair on the other side of his desk.

'Thank you, my lord.'

The dreams Colm had had last night made him angry with his mind for the fantasies it indulged in when he wasn't looking, so he hated to think what Miss Winterley's father would have to say about them if he knew. He met the man's almost-smile and waited for his host to say what he wanted.

'I suppose you think me rude for summoning you here like this?'

'You have something to say and I am here to listen, my lord.'

'You don't give much away, do you, Hancourt?'

'Not if I can avoid it, Lord Farenze.'

'It's all right, I didn't ask you here to warn you off again.'

'Thank you,' Colm said tightly.

He felt as if he was turning his back on something unique, but he would ignore this need to spend any moment he could contrive in Miss Winterley's company. They didn't have the mutual need, courage and passion to seize the present and damn the past. They were not in love and they would have to be fathoms deep in that to find a way round the obstacles that lay between them like razor-sharp rocks waiting to scupper them.

'I thought you would want to know what I learned from my late wife's diaries, since you found them and have a valid interest in parts of them.'

Colm wondered what good could come from Pamela's incendiary outpourings, but kept silent and waited.

'I have read them and the papers her landlord sent here after her death,' Lord Farenze said stiffly. 'There are questions about your father's affairs nobody seems to have picked up when he and my first wife died together and some secret he refused to reveal even to Pamela and she found that very irritating needless to say. I have presumed and asked a friend to find out when your fortune went missing and if some of it might be recoverable so many years on.'

Colm hated the idea of someone else knowing the full depths of his father's folly, but was almost convinced Lord Farenze meant well, as long as Colm avoided his daughter.

'You think me interfering?' his lordship asked with a cool look.

'I'm not sure I want to know how my father wasted my money. I don't want the old scandal woken up again and would not have thought you would either.'

'The man I speak of is so close mouthed he hardly lets his right hand know what the left is doing.'

Colm thought through the formidable set of noblemen this man belonged to. Sir Gideon Laughraine trailed a bigger scandal than even Colm had behind him, but the one-time lawyer was said to know more secrets than the whole of the government put together. If he was the man Lord Farenze was refusing to name, Colm had little reason to fear his father's secret would leak out by accident.

'I don't want my sister to suffer any more than she already has from our father's idiocy,' he admitted gruffly.

'Yet if there's a chance of recovering a competence you must take it. I doubt a lady spirited enough to rescue her brother from a battlefield will quail at some ancient gossip surfacing if it puts you both back where you should have been all along.'

'I don't know how you knew about what she did this summer; I hope you won't expose her to gossip.'

'I admire her too much for facing the slaughter after Waterloo for your sake to do that. You must be very proud of her.'

'I am, she is a sister in a million,' Colm admitted.

'So you should read my late wife's papers without prejudice for her sake.'

'I'll try, my lord.'

'Nicely non-committal. There's only one key to the Italian cabinet in your room,' Lord Farenze said as he handed it over. 'Don't mislay it or leave it in the lock.'

'Neither of us would want your first wife's papers out in the world, but they will keep me neatly out of your daughter's way until the Hancourts leave Darkmere, won't they?'

'Eve is always my first consideration.'

'My sister is mine,' Colm said, but Nell had looked after herself *and* him this summer and he was beginning to doubt she would give up her independence, even if he had everything back his father took from him by some unlikely twist of fate.

'The day someone lays your first child in your arms that will change,' his lordship warned as if that explained everything.

Colm supposed his host was right when it came to his firstborn and he ordered his stupid imagination not to show him any more images of Eve Winterley wearily smiling at him from their bed as a nurse handed him *their* firstborn. It was a twist of the knife that made him want to rub his belly just to make sure there wasn't one sticking in him.

'Maybe,' he said and took the key Lord Farenze offered.

It took him two days of snatched hours to read everything, since the entire neighbourhood was vying to entertain the Duke and Duchess in their midst. In the time left over from dinners and dancing parties and sightseeing trips Colm plodded through every word. When he sat down to read he had to call on all his self-discipline not to sit and dream of what might have been, if this woman had never met his father. The more he read, the less he believed the jewels were lying about somewhere waiting to be discovered. The instant he heard of Pamela's scandalous demise, Derneley would have plundered the house where Lord Chris kept his mistress for any remnants of Colm's fortune to bankroll his own wild lifestyle with.

Colm paced the airy guest room he'd been allotted with a letter in his hand he would love to rip up and throw on the fire. It was obvious how Derneley kept his head above water so long. When he thought of all the waste and dissipation his mother's jewels must have financed Colm wanted to strike the man down, then dance on him. How had he not seen the obvious before? But he supposed he had no chance to grow up knowing which of the *ton* were sharp as knives and who was rackety and wild, or light in the upper storeys. After his stay at Derneley House Colm knew very well that Derneley cared for nothing but cards, brandy and loose women. It would never occur to Lady Derneley to argue Pamela's jewels rightfully belonged to Colm, but Colm hated his eldest uncle anew for what he had let happen because he was indifferent to, if not plain neglectful of, Lord Chris's children. Pamela was right for once; jealousy lay at the heart of it, Colm decided hotly, wondering how the last Duke let such a petty emotion twist him into the mean-spirited man Colm remembered.

He frowned out of his window at the gathering clouds and wondered if the gems Pamela loved so much had been cut up and reset to crown the Empress Josephine or even her martial husband, since they disappeared a year or two before he crowned himself Emperor of France. He grimaced and wondered if the old legend that the rubies were cursed was true and perhaps he and Nell were better off without them.

Which left the diamonds as his father had had no time to hand them over to his greedy mistress before they left England. They would buy a small manor and dower Nell, if his eldest uncle hadn't given them to his mistress as Pamela claimed. Even the most discreet and retiring kept woman would have worn the confounded things now and again though, wouldn't she? Whispers she had them would leak out, since legend said they were too spectacular to go unnoticed and his early memories of his mother wearing them agreed. If the last Duke had kept them, how dared he preach of the poverty and shame Lord Chris had left his children while he robbed them of their last chance of security?

For a moment Colm wanted another battle to fight or a wild horse to tame as a way to wear out his frustrated fury. Or perhaps he should gallop off to Linaire and demand access to the safe in his elder brother's private apartments that Uncle Horace had no desire to move into. They wouldn't be there, because open possession would mean his eldest uncle admitting he was a thief from beyond the grave. Any chance of seeing the diamonds again seemed like a mirage as he stared out of the lofty windows of this elegantly furnished room. Did he really want to drive himself mad chasing one of those?

Chapter Fourteen

Eve found out how humbling it felt to be less interesting than her dead mother when her father cunningly gave Colm Hancourt access to Pamela's papers in a way she couldn't share. Perhaps she was more like Pamela than she wanted to be, since she had this urge to rage and sulk until both the managing idiots admitted she had more right to see those diaries and letters than anyone else. Not that she *wanted* Mr Hancourt to consult her about his lost fortune and neither did she want to enslave a lover as her mother did every man she ever met so far as Eve could tell.

She wandered over to the windows of her favourite sitting room to stare into the driving rain at the restless grey sea being lashed against them by a fierce storm. Her mood fitted the day to perfection, but she must pay more attention to those around her and forget about Colm Hancourt. And as for that wretched, ridiculously haunting kiss they had exchanged in London, it wasn't even as if he meant to kiss her, she told her inner siren crossly. He had done it to pretend they were a man and wife looking for a little illicit privacy on a mad and mysterious night when everyone was masked. How could she feel so hot and confused by the very idea of that intimate encounter so many weeks after he'd turned away from her as easily as if it was only a means to an end?

'Is Miss Revereux's papa expected to join her for the Christmas season?' Alice asked her so casually Eve tried to forget her own blue devils and look harder at her friend's averted face. Of course, Alice must have a *tendre* for the gallant captain. How could she have missed that for so long?

'I am sure he will do his best to spend it with his beloved daughter, even if he has to row in a ship's boat up the Channel by himself,' she said as she recalled all the little signs she'd missed that Alice longed for a man she thought she couldn't have.

She was a fool not to have seen it sooner—pretty, clever Alice had neatly dodged a pack of eager suitors and fortune hunters over the years and done it so well nobody realised how odd it was that she hadn't married years ago. So how did Verity's father feel about Miss Clempson? He learnt to hide his feelings in an even harder school than Colm Hancourt, but was he indifferent to Alice? Something told her he was not, but thought he ought to be.

'He is touchingly devoted to Verity, isn't he?' Alice said so carefully Eve was sure she was right, if feeling stupid not to have seen how the land lay long ago.

'I don't think there's anything he wouldn't do to

make sure she's happy, even when it means seeing less of her and leaving her with us when he's away.'

'He's endured a great deal for love over the years, has he not? Lady Farenze is so lovely I suppose her sister was a rare beauty as well and he will never look at another woman as he must have done at his wife.'

'You only have to look at Verity to see how lovely her mother must have been, but I suspect Lady Daphne's character chimed well with the Captain's as well. Papa and my stepmother are very definite people and suit each other to the finest degree. I dare say Captain Revereux and his Lady Daphne loved as fiercely, however young they were at the time.'

'And a man who once felt such deep and passionate love might never settle for a lesser one after losing his wife so tragically and at such a young age,' Alice murmured so softly Eve wasn't even sure she was meant to hear.

Adam Revereux was a warrior and a man of real substance. Eve regarded him as an honorary uncle to match his daughter as her sister of the spirit, but her friend must see him in a different light. Trying to adjust her ideas about both parties, she realised Adam Revereux could only be about four and thirty and Alice was almost four and twenty. Of course Alice saw him as a handsome hero and Eve had just been mentally bemoaning the lack of potent single gentlemen to distract her from Colm Hancourt. Why wouldn't Alice look hard at the one under her nose as often as he could get to Darkmere to spend time with his daughter?

Eve preferred less dour and aloof gentlemen herself.

One a decade younger than Captain Revereux, and at the same time tried and tested by war and experience, appealed as that hard-edged commander never could. A man with unruly golden-brown hair that constantly disobeyed his attempts to keep it in military order and eyes every shade from defended dark brown to sparkling golden merriment when he remembered he was young and glad to be alive. The Eve she was trying to push into a corner and ignore sighed for her chosen hero and stuck out her tongue at the woman living in the real world, where she had no right to prefer Colm Hancourt to any other man and so many reasons not to.

'Maybe a person loves differently a second time, but that doesn't mean it must be a lesser feeling,' she finally managed to say and hoped it was what Alice wanted to hear. She certainly wanted to believe it herself, because if it wasn't true she might be in for a lonely life.

'I suppose I could be happy with the respect and companionship of a husband if he was content with me. It's more than most young women in my position expect from marriage. My parents want me settled and happy with a family of my own, but they will be disappointed if I don't wed above my station,' Alice said with a resigned shrug. 'Love is probably too much to ask.'

'Why would a husband *not* love you, Allie? You are clever and lovely and easily as accomplished as any of our neighbours. I like you a lot more than most of them as well, which must make you a paragon of all the feminine virtues, don't you think?' Eve joked in an attempt to lighten the atmosphere, lest they both sit here being brave about gentlemen they couldn't afford to love.

Wanting was a different matter; she couldn't seem to stop doing that so much her body felt as if it had taken on a life of its own the day she met Colm Hancourt and now went its own way, despite her resolution to stop wanting any more of his hot and mind-stealing kisses and this time with nobody watching.

'Good afternoon, Mr Hancourt.'

Colm hesitated, then decided he couldn't pretend not to hear and hope she would pass on when this was the only shelter easily available. 'Good afternoon, Miss Winterley. You should have stayed indoors and paced the long gallery rather than come outside in this.'

'Being used to a daily dose of bracing northern air I felt in need of some before dark. This is only heavy mist by our rough standards,' she said with a wry smile that did unfair things to his insides.

'It looks like rain to me,' he grumbled with a jaded look at it lashing past this colonnaded summerhouse he dearly wished he hadn't sought refuge in now.

'Aye, it does know how to rain here, which is one reason we normally spend this time of year in Somerset, but my father misses Darkmere and Chloe is happy where he is. I hope to persuade them I have no wish to spend the next Season in town and would far rather be here when my next little brother or sister is born.'

'If you can convince them they will be content to stay,' he said and wondered how he managed to sound cool when he was so hungry for her it hurt. It felt private and intimate in here watching the rain and cut off from the real world. Lord Farenze's warnings were so much thistledown in the wind with her standing far too close and his inner savage roaring for more than a stumbling conversation about the weather and her plans for next Season.

'I love it here,' she said with a glance out at the downpour that looked almost affectionate, as if she realised it meant privacy as well. 'I spent my first sixteen years living at Darkmere most of the year. How can I not when it's rugged and beautiful and my home into the bargain?'

'It is a magnificent sight, even in the rain,' Colm conceded with a glance at the view of Darkmere Castle even a fine landscape gardener couldn't tame.

It stood rugged and undefeated against a lowering sky and the wild roar of the waves at its feet he could hear even from here. A tamer family might have retreated from the thunder of storms that churned up the sea under the curtain wall night after night, but he suspected the warrior race she stemmed from gloried in the constant battle of sea and rock-hard shore. The Winterleys probably regarded it as their family lullaby. Even as the product of a far tamer line, Colm felt the tug of primeval nature the Winterleys had breathed in since they were born. If he could sense something wild and restless in the air today, how could he expect Eve Winterley not to? She had been feeling and probably fighting the unlimited passion of it all her life.

'It's a lot colder here than it is in the south,' she said as if the battle of reason over feeling was almost won for her. He wanted to yell out loud it never would be while she held such heady passions inside her that to kill them was an affront to nature. 'Even my father has been heard to admit the weather can be dour and relentless, so if my stepmama finds it too much we will decamp for the winter, I suppose.'

'Your people seem very happy to have the family here for Christmastide and I dare say spring even comes here some time before July.'

Now he was the one being polite and impersonally light-hearted. Even as the words left his lips the wild energy in the cold, wet air, the feeling fire was flowing through his veins and calling out to the same heat in hers was as real and primeval as the heavy beat of the waves against the shore. In this shadowy little shelter from the worst the elements could throw at them the battle between reason and unreason, the possible and the impossible but infinitely desirable still raged unspoken between them. Lucky he had so much experience of the fear and exhilaration and sheer terror of war, then, because this time he was fighting himself and part of her she didn't want to admit existed.

Miss Winterley shrugged and looked as if she didn't quite understand why he asked her if family came before her own wants and needs. He felt a stab of envy at her conviction kin were more important than everyone else and reminded himself not all families were like his. He had learnt to live with what was and what a timely reminder she was as remote as the moon. He couldn't reach for her and kiss her with a pinch of honour left to him.

'What were the winters like in Portugal and Spain?'

she asked as if she had no idea he was on the edge of a wildness close to the unleashed elements.

Yet there was tension in the very air that said she knew and felt it too and this was her way of keeping it under control. He tried to follow her lead. Those days seemed so long ago and yet so close it was as if he had just disembarked from a troop ship and couldn't quite grasp the new life he was stepping into. Men he thought of almost as brothers were dead; or with the regiment; or doing their best to fit the puzzle together of family and friends who didn't know how it felt to live each moment as if it was your last.

'In winter quarters we acted in plays, kicked up the odd lark, and did our best to keep the men occupied with shooting practice and any sports we could persuade them to take an interest in. It was an uphill battle with most. If they could get hold of liquor, drink their days and nights away and cavort with the local women they were content, if nigh ungovernable. In some ways Old Nosey is right about them being the scum of the earth, although most fought like demons. They were capable of heroism and even compassion, when not disgracing the uniform they wore and making me ashamed to be a British soldier, but I should not share all that with a lady.'

'Oh, stuff! Am I to pretend I'm blind and deaf to the world around me? I refuse to not listen and not see and hope to blast such silly expectations of me out of the water.' She paused, shot a look at him that said she suspected how grim and haunting some of his memories were, even if she had plenty more to say on the subject.

She still turned the subject. 'Rumour has it the Duke of Wellington loves the chase and hunted as often as possible—did you join in?'

'He and his staff did go out whenever they could, but only a few Light Bobs had horses of any sort, let alone beasts fine and fast enough to keep up with the beau's entourage.'

'That must have been galling,' she said carefully.

Colm wondered if he was too touchy about his strange status as not rich enough for the *ton* nor plain enough for a secretary. 'Not really, my parents preferred London to the country, so my sister and I didn't grow up longing to join in the chase as we might have if we spent more time at Linaire Park. It's a privilege I am happy to have been denied after hunting men for too long.'

'You ride as if you were born in the saddle.'

She had noticed how he rode then, had she? Devious Miss Winterley, he silently accused as he recalled her queenly indifference to him when she rode ahead of the pack on those sightseeing expeditions and left him to his fate as squire to more nervous lady riders. 'Trust my father to make sure his son could ride, even if he was less proud of my love of books and scholarship.'

'I dare say he couldn't understand the lure of learning when his own father and eldest brother despised it so deeply; your uncle has my sympathy.'

'Mine, too, now I know him better. As a child I heard tales of my father's useless scholar brother and thought he sounded more interesting than the rest. My eldest uncle raged about Aunt Barbara whenever he heard her name mentioned and she sounded much more fun than my other aunts as well. I admire them for ploughing their own furrow and leaving the rest of the family behind to wear themselves out with rage and endless arguments. Nothing he could say or do would alter things one iota and I suspect my Uncle Horace is more of a realist than the rest of us.'

'Whereas I suspect the Duke regrets not being here to fight for you and your sister when Lord Chris died and left you two at the mercy of his brother.'

'He would have wasted his breath and serenity and my uncle would still not have let him have any say in what happened to us.'

'And you were already too proud and stubborn to ask for his help? Be careful, Mr Hancourt, one day you might wake up and find yourself so alone you are no more than a rocky outcrop of humanity marooned in the midst of a desolately empty sea.'

'Like a latter-day Robinson Crusoe in the cold?'

'You can make a jest of it, but it sounds a very lonely existence. Be careful of hugging your past ills so close they blind you to the joys you could have in life, sir,' she said and something in her stormy gaze made his heart plunge, then race as the elemental forces around them seemed to crackle and shimmer and he heard a real peal of thunder over the harsh rhythm of the waves this time.

'You know how stupid of me it would be to expect more.'

'And you never take risks, do you, Mr Carter?' she taunted, knowing he had done so every day of his military career, but that wasn't the sort of risk she was talking about, was it?

'You don't know me,' he told her gruffly.

'You don't know yourself, so how can I?' she said and refused to take the warning.

'You won't want to know this, then,' he said gruffly, reaching for her as heat flared between them despite the December rain. The half-worn-out blast of the sea's fury on to the rocks below Darkmere stirred something forbidden and desperate in him and he was so weary of fighting it.

'Dare,' she ordered provocatively, no longer cool and composed Miss Winterley, but the warm and passionate Eve he longed for every night in his dreams.

What else could he do in the face of that but let go of his chains? He shaped her close, breached the chill and felt her warmth with a shiver that ran over his whole skin like fire. They shared heat body to body against the seeping cold of damp air salty from the sea. 'Lovely, reckless fool,' he chided as he gazed down into her challenging green-blue eyes and spoke the words against her mouth. Sharing air only added to the heat, however wet and cold it was outside. How could he care right now who might happen on them, then stumble back into the lowering afternoon upon finding out what Miss Winterley and young Hancourt were doing to pass the time?

'Yes,' she murmured by way of encouragement.

He was so strung out with hot curiosity he broke first. He bridged the final gap between them with a kiss that healed yet burned like wildfire at the same time. Haste, heat, fury, excitement, and a pinch of doubt, roared through him in a heady tangle he couldn't begin

to sort out. Then she kissed him back and that wild rush
of feelings melted into just her, just them.

'Closer,' he urged until they shifted together so the
back wall of the summerhouse stopped them. He braced
against it to keep her from the cold hardness of it and
they were locked together now as if they might dissolve
walls and pillars and damp December with their own
version of summer heat and never mind hard angles,
chilly marble and the ever more ferocious storm outside.

'Again,' she demanded back and he spared a moment to marvel at the insatiable recklessness of her
as he shaped more of her delicious curves to him,
sure enough of his damaged knee with all this solid
masonry at his back to draw her up on to her tiptoes
and feel the blessed suppleness of her against his body
as she stretched sensual and catlike against his longer
limbs and thundering heartbeat. She felt like silk and
moonbeams and at the same time as real and supple and
alive as if she was the embodiment of all womanhood
as her name suggested.

'Eve,' he whispered reverently, then plunged them
straight back into a passion he had never before dared
imagine with another, even deeper kiss.

He was rampant by now; he tried to shelter her from
the blatant fact of his manhood rigid and desperate for
a virgin the last whispers of reason reminded him he
could not have. A little feminine mewl of protest and she
shimmered her body closer still, blasted that last shred
of caution clean out of him and denied his never into an
urgent maybe. Deepening his hungry kiss against her
eager mouth, he felt every inch and sinew that marked

him from her dissolve in a white-hot blaze. Was heat, need, possession or sheer madness first and foremost and which was his and which hers? Why would they want to know? Best if she didn't ask questions while he still had a faint rag of sanity to hang on to. Still he plunged his tongue into the depths of her mouth and she met it and played and parried and demanded right back, as if she had embraced this madness completely and wanted to know every inch of him intimately at this very moment.

He felt her curiosity, her dangerous wonder about the heat and need burning deep inside her and his heat and more obvious need against her. He groaned and heard all the warnings he should have sounded before this happened in his need as she shifted her long and slender limbs again. The beast in him roared and he had to clench his fists against the intriguing hollow at the small of her back to stop his hands lowering and moulding her neat buttocks as they strove towards risking a climax Miss Winterley and Colm Hancourt could not afford to reach.

'We can't,' he said his voice rusty and reluctant; the words making his throat ache at having to say them even this softly against the heat and reality of her sweet, teasing, daringly bold mouth and all the promises they couldn't make each other.

'I have to argue with that statement, Mr Hancourt,' she said as she lowered one wickedly wondering hand to shape the undeniable fact of his need and passion for her where it reared its eager length between them and made him a liar.

Once she gave, she gave everything, didn't she? She knew this was impossible just as grievously as he did, but she still refused to let him get away with pretending he didn't want her to the edge of madness and made him face the truth. The fact she trusted him so much humbled him and made him realise how vulnerable she had made herself. For a woman who spent her life doing her best to avoid scandal she was courting one right now and that made her braver than he was. Could he be more than a passing passion for a reasonably fit and healthy young male? He physically shook with the effort of not making that question irrelevant and taking everything she had so recklessly offered.

'We could,' he admitted in a voice so rasped with that admission he hardly recognised it as his.

She shivered with the awe of it, he could see that in her eyes, even if he didn't dare read more in the wide, dazed depths of the blue-green mystery looking back at him. He knew her so well and yet not at all. Even as he stared down at her spellbound and on the edge of something life altering, he saw her come back to the real life all around them and Mr Hancourt and Miss Winterley being heedless and wild together. Which would never do; he saw the fact of who he was reaffirm itself as her gaze sharpened and the misty blue of her passion-blurred gaze faded to sharp Winterley green. She had thrown off the spell and somehow he could not. He felt as if part of him was being ripped out and might bleed all over the fine resolutions he'd made never to let another human being hurt him again the day his eldest uncle told him his father was dead and he had no home and no fortune but what the latest Duke of Linaire chose to give him and he chose to give him very little. This wasn't about him right now though—it was all for her. He felt enough for Miss Eve Winterley to care more about her hurts than his own.

'But I never want to need this as desperately as my mother did and you don't dare love me insanely, the way your father loved her,' she said huskily, sounding so unlike her usual cool, clear self he knew it was an Eve no other man had heard, even if she was saying things he didn't want to face right now.

He clung to that with a sort of desperate, selfish possession; the owning of that once-in-a-lifetime intimacy for only a second or two was more than he had ever expected. *Let yourself rest here just for a moment*, the lover he might have been whispered, and he intended to gloat over it while he had the chance, *the chance of this is all you can have. One day she will rediscover this Eve for the man she can wed and bed and respect and how I wish he'd envy me the first sounds and sight and scent of her that he can't have, but won't know he's missed. He will have every other moment as her husband that I can't, but not this one.* Which only went to show how unworthy of her he really was, he told himself sternly, and prodded his conscience back into life.

'That sounds like a problem with no solution to me,' he admitted grimly and all the dank chilliness of the month and the place and the brooding bulk of Darkmere Castle in the rain lined up to shout *No* to the sensual meeting their bodies still longed for as they clung to each other as if they couldn't bear not to feel their heat and all the chances they were about to let go. An essential part of him he'd almost hoped was dead yearned for her with a want that seemed to go on for ever. Perhaps he was Lord Christopher's son in every way after all, he reflected bitterly as frustrated need jagged through him as hard as the French bullet that hit him six months ago.

Chapter Fifteen

'Eve Winterley! Whatever are you thinking of?' Lady Chloe's usually mellow contralto voice rose almost to a squeak from the other side of the fine curtain of rain and then she was in here with them. There was no need to wonder what the world thought of them kissing in the rain, it was there in her ladyship's pale face and wide, shocked eyes.

Eve pulled herself out of his arms at last and turned to meet her stepmother's horrified gaze. Colm tried hard to force his will on his body as he stood where she left him, like a piece of wreckage cast up by her wild northern sea. His heart stuttered with something he told himself must not be love when Eve deliberately stayed in front of him to hide his blatantly aroused state from her father's wife. Nobody had protected him so rashly since his mother died and that realisation threatened a hard place he didn't even know he had. To feel Eve put herself between him and Lady Farenze's appalled stare made him feel wild emotions that threatened to burst out in unsayable words and deeds that would make Eve's choices narrow unforgivably. He couldn't do that to her, so he tried hard to control unchained Colm while Lady Chloe's face revealed her search for words powerful enough to express her shock and disquiet.

'Probably what every healthy and unattached female thinks when she looks at a handsome young man,' Miss Winterley said as airily if they had been discussing the weather, or what they might have for dinner. She was Miss Winterley again now; warm, wanting Eve had been put in the corner until she said she was sorry.

'Well, you can't think any of those things about him,' Lady Chloe said with a helpless shrug and a gesture at Colm that said so much a lady like her did not want to speak out loud. 'What if somebody else saw you, Eve? You were kissing Mr Hancourt, nobody could think you reluctant the way you snuggled in his arms and gazed up at him spellbound like that. Your reputation would be in shreds right now if anyone but me had caught you and I can't bear to think what your father would say and do if he stumbled on you instead,' she added with a horror-struck shiver. The fear in her eyes at the thought of her husband duelling with a sharpshooter made Colm feel guilty and wonder if such terror might endanger her unborn child.

'I'm quite sure Mr Hancourt would offer for me if things were that dire,' Eve said soothingly, looking as if she thought he'd have to be horsewhipped to do so. He wanted to protest he could think of nothing he'd like better than to marry her right now, if she wasn't so horrified by the idea and he wasn't as poor as a church mouse.

'I would, that is I will. Will you marry me, Miss Winterley?' he heard himself ask like a simpleton.

'No, thank you, Mr Hancourt. My stepmother is not going to gossip and I refuse to wed a man who doesn't even want to love me,' Eve Winterley said with a bitter irony that lashed at his heart, because it sounded as if he'd really hurt her and he thought it was she who didn't want to love him.

'You are a Winterley, Eve, and I know by now every one of you is born reckless and bold, despite the years you spent pretending to be the exception, but I'm shocked at you, Mr Hancourt,' Lady Chloe scolded as if she couldn't quite cope with her stepdaughter's bleak logic and found it easier to blame him. 'I thought you far more honourable than your father until this very moment.'

'I'm quite shocked myself,' he admitted unwarily and felt Eve stiffen, as if she thought he was disowning their hasty, soul-branding kisses when they felt as if they'd altered him right down to the bones. 'Miss Winterley is everything a man could ever dream of in a wife, of course,' he added as if some demon was prodding him to make bad worse, 'but I can't make her marry me,' he said to her now rigid back. Even through her cloak and the gap rapidly growing between them he felt her fury at him for being such a clumsy great idiot and his father's son.

'We exchanged a curious kiss when trapped here with nothing else to do, Mama Chloe. Right now I really can't imagine why; maybe I wondered how the world might look if I actually liked you, Mr Hancourt,' she informed him regally, without bothering to turn round and glare at him.

'You do know I would never condemn you to wed a stray gentleman you happened to kiss so lightly, Eve?' her stepmother said earnestly.

Colm felt the dart her ladyship probably didn't even know she fired hit home and cursed opening his secret self to Miss Winterley's scorn. He must get that Colm back into the cage the idiot would just have to live in from now on and like it. Such joyous vulnerability was out of character and would soon wear off, he assured himself bleakly, but deep down he knew he was lying. Bidding Eve and Colm a final goodbye and a *No, never* would hurt for the rest of his life, but he'd do it for her sake. He straightened his shoulders and thought chilling thoughts before he was fit to step past Miss Winterley and meet Lady Chloe's bewildered gaze. She was far too much of a lady to look lower and remind them how eagerly he and Eve had been trying out that 'impulse' for size before she chanced on them anyway.

'Of course I do, darling.' Eve's queenly gaze softened for her stepmama. 'It took you ten years to wed my father for love. How could I expect you to push me into a lesser marriage because Mr Hancourt and I were silly enough to explore a fleeting urge when we were trapped here by the rain?'

'I doubt any gentleman likes to be dismissed so lightly, but for both your sakes I hope you were truly curious about that impulse and nothing more?'

'You arrived in good time, my lady, so I presume that will be that? What with me being who I am and Miss Winterley being a lady of high birth, good character and comfortable fortune,' Colm said flatly, deciding the best thing he could do was remove himself before any more distress was caused.

A stiff bow in Eve's direction and a slightly more graceful one for her stepmother and he left them to decide what to tell Lord Farenze. He'd seen enough of Lord and Lady Farenze to know the lady would not keep such a secret from her lord and Eve would not ask her to. Now he must wait for an order not to darken his lordship's doors again, or to eat grass before breakfast with him.

'You know how foolish it was to kiss Mr Hancourt where anyone might have seen you, Eve. I'm sure I don't need to tell you again how shocked I am,' Chloe said as Colm Hancourt's stiff-backed figure limped into the driving rain.

Eve could hear the lingering astonishment and horror in Chloe's voice and spared a moment to regret Chloe had come upon them when she did for her own sake, not just because she felt cold and forsaken standing here watching Colm limp off to brood alone. He hadn't taken the path back to the Castle, so he must be heading for the cliffs above the raging sea Eve could hear thundering against them from here. She hoped he'd be careful and realise how dangerous Darkmere was for the unwary on a day like this, then sighed for her own stupidity. The man had survived troop ships crossing the Bay of Biscay in winter; who knew how many skirmishes and pitched battles; forced marches and desperate retreats over far worse terrain than any peaceful England had to offer, and then there was Waterloo. He didn't know this sometimes wild and capricious coast, though, and part of her seemed to have gone with him, to stand at his shoulder and fret over slippery paths and shifting soil. How was a man as proud and prickly as Colm Hancourt going to look out for them as he should when his thoughts were occupied with what they had not quite done today?

'Papa is sure to have warned him about the cliffs and the danger of losing his footing in the rain,' she reassured herself softly.

This time she actually felt her stepmother's acute mind focus sharply on her as she wondered how deep the damage had gone between her stepchild and the stubborn, bungling great idiot of a man. Right now Chloe must be thinking she should have kept Colm away from Darkmere, rather than invited him here as if he were a harmless youth. Anxiety for his safety nagged at Eve like a sore tooth and argued she should not have been so bitter and angry when he fumbled out that forced proposal. If she hadn't lashed out at him in hurt and frustration he would have gone to find her father to make that ridiculous offer real and he wouldn't be out there on the cliffs in a raging storm right now.

'And before you ask, no, I don't know what I feel, Chloe,' she added absently. Those devastating kisses must be shut in a corner of her mind to think about after she had coped with here and now.

'I might be able to help you,' Chloe said, an unexpected thread of laughter in her voice. 'Such feelings can creep up on you all unwanted and unlooked for, but pretending they don't exist is a waste of time.'

Chloe was obviously thinking about her own gruff, tardy and reluctant suitor from the faraway look Eve had become familiar with—Papa and Chloe always wore it when they were thinking about each other and wondering why they had been such idiots for so long. Then Chloe's acute violet eyes focused on her and Eve fidgeted at the thought of all the uncomfortable questions that would probably come next.

'I suppose if you take his father and your mother out of the equation, Mr Hancourt *is* a brave and honourable man,' Chloe said as if logic had overcome her initial shock. 'Don't look at me as if I've grown two heads, Eve; you must like him to have done what you did with him this afternoon.'

'I really don't see what that's got to do with the price of fish,' Eve muttered.

Whipping up her own fury at his clumsy proposal and unspoken rejection of all they could be to one another might block out this feeling she had lost something crucial to her future happiness this afternoon. He kissed her as if she was all he ever wanted in a woman, then limped away with that tight, closed expression she recognised from the night she met Mr Carter. How dare he make her feel so confused and shaken and confoundedly empty as she did right now, standing here agonising about whether to follow him or stay with Chloe?

'You weren't exactly struggling in his arms, my love,

and you must know your demons if you want to banish them,' Chloe cautioned with an anxious look down that sodden and rain-blurred cliff path as if she was afraid Colm meant far too much to her stepdaughter as well.

'As you did, I suppose?'

'Refusing to admit our feelings cost your father and me so much I can hardly bear to look back at all those wasted years.'

'But this is different and you saw how completely Mr Hancourt was himself again when he walked away. Neither of us can change the past.'

'So it's as well you don't love him then, isn't it?' Chloe said with the stubbornly practical logic Eve usually valued, but didn't feel in the least bit soothed by right now.

'Except if he wasn't Lord Chris's son, I think I might,' she admitted on a long sigh that did justice to this grey and sodden day.

'Then he wouldn't be the man you could fall in love with in the first place, would he?'

'True, a Lord Chris with all his flash and glamour and selfishness would never do for me. He was the perfect mate for my mother though, wasn't he?' Eve said bitterly, thinking the worst crime those two ever committed was happening now.

Their shades were standing between her and a man of such depth and character it was impossible not to want to be closer to him somehow. Because of what they did, she had to say goodbye to a *perhaps* that could have been wonderful. Because of them Colm didn't trust himself to love Pamela's daughter.

'I think they both deserve to be forgotten,' her step-mother said as sadly as if she knew exactly what Eve was thinking and it was impossible to make life easier for her.

The fact she wanted to made Eve love her more and she forgave Chloe for coming on her and Colm a little too soon for the tortuous ache of unsatisfied need that still ground inside her. It felt like a warning she might never recover if she thought too hard about what had happened, and what had not.

'Yet as long as Mr Hancourt exists they never will be and I refuse to live in their shadow any longer,' she said practically.

That was it, then, she would soon be her old sensible self again and might even be safe from feeling too much once again. Except she doubted folly worked backwards like that. This tender ache inside said being sensible never felt as glorious as being reckless and headlong and... Her supposedly clever mind took over at that point and told her not to listen to her inner wanton.

'Your mother and Mr Hancourt's father are so firmly lodged in both your heads I wonder if you can see past them,' Chloe surprised her by saying and now she had to revise her prejudices through her stepmother's eyes.

'Then you think I exaggerate?' she asked, the shock of wondering if she was the person she thought she was jarring through her for the second time today, joining the tension of watching that dratted cliff path in the hope Colm would come back down it and relieve her mind of its greatest anxiety to date.

'No, what they did and how they died was dreadful,

in both senses. But that was fifteen years ago and this is now—your life, Eve, and not theirs. If you did happen to love Mr Hancourt it would be hard for you to be watched by the gossip mongers all the time, but it would be worth it, believe me.'

'Luckily we don't love each other,' Eve said flatly, feeling as if she was the one standing on an imaginary cliff looking down at awe-inspiring stormy waters, as she suspected Colm was doing in reality right now, and refusing to even consider that disaster. 'Do you think he'll be safe on a rocky path with a bad leg and all that spray and rain buffeting at him?' she added unwarily.

'Since you don't love him, why would you care?' her cunning stepmother asked and anyone would think Chloe wanted her to love the stubborn great idiot.

'He is a guest here, of course I care about his welfare. Think of the scandal if Lord Chris's son fell into the sea from a cliff near Darkmere and drowned.'

Even saying such a terrible thing out loud made her want to scream a denial at the gods and rush after him, pull him to safety and rage at him for taking such a risk with himself in the first place.

That Eve whispered, *To hell with any risk that we might compromise each other once and for all by returning to Darkmere sodden and storm-wild together with our clothes so wet we might as well be naked.*

The real Eve still wanted to be with him, but she cursed her doubts for not falling away in the face of the tragedy it would be if Colm Hancourt fell to his death from those rocks because they wouldn't have each other as lovers, despite that life-changing kiss.

'Think of his poor uncle and aunt rather and he's more than his father's son to the rest of us now we've met him. We had best go back to the castle and send out a rescue party, don't you think?' Chloe said practically.

'Yes, I thought he would come back when he saw how wild it must be out there, but he's not going to until someone talks some sense into him, is he?'

Eve sighed at her own cowardice for not admitting how desolate she would be if anything happened to him and set out with her stepmother through the gloom of the December afternoon as fast as she dared with Chloe's pregnancy and this terrible heaviness in Eve's heart to slow them down. For some reason every step she took away from the cliff path and Colm felt heavy and wrong, as if she was the only one who ought to go after him and risk what he was risking. They were both too stubborn to let themselves take that last step into loving one another together, but he was lodged so firmly in her head and heart it felt as if any fate that befell him would stay with her for ever as well.

She felt… Eve paused her thoughts and wondered if she even knew how she felt about this tangle of emotions fighting for breath inside her. She felt desperate, she finally realised with a shock of horrified honesty. So she made a breathless apology to Chloe, then ran ahead as fast as she dared go. It would do Colm no good if she slid into the nearest muddy hollow and hit the ground at speed and needed rescuing herself, so she concentrated on remembering every path for hazards and sped on with heart racing and a suspicion she cared more about Colm Hancourt's well-being than was good for either of them.

* * *

Standing brooding about things he couldn't change wasn't doing any good, but Colm couldn't seem to up-root himself and tamely plod back to the castle in order to get out of this infernal rain. That would mean facing the world as if nothing much had happened and it had. The hypnotic boom of furious waves pounding the sternly indifferent rock Darkmere was built on beat in time with his busy heart and made him wish he had even a thread of poetry in him. He thought it a blessing he lacked the sensitivity of a poet as he struggled to live the life his eldest uncle and the Almighty had laid out when he was little more than a child. Now unformed words beat in his soul and he'd love to shout them at the angry sky, launch fury back at the mighty sea and defy stars he couldn't see through the depth of rain in the clouds and an early dusk.

Damn fool, he railed at himself instead. *Careless, reckless fool.* The feel of her in his arms still haunted him, as if *Evelina Winterley* was printed on his skin. To open himself up to so much pain, such needless hurt; didn't that make him as guilty of stupidity as their parents? He had made the idiot's move that let her inside his barriers and she walked into Fort Colm as if she belonged. He left her behind now with an effort that still tore at him like a wound, but she was still doing something strong and deep to him he dare not define. Part of him wanted to get away, to ride into the storm, mud, danger and darkness; a saner part refused to put his horse through so much and so he stood here like a monument to folly and glared down at the pounding sea.

A vast wave broke on black rocks that seemed even further away now it was almost dark. The mighty surge of spray even reached up here as a wave broke on the cliff edge to soak any part of him not already drenched in salty fury. He shook his head like a wet dog and roared back at the storm in wordless outrage. All this majestic madness was going on around him and he was so wound up in Eve Winterley and wanting, needing, demanding things he could never have from her. Even vast, angry nature seemed smaller than the maelstrom inside him. Pain stretched from his head and heart to his gut and shook him with a powerful longing he didn't even want to think about.

By now discomfort should have driven her out of his head, but she was still there. Still unattainable, still herself, still uniquely alive for him as no other woman ever would be now, thanks to her. If the ancient, capricious gods of Olympus still ruled the world he might think his birth offended one of them—Poseidon himself perhaps, the cross-grained old thunderer of legend.

'What the devil are you doing out here, you young fool?' his host demanded, sounding almost as furious as that imaginary god of the sea.

'Being a damned fool,' he shouted above the storm.

Lord Farenze shook water out of his own rain-plastered dark locks and motioned Colm impatiently inland. 'Grab my hand and make very sure you don't slip and pull both of us to our deaths. I have no mind to chase you into hell for taking such a risk,' he said dourly, but still held out that hand and defied Colm not to step away from the cliff edge and the towering spray sniping at them from so far below he was dizzy and a little sick at the thought of the rocks waiting if he put a foot wrong and Eve's father made a hasty grab, then plunged in after him.

Feeling the locked agony of standing too long on his bad leg and waving the man away, Colm flexed his abused limb until it felt strong enough to bear his weight again. He backed slowly away from perdition, ignoring the angry lord at his back until they were safe and could yell at one another in relative peace.

Chapter Sixteen

'Why?' Lord Farenze demanded. 'Why did you take such a stupid risk?'

'It wasn't much of a risk until you came,' Colm replied, sounding like a sulky boy even to himself.

'You're not immortal, despite managing to survive more battles in your short life than most men have nightmares about in three-score years and ten. What about your sister and aunt and uncle? For some odd reason they seem fond of you. How do you think they would feel if you lost your life for the sake of an urge to dare the devil?' The angry Viscount paused and shot Colm an even more furious look through the increasing gloom and lashing rain. 'It *was* only recklessness, wasn't it?' he added, looking as if he'd land Colm a facer if he'd been working himself up to launch into the abyss and end his time on earth.

'I survived death in battle too many times to court it lightly now.'

'Nice to know you're just an ordinary looby and not a coward then.'

'I should save your praise until you hear why I *am* out here,' Colm shouted over the receding thunder of the waves as they walked cautiously away from immediate danger through this incessant rain and the ever-thickening gloom.

'Never mind that now, we need to get warm and dry and call all the other wet and cold men looking for you back in before you have them on your conscience as well.'

'You should have left me to take my chance with the sea, idiots like me rarely come to harm.'

'And have the world whisper I did away with the son of my first wife's lover one dark night on the cliffs of my sinister northern stronghold?'

'I refuse to let every turn in my road lead me back to them,' Colm railed uselessly against fate, then shook his head and signalled that he could match whatever pace the Viscount set and wanted to get those searchers in too, since it was his fault they were out there in the first place.

'I doubt even they were this mad,' the man said grimly and set such a punishing speed neither of them had breath to argue.

Colm had to add several cans of hot water to his bath water before he felt even close to warm again. Now he was fighting the last hint of a chill in his bones to reassure his uncle and aunt all was well with him. Aunt Barbara had put aside her latest picture to concentrate on him like a hen with one chick. Uncle Horace used the excuse of escaping her fussing while he helped his nephew strip off his soaked clothes and climb into the bath as if he was a boy again. Colm watched them with rueful affection now and decided he had family beside his stubborn sister after all. He might not have much in material terms, but their love and respect was priceless to someone who had walked alone as long as him.

'Better?' Aunt Barbara demanded once he was dressed and furnished with a brandy. Only when he finished the fiery spirit did he finally feel warm again.

'Yes,' he agreed with a sigh.

'Then you had best have good reason for giving us such a fright, lad,' his uncle told him sternly. 'And your aunt will lose her temper if it isn't up to scratch.'

'I kissed Miss Winterley,' he admitted baldly, then wondered if he was still in a state of shock to admit it out loud. No point pretending it wasn't a calamity and, if he was about to be evicted from Darkmere, they ought to know why.

'Oh,' said his uncle blankly, as if he understood why Colm had to stand on a cliff edge in the middle of a storm and brood now.

'Was the young lady shocked and angry, or frightened half to death, perhaps?' his aunt asked him sharply.

'Not at the time, although I suspect she may be by now.'

'She didn't fight you off or demand you desist immediately?'

'No, she did neither of those things,' Colm said carefully, trying not to revisit the way she had reacted to his kiss in this quiet room with all their attention centred on him and something deep and painful in his heart he'd best not think about.

'She put her face aside as soon as she was able to and treated you with frigid disdain, perhaps?' Aunt Barbara persisted and he had to control an urge to shout *no*, then go and find Miss Winterley to rage at her for not doing exactly that.

'No,' he answered as blankly as he could manage.

He felt confused and on edge, but there was no point blaming Eve. He couldn't let himself believe a woman like her could love a man like him. With his father's example in front of him he wasn't sure he knew what love was anyway. He didn't want to ignore the rest of the world or wrap Eve up in a cocoon where he could worship her all day and every night and to the devil with everyone else. He could still see people around him and responded to them perhaps a little more than before he met her. So he couldn't possibly be in love with her, could he?

And what were her feelings about him? Maybe the passion that exploded between them in that confounded summerhouse had made her hate him. She feared her own desires; he knew that because she guarded her true self so fiercely. Now he knew about the passionate, desirable, vulnerable creature behind that careful shield of hers he could quite see why. Again, he wanted to find her and shake her, then make her listen when he told her she was her own woman and totally desirable in her own right. She had no need to look for her mother in herself and say a polite, *No, thank you*, to a side of her she had kept walled up for too long.

Not that he wanted her to go about the countryside kissing any fool who forgot to ask her if she minded, of course. The thought of Eve in another man's arms made him wish he'd stayed on that cliff until the fierce night cooled his ardour *and* his temper. He had to get away from Darkmere, he decided with a shudder. The frown of concern on his uncle's face after that giveaway shiver brought him back to here and now and reminded him he was trying to look warm and recovered from whatever ailed him. Calm and collected might take longer.

'If Miss Winterley did none of those things I conclude she kissed you back,' Aunt Barbara broke the near silence in this comfortable fire-lit room to quiz him.

How could he admit that a young lady he wasn't going to marry had done anything of the kind, even to his aunt? Somehow he couldn't quite lie to her either.

'Ah, so she did exactly that,' she said as if his silence explained everything.

Colm wondered what she was up to when she looked quietly satisfied with the results of digging about in his most tender places. Aunt Barbara knew perfectly well he was no fit mate for the daughter of the house. The best thing he could do was leave now he'd made such a damned fool of himself, so why was his aunt happy he must struggle to forget Eve Winterley and those fiery, unique kisses? He had been almost ready to admit this part of his family liked him as well.

It was beginning to dawn on him how much he had changed these last few weeks. He'd dreamt of living secure and respected in a quiet country house so often when the Duke of Wellington's army waited on the verge of battle, but was that really all he wanted out of life? On retreat from unbeatable odds, when any sort of home seemed a million miles away, he would dream his sister was restored to her proper position in life in that neat little manor house and he was free to court a quiet and contented wife to share it with them.

In the real world Nell would be bored in a month and their respectable neighbours would still look down their noses at the progeny of the most scandalous lord of his generation and avoid them. Colm's faceless dream wife would have grown shrill and a lot less content when the gossips mulled over the past and speculated how long it would take him to fall in love with a painted hussy and run off with her. Ah well, none of it would happen now and he was sure his grandfather's fabled wealth had been spent, whatever Lord Farenze said to the contrary. Even the jewels had gone to fund Derneley's extravagant lifestyle, so the fact it was all a castle in Spain didn't matter now. As long as his uncle was alive Colm had work and a chance to invest his salary and make his own money. He was the grandson of a nabob; he ought to have some of Joseph Lambury's fabled luck and cunning in him. It was high time Colm Hancourt became his own man—he was beginning not to like the one his father and eldest uncle made him into.

'Miss Winterley is not at all like her mother,' he said carefully into a thoughtful silence. Eve had a generosity of spirit, an untapped warmth and joy that argued she was the very opposite of her faithless, heartless dam.

'Perhaps you should explain that to the young lady herself,' his uncle said with a weary sigh, as if he was tired of tiptoeing round the subject. 'And why do you take your father's sins on your shoulders, Colm? Chris didn't feel the burden of them, so why do you?'

'Probably because he didn't,' Colm admitted after thinking carefully. 'Miss Winterley's mother refused to own up to a single flaw, let alone the cartload she rejoiced in, but because of those two heedless idiots Miss Winterley and I cannot afford to look at each other as we did this afternoon.'

'Why ever not?' his aunt challenged, looking as if she would shake him if she could reach. 'Because society says so? That's no reason not to do whatever needs to be done in the real world we live in day by day, Colm. Society is only for best and God judges our actions, not them. It's high time you stopped letting your father and Augustus spoil your life and as for the opinions of shallow idiots who never did a proper day's work in their lives, I can't believe you listen to a word they say, let alone allowing them to dictate whom you can or cannot love.'

'Best not let those idiots hear you, my dear,' the Duke of Linaire said placidly, as if he agreed with everything else his wife said.

Loving Eve, if she loved him back, would risk cutting her off from her family and secure place in society. Even if he wasn't Colm Hancourt, he was still a nobleman's secretary, not the match her family must have hoped for all her life.

'So you think I let the gossips rule my life?' Colm said, wondering if his aunt wasn't right.

'Not just them, but you were too young to fight what

my brothers did after Chris died,' his uncle put in sadly. 'They bundled you off to some charity school, then the army without giving you a chance to make sense of any of it, so I suppose it's little wonder you got things out of proportion. Yet you endured all that and emerged a hero and I don't know how to make you see yourself as you really are.'

'I'm no hero; all I did was survive.'

The thought of all those who did not made Colm shake his head and frown at the fire. None of them felt anything now, not the warmth of a fire, or the elemental passions of the storm raging outside the castle walls. He sat here warm and cosseted and feeling guilty about Eve and they were in the cold ground. Somehow the thought of what they had lost so young made the weight on his shoulders feel heavier than when he only had Eve to feel empty and protective and wretched about.

'You shrug off that description and claim other men behaved better in the Peninsula and during that terrible business last summer, but your aunt and I have come to know you, Colm. A good man stands in those shoes you fought so hard not to have, along with the few clothes fit for my nephew we nearly had to force you into when you finally came home.'

'Thank you for them and I admit Carter was a mask I hid behind.' The business of killing and surviving had gone on so long Colm refused to think beyond Carter and his next march or the best shot to take with the Baker rifle no true gentleman would carry as he skirmished with his men beyond the main army.

'I suppose you were too busy staying alive to be Colm Hancourt at the time,' his aunt excused him.

'There was plenty of time to think when we were in winter quarters, too much at times, but I refused to do it,' Colm admitted.

'At a time like that a young man needs to get through the next fight, not worry about things that might never happen,' his uncle said and Colm realised these two would always find an excuse for him.

'You may be right, Uncle,' he said lightly. He was lucky to be loved by three good people, but the reason they were having this conversation in the first place almost robbed him of joy. 'I can't replace one fantasy with another though, can I?'

'You could if you loved the girl,' Aunt Barbara argued.

'We Hancourts make such a poor fist of love it's probably best if I don't attempt it,' he said with a weak attempt at a smile, 'I'm sure the lady agrees.'

'Oh, I don't know, I once met a stubborn idiot who wore a hair shirt that didn't belong to him either and I fell deep in love with him, despite his bad habits. Who is to say who will appeal to a young lady weary of the ordinary sort of fool she can meet every day on the marriage mart?' the Duchess of Linaire summed up the younger gentlemen of the *ton* with magnificent contempt.

'Thank you, Aunt Barbara.'

'Don't mention it, my boy,' she said smartly, rose to her feet and tucked her hand in his elbow when he did the same, then she nodded as if it was the right thing to do when the Duke of Linaire stepped back to let his family precede him.

So they went down to dinner and whatever declarations his aunt and uncle made about his place in their lives with that touching gesture, Colm was no more than a duty acquaintance for the notice Miss Winterley took of him. Everything they almost were this afternoon made Colm wonder if he might choke on the fine dinner he worked his way through as if his life depended on it. Refusing port and painfully polite conversation in the drawing room afterwards, he retired to his room to brood about young ladies who kissed as if their hearts were in every ragged breath and racing pulse, then sat down to eat their dinner a few feet away and ignored him as if he was part of the furnishings.

'We'll have to stay until Monday, my boy,' Colm's uncle told him the next morning when he suggested leaving as soon as everything could be packed and ready. 'If we scramble off on a Saturday we must stay at an inn tomorrow and it will seem as if we fell out with the Winterleys. Since we came here to mend a quarrel, we can't set tongues wagging again and if we leave on Monday we might even seem sensible if we're not careful.'

'I could paint something special on our way home. An icy waterfall, frozen in its tracks would do nicely,' his aunt said with a dreamy smile.

'The boy's not a miracle worker, Barb, and it'll be too mild to freeze a millpond this side of the New Year,' the Duke argued.

'Will it? What about the Pyrenees, then?' she asked Colm half seriously.

'At this time of year they are bitterly cold, treacherous and unfit for man or beast after so many years of all-out war.'

'Maybe the Alps would be better,' she said with a thoughtful frown.

'Perhaps next year,' the Duke said as if he meant it and Colm only just bit back a groan.

Now Bonaparte was truly beaten travellers had no limits except the depth of their pockets and the strength of their nerves. If his aunt and uncle chose to travel he would have to go with them and never mind this feeling he'd seen quite enough of the world to be going on with. He couldn't let them be exploited by renegades and rogues posing as couriers or interpreters to the unwary as British travellers flocked over the Channel after so many years pent up on their own island.

Somehow the thought of being hundreds of miles and several countries away from Eve Winterley made him feel cold to his bones and that was ridiculous. Staying here another two days with that passionate encounter looming over him like the sword of Damocles should horrify him. He had two days to feel sheepish and silly under her father's vigilant gaze and take in enough of Miss Winterley to last him a lifetime. Best if he avoided her then; he didn't need any more images of her to haunt him as if they had truly become lovers.

'Aunt Barbara, can you endure company on one of your sketching outings this morning?' he asked, rather desperate to avoid Eve and her family until he could ride away from this place she loved so much.

'Of course, I haven't caught the sun on the sea as I'd like and it looks as if we shall see more than a glimmer of it this morning at long last. We might as well find out if you remember anything you learnt about drawing as a boy while we're out there,' she agreed happily, but could he really afford to open himself to another way of feeling when he had so many of them to cope with already?

Chapter Seventeen

'I have lived at Darkmere most of my life, but still don't understand our weather,' Eve told the Duke of Linaire as they strolled down to the beach below the castle in placid sunlight later that morning.

'It is a fine day after that impressive storm last night,' the Duke answered with the vague smile that hid his true thoughts about yesterday quite beautifully.

'The wind from the sea is cold though,' she persisted, determined to talk about the elements as they took the gentlest path to the sea with a small procession of servants picking their way down it some distance behind them.

'You really don't need to worry about my wife, Miss Winterley. I may seem preoccupied to a busy young lady like you, but I make sure Barbara is well wrapped up before she goes outside. She's too eager to be out and about to bother with aught but her paintbox if I don't watch her. She will be glad of that coffee and soup your people are carrying so diligently by now though, for all she claims not to notice anything but the scene in front of her when the muse is upon her and the light just right.'

'The Duchess is a dedicated artist,' Eve observed, cross with her own inability to go beyond the obvious this morning. The simple mechanisms of every day got you through bigger things and what had happened yesterday seemed almost too big to think about right now.

'She is and I'm proud of her. It's as well neither of us enjoy the state my late father and brother always insisted on though. We couldn't afford it and we're far too old to learn after years of going our own way. We did well enough with my wife's portion and our earnings after my father cut me off when I ran away from an arranged marriage and wed Barbara instead.'

Now why did she think that was a veiled reference to Colm and who her family thought was a suitable husband and who wasn't suitable at all? Not that Mr Hancourt would offer again and she wouldn't accept him if he did. So why was the Duke quietly letting her know love was more important than money and family expectations?

'What a hard man the last Duke was. He stood by while his father treated you so coldly, then he rejected Mr Hancourt and his sister after their father died,' she said impulsively then she thought a little harder about what she had said. 'I'm so sorry, your Grace, your brother has hardly been dead a twelve month and I dare say you are still mourning him.'

'Oh, no, I don't pretend to be grief-stricken. Gus did his best to control us all while he did what he pleased and pretended to be saintly as an archbishop. My young-

est brother's actions were deplorable and I'm very sorry
for the shadow they have cast over your life and my
nephew's, but I liked Chris a lot more than my other
two brothers.'

'He wasn't a very reliable parent though, was he?'
she said, thinking how lucky she was her father had put
her welfare ahead of his own.

'I can hardly imagine a worse one, Miss Winterley,'
the Duke replied quietly. 'But at least my wife filled the
dark corners in *my* life with her verve and imagination.
Would my nephew could be as lucky in a wife, if he'd
only get on and marry one.'

'I suppose most of our kind wed for the sake of a
family and connections,' she managed casually. The
thought of Colm loving and marrying another woman
stung her bitterly. She felt wrapped up in darkness on
a day when low December sun slanted down on a sea
blue-grey and silvered in the sun with the sky serene
and clear above it and yesterday's storm and fury impossible.

'I hope you don't expect so little from marriage, Miss
Winterley,' the Duke said a little too seriously.

Eve stayed silent, struggling with how she might
feel if Colm married a rich young woman who considered him too fine a catch to get away. Thinking about
heiresses made her consider Alice and understand her
friend's rather wistful cynicism about the world. If Alice
had really loved Verity's father from afar all these years,
how painful it must be to love a man who didn't seem
to have noticed her. She didn't want Alice to give up on
her dream and settle for someone poor and well con-

nected like Colm Hancourt. Eve wanted him too much
herself to make that idea at all acceptable. She struggled with the dilemma of trying to stay away if one of
her closest friends married the man she longed for so
much, try as she might to ignore him. Now she and the
Duke were picking their way over the rocks newly rearranged by the storm as the path began to broaden out
and she should stop worrying who the wretched man
might marry and watch her step. Excellent, she would
learn to be grateful for that storm yet.

'Your papa and stepmother seem blessed in their
marriage, so mutual love cannot be that rare among the
ton,' the Duke persisted gently.

'Ah, but I have my mother's poor example to make
me a doubter, your Grace,' Eve said with a would-be
careless shrug. 'I would as soon not wed at all as waste
my life searching for a perfect lover and never find him.'

'You fear the marriage bed will wake similar demons in you to the ones that drove your mother then?'
the Duke asked a question nobody else had ever dared.

Eve gasped in shock and was very glad the servants
had fallen behind to flirt and laugh with each other out
of earshot. Even Chloe would think twice about asking her that and it was outrageous of the man to even
mention such a possibility, but the memory of how it
felt to burn in Colm's arms whispered was his uncle
right? Did her shame and contempt for Pamela stand in
the way of accepting one of the eager young men who
asked her to marry him? No, she decided, as she con-
ducted a mental review of her suitors and couldn't consider being intimate with a single one without a shudder.

Her next silly idea about wedding and bedding Colm instead sent a shudder through her that had nothing at all to do with being cold.

'Perhaps,' she said at last, because how could she take offence and storm off when the idea of being scandalously close to this man's nephew and enjoying it as much as she had last time crept into the least-visited corners of her mind and settled in as if it belonged? He seemed so concerned for Colm's happiness and well-being it would feel hard and brittle of her to snap a ladylike denial, then stalk off in a huff.

'You seem very much yourself to me, Miss Winterley,' the Duke went on gently. 'So why do you allow your mother's past sins to shape your future?'

It was a fair question, considering they had wandered so far from the nothings that usually passed for polite conversation. The Duke's good intentions practically shone out of the brown eyes she suddenly saw were very like his nephew's and far more acute than he let most people know.

'Your particular demon looks the opposite of Pamela Verdoyne's to me,' he continued. 'Could it be you risk loving the right man too much, my dear? The first Lady Farenze wasn't capable of love and it was my brother's tragedy to love her even so, but your father and stepmother's story proves there are very strong passions in the Winterleys and I doubt you're immune to them. Don't let the life you could have with the right man slip through your fingers simply because your mother died with her lover a decade and a half ago.'

Silence fell between them and how could she fill it

with neat little observations on the day and the scene in front of them now?

'It isn't what we do that sometimes haunts us like fierce ghosts; it's what we don't do,' the Duke added soberly.

She watched his gaze focus on the shore now they were past the last curve in the cliff path and she finally saw the Duchess of Linaire sitting next to her husband's stubborn nephew. She should have known, she decided, wanting to glare furiously at the devious man who brought her here as if he had no idea how she and Colm were together yesterday. Yet how could she condemn the Duke when he was clearly a good man with a bad conscience about his nephew? She let the tug of simply looking at Colm off the leash for a weak moment. Standing next to a man who had already seen too many of her secrets, she still let herself appreciate the way sunlight picked out the gold in Colm's unruly mane and outlined his lithely powerful shoulders and lean hips. His gaze was fixed on the wonders of nature with a fierce intensity Eve let herself know she wished was focused on her instead. He had no idea she was here; that she could stand spellbound by such a vigorous young man when he forgot to be humbled by war and life for an hour or two. The footmen and maids catching up with them at her back would see how her eyes lingered on Colm Hancourt's finer points and vivid presence if she wasn't careful, so she wrenched her gaze away from him and gave her companion a look of queenly reproach.

'Is Mr Hancourt your ghost, sir?' she demanded, but

he had brought her here and asked outrageous questions, so she had the right. 'If so, he haunts you and not me.'

'Ah, but the boy hasn't left Darkmere yet, has he?' the Duke said, as if he knew gaps would yawn in her life the very moment that happened.

She almost wished Colm really was plain Mr Carter, except then he wouldn't be himself and she wouldn't have this fear gnawing away inside her that the Duke was right. She *would* miss the wretch when he left, as if someone had cut away a vital part of her and the rest was limping on as best it could. She refused to be the woman he wished he didn't want, though. He refused to fall in love in his father's footsteps and she had too much pride to chase after a man and make him want her as her mother would have done, so thank goodness she didn't know the full complement of pleasures a woman could ache for in a man's arms. Yesterday afternoon they had stopped, or been stopped, in time for marriage to be a choice and not a necessity, so she chose to let him ride away.

'Monday will remedy that,' she said coldly. 'Since my stepmama tells me you are leaving us on that day, your Grace,' she added and she shouldn't be hurt Chloe heard about it before she did. Her stepmother was mistress of Darkmere Castle and had every right to know when their guests were going home.

'Yes, I think we must before more damage is done,' he replied with a frown of concern for his nephew that made Eve squirm. 'I failed him as a boy, you know. His sister as well, although my mother did live long enough to make sure young Eleanor went to a school where she could be happy. She considered a boy the province of the men of the family, unfortunately, and I was hiding on the other side of the Atlantic. I let my brother take out his fury on two helpless children, Miss Winterley. Somehow Colm and Nell managed to grow into two of the finest beings I know, despite the efforts of their family to ruin their young lives, but they did so on their own.'

'I'm sure they don't see things that way,' she said uneasily.

'I did say they were fine people, didn't I?' he insisted with gentle tenacity, then smiled and seemed to realise he was being an awkward guest. 'On a bright and hopeful morning like this one old misdeeds should not cast such long shadows.'

'Yet still they do,' she said with bitter resignation.

Now the Duchess had seen them and Eve wondered what kindly meddling to expect from Colm's next partisan relative. She ought to be thankful his sister was not here to take over once the Duke and Duchess had finished with her.

'Ah, coffee and soup, how very welcome. And you have been so careful with it that I dare say there will be enough for all of us,' the Duchess said to the footmen as they solemnly set out stools for the quality to sit on and the maids laid a cloth and cutlery on the biggest one before decanting soup into rougher bowls and mugs than usually graced a lord's table.

Impossible to sit stiffly aloof while everyone enjoyed an impromptu luncheon on a beach in December, cocooned against a cold wind from the North Sea and warmed by the sun still shining so serenely the cloud and tempest of yesterday might have been a dream, but for the forbidden tingle in her belly whenever Eve met Colm's eyes by accident. Impossible to dismiss that as imaginary when she could feel his touch echo through her again simply by being within ten feet of the wretched man, with enough chaperons handy to satisfy a convent nearby.

Once the food was eaten and the coffee flasks empty, the servants sat and enjoyed a few moments' rest on sun-dried boulders. Eve had to stay here or look as if she was avoiding the Hancourts, but she eyed the maids and footmen heading back to the castle in a merry gaggle rather wistfully. The Duke seemed hell-bent on inter-fering today and next he insisted on taking his Duchess for a walk to shake the stiffness out of her legs and get her truly warm again. Soon they were out of earshot, yet close enough even to satisfy Eve's papa no more mischief could be done.

'It seems we must talk, Mr Hancourt, your uncle is almost insistent upon it.'

'I'm rapidly finding out he can be very stubborn under his act of the mild-mannered scholar,' Colm ob-served with a distracted smile as he watched his aunt and uncle and refused to centre his brown and gold gaze on her.

'He's quite right, of course; it *is* foolish to pretend yesterday didn't happen when we both know it did. It was a moment of madness and that's all. So there, I have said it and now we can forget it ever happened. If we don't, the good our families did each other by this visit will be wasted.'

'And we can't have that, can we?' he asked gruffly and Eve felt as if Mr Carter was back and had little to say to the daughter of a viscount.

'No, it would waste a great deal of effort by my parents and your aunt and uncle to put the past behind us,' she said briskly and wondered why she cared which of his masks he was wearing today.

'It's not though, is it? The past, I mean,' he added as if she might misunderstand and heaven forbid she thought he was talking about their long, sweet kiss in the rain.

'If we take yesterday out of consideration it is. From now on our families can meet and be at ease with each other, if we forget that particular idiocy.'

'What if I can't forget?' he demanded roughly, as if the words forced their way out of his mouth against his better judgement. 'What if the memory you kissed me back so passionately got inside my head like a burr that won't go away however hard I try to rip you out of my mind, Miss Winterley?'

'That's not a flattering comparison,' she said with a weak attempt to make light of things that felt wrong even as she said it.

'Damn it, woman, why should I flatter you? I didn't want that folly to happen any more than you did. There's no future in us feeling anything for each other and whichever way I turn I always end up wanting and never having. I thought I was used to being Lord Chris's son and living with that lack every day of my life, but

it's all you see when you look at me, isn't it? My father
and your mother. So be careful how you tweak my tail,
Miss Winterley, because I'm not sure I'm quite as tame
and resigned to it as I thought I was.'

'I didn't intend any of it to happen,' she whispered
because saying it out loud seemed dangerous. 'Chloe
wanted peace between us all and her intentions are so
good. Anyway, I had no idea you were not a Mr Carter
but a Mr Hancourt when she asked me if I minded
your aunt and uncle and their nephew coming to Darkmere for a week or two. If I had known he was you, I
might have gone to stay with my Uncle James and Aunt
Rowena and saved us the ordeal of sitting here trying
to be civil today.'

'My aunt and uncle wanted to bridge the gulf as well
and we have made it bigger. We might as well be Capu-
let and Montague for all the good we will ever do each
other, Miss Winterley.'

The way he said her family name hurt as if he'd
aimed a fist at her heart. The Duke's warning not to
throw love aside went directly against her father's wari-
ness about Colm and that balance felt too hard to think
her way around right now. She had to keep the chaos
of feelings she didn't want or understand at bay somehow and that meant making sure the unsayable never
got said.

'Then we must learn not to want each other,' she
said and tried not to look at him again. She might find
him too vital and grumpy not to want more from him
than words could say if she did. He didn't trust love and

mere passion would never be enough for her, so all they could do was hurt each other more.

'Do make me a map of that, then,' he demanded urgently, as if she was the one refusing to let go of her prejudices when she felt it was the other way about.

'When I have one myself, I will send it to you.'

'I spent all morning trying to draw one and look what came of that.'

He thrust one of the little books of drawing paper she had seen the Duchess take out of her reticule and make lightning sketches on at her, then he strode away, as if only by removing himself from her presence could he breathe freely. Insulted that he wanted to get away from her so urgently he couldn't stay to be seen to part friends by anyone who might be watching, she held the little book at arm's length, as if it might explode and stared at his retreating back. She told herself it didn't matter if he loved her or loathed her, he was the most infuriating and stubborn male she ever encountered and she almost wished she hated him.

Chapter Eighteen

'In a month or two this will be no more than a half-forgotten nightmare, Evelina,' she whispered to herself as Colm disappeared round the headland and her hungry eyes couldn't follow his halting gait any longer.

How dear a dream he could have been, she acknowledged in the privacy of her own head. She smiled to herself at his stubborn refusal to admit his leg still hurt barely six months on from Waterloo and all the terrible danger he had somehow survived that day. Any other man would cosset himself and use a cane to ease the stiffness that must plague him badly today, after that reckless dare against the churning sea and her father last night on the cliffs. Colm Hancourt was far too proud and obstinate to do anything of the sort, she accused him crossly, as she turned her gaze back to the sea, where the sun still shone on playful little wavelets, distant cousins of the wild ones that thundered against the cliffs as if they meant to tear them down last night.

There, he'd left his borrowed sketchbook in her hand

with a driven invitation to look at it and she was wasting her time watching him go away as if every second she could still see him was precious. She eyed the book dubiously, expecting to see furious lines and harshly scored portraits of this place she loved so dearly, despite its capricious moods. Well, she defied him to spoil Darkmere for her and opened it anyway. Oh, Heaven, how could he do such a thing to her and then stump off as if he couldn't wait to get away from her? She stared down at first one page, then another and another of quick images and one or two more finished drawings of nothing but her. Except how could it be her when he seemed to see her as her mirror had never shown her to herself? There was Eve Winterley looking pensive and a little bit sad; here she was smiling as if greeting the most precious person in her life; now she was frowning and here looking offended.

Her heart jarred, then galloped as she came to the final page and found out he'd drawn her a picture of yesterday—Eve undone. She admitted the truth of that image to herself as he shot down hers of a lady who had only let herself forget who she was for a few moments. She looked soft mouthed and heavy eyed, a world of possibility in her kiss-swollen lips and avid gaze as she stared back at the man who had woken her up to so many things she wanted to cry just looking at herself. This was the chance they must never risk again, the Eve and Colm she longed for yet dreaded with all the caution in her after growing up not just motherless but with Pamela's example to say, *Don't take her path through life. Never allow the scandalmongers to whisper in corners about you as they still do about her.*

How she would miss the lovers this drawing showed her. Even now she felt as if half of her life had gone with them and she would always be less than her full self because she would never be the woman in his drawing again. It hurt, but the Duke and Duchess would soon complete their tactful circuit of the beach and she had to meet their acute gazes as if she hadn't seen this portrait of herself as she might have been, if only Colm let himself love her. So she tucked the little sketchbook into her shawl and turned to greet them with a social smile.

'I see my nephew has flown the scene,' the Duke said by way of greeting.

'He is such a restless soul at the moment. I think he could make a fine artist if he would only sit still long enough to apply himself,' the Duchess observed with a sad shake of her greying but still handsome head.

Eve wondered how brilliant Colm might have been if he had application since that little book seemed to burn her inside its sensible wool wrappings as she met the lady's eyes as serenely as she could. 'Mr Hancourt must be used to a very active life, considering his occupation these last few years,' she said blandly.

'All the more reason to calm down and fulfil his potential now he's home,' the lady said forthrightly.

She would miss the Duchess, Eve realised. The Hancourts were nothing like the proud and snobbish people her childish imagination had painted them when she learnt of her mother's nightmare death at her lover's side. She tried to imagine the sort of man Lord Christopher Hancourt must have been coolly, but it was no good. She couldn't be dispassionate about a man who deserted his children and spent their inheritance on his selfish and greedy mistress. He would be a soft version of Colm, without his son's bone-deep integrity and with a flashier version of his son's quiet good looks. Eve suddenly realised her father had recognised Mr Carter as Lord Chris's son when they were still in London. She would have words with him about that, but for now she went back to the differences between Colm's father and his son. Lord Chris would lack the rock-like chin and stubborn courage of his only son, but have an easy charm and a way with the ladies Colm lacked. Colm was much more trustworthy though, wasn't he? He hadn't run off with anyone's wife so far either, but this wasn't being dispassionate, was it? She put all the strength and integrity on Colm's side of the balance, weakness and neglect on his father's.

'What was Lord Christopher Hancourt like?' she asked the Duchess after the Duke had wandered back to the castle and his beloved books.

'From what little I remember of him before Horace and I fled London and his family, Chris was much like any other spoilt youngest son who refused to grow up.'

'He was a decade older than his son is now when he met my mother though, wasn't he? And he'd been married and had children,' Eve said, feeling she needed to understand how his father's desertion changed Colm's life.

'You won't get an impartial opinion of them from

me, Miss Winterley; if you're looking for one of those, you must go elsewhere.'

'Any interest I showed in your nephew would stir up gossip enough to deafen us,' Eve said stiffly.

'Then trust the evidence of your own eyes, girl, and stop letting the actions of a pair of long-dead fools cloud your judgement.'

'I have two little half-brothers, your Grace. What if the next child my parents produce is a girl and I go about proving the gossips right? My bad blood will taint a little sister, or even put off the girls my brothers might one day want to marry if I am not very careful about any risks I take with my good name now.'

'Can you really intend to live your life chained to a set of maybe happenings years in the future? Or let it be dictated by the past? Your mother had no blood in common with your brothers and sisters and there's little to connect her to you but the bare fact she gave birth to you. I pity you if you intend to let Pamela Verdoyne's shade overtop you for the rest of your life.'

'How can I not have a care when she was so notorious?'

'By living your own life—there is no better proof I can think of that you take after your father and not your mother. With Colm the sum went the other way, but it adds up to the same total: he is not his father and you are not your mother. All you two have to do now is see yourselves as you really are, before you miss out on a happy life, together or apart.'

Which was all very well, but, even if she wasn't her mother's daughter, Eve would still flinch from loving a man so self-sufficient even he didn't seem to know what he was feeling most of the time.

'Ah, Hancourt,' Viscount Farenze observed as he looked up from some ancient estate map later that morning and met Colm's eyes with a cool challenge in his own. 'I wondered when you were going to explain what happened yesterday.'

'I am sure you already know, my lord,' Colm said, standing stiffly on the other side of the desk even when the man waved imperiously at the chair opposite his own. 'Lady Chloe has a clear-minded command of most situations she stumbles across and will have described it to you in detail.'

'So, what do you intend to do about it?'

'I will meet you whenever and wherever you choose, my lord.'

'And that would damp down any gossip about you and my daughter quite wonderfully, wouldn't it?' the man asked with the cynical irony he was once famous for. 'You could pick your spot and put a bullet through me wherever you choose. I know what a fine marksman you are held to be by your peers, Hancourt, because I made it my business to find out all I could about Captain Carter of the 95th Rifles, so please don't try my patience by pretending otherwise.'

'Another sign I am no gentleman, don't you think? As if you really needed proof,' Colm said quietly. No ordinary infantry officer would dream of carrying a gun at the head of his men instead of his sword. Only among the Rifles did an officer occasionally do so, but it was considered eccentric even there.

'You're a young fool if you think I'll meet you. I have no mind to become a murderer when you send your bullet into the nearest tree, so keep your challenge and I hope it eats into that prickly conscience of yours when you next feel the need to kiss a man's daughter you have no intention of marrying.'

'I shall not,' Colm said stiffly.

'What, develop a conscience or kiss disappointed girls?'

'The kisses, of course.'

'You trust your will to triumph over base nature a little too easily then, lad,' Lord Farenze warned him as if that kiss was nothing more serious than a moment's misjudgement on his part.

'I have nothing to my name but a few decent clothes provided by my uncle and a Baker Rifle there is very little use for in civilian life, my lord. I am in no position to keep a wife and family, so I must learn to keep my more unfortunate longings under strict control in future,' Colm said, like some spotty youth who was ready to launch himself on any halfway-willing female simply because she was one.

'Isn't that something you should have remembered before you kissed my daughter?' this slippery lord demanded.

'Yes,' Colm said, driven to brevity by the lie he was a knave who had been caught kissing a desirable young lady he couldn't aspire to marry.

'Don't be a fool, lad,' the Viscount surprised him by

saying on a sigh. 'We both know you are mature beyond your years and little wonder, so please don't treat me like a flat and pretend you feel nothing for my daughter but a little misplaced lust you will both get over quickly.'

'I could never be that deluded, my lord.'

'I don't want to know the deepest and darkest secrets of your heart, Hancourt, but please don't imagine I would agree if you demanded Eve's hand in marriage. I told you in London only the most dedicated and determined sort of love between you would make me let you marry her and you don't look like a man who thinks the world well lost for love.'

'I am not my father,' Colm said, hanging on to his temper by a whisker.

'Which is the only reason I'm not brandishing a horsewhip at you like the indignant father out of a bad farce right now; Eve is not like her mother either.'

'Well, of course she isn't,' Colm said impatiently. 'She is the most extraordinary young woman I have ever met,' he caught himself saying and felt a foolish grin on his face at the mere thought of her.

Yesterday afternoon she watched him with so much in her turquoise eyes he'd hardly dared breathe. No, best not to think how she looked after that kiss in her father's company, he remembered, as enchantment threatened to make a fool of him all over again.

'And the world had best be ready for a shock when she finally steps out of my late wife's shadow,' Lord Farenze said.

'I expect she will dazzle it. I promise to do my best

to avoid your daughter from now on, my lord,' Colm said stiffly.

'Ah, but what if she seeks you out?' the man challenged.

'I learnt to retreat in good order as well as to advance in the Light Division,' Colm admitted with a self-mocking smile.

'You're a stiff-necked young idiot, Hancourt, but I suppose you're young yet and might learn to do better if you live long enough.'

'Thank you, my lord,' Colm replied and took it as permission to go away and leave the puzzling Lord Farenze in peace.

Breakfast was served a little earlier than usual on Monday to allow the Winterleys' guests to depart in good time to reach comfortable lodgings before dark now that it was so close to the shortest day of the year. Colm wondered if it was more tactful to take a tray in his room, but when did tactfulness become cowardice?

'How wonderful, here's a letter from Papa,' Verity Revereux said as she danced into the room and took her seat, holding out her cup for chocolate as Eve took her stepmother's place as hostess, until Lady Chloe felt equal to greeting the day. 'Would it be very rude of me to read it, Uncle Luke?' she asked with a hopeful look towards the Duke and Duchess, since they were more likely to tell her of course not and she must read it as she was clearly longing to.

'Yes,' Eve said austerely and Colm felt small for hoping her pale face and lack of breakfast conversation gave away a disturbed night almost as hellish as his own had been. 'But no doubt you will do so anyway.'

'I do hope he will get here in time for Christmas, so you are quite right, step-cousin of mine. You have a letter from Sir Gideon, Uncle Luke. It looks very long as well, so what a good thing Lord Laughraine franked it so as not to bankrupt you,' she said with a solemn face and mischief in her eyes at the idea any Winterley need worry about paying for a letter, especially when a member of the Lords.

'I have been waiting for his answer to a question, so I hope you will forgive my appalling manners as well, your Grace?' he asked the Duchess, who waved a hand to say of course and went back to discussing the Lake poets with Eve and the Duke.

Colm sat and brooded about his latest glimpse of family life. Verity had got over her youthful infatuation with the youngest Louburn very quickly and was happily absorbed in her father's letter just as if she had never taken that false step into adulthood. The resilience of youth struck him as he visualised the pale, pensive and woebegone girl he saw at the Warlingtons' masquerade only a few weeks ago and felt older than his rightful four and twenty. He wouldn't bounce back from whatever he felt for Eve Winterley like that. Somehow he doubted he'd ever be able to put his hand on his heart and say he felt nothing for her. He gave himself the luxury of furtively watching her as she discussed poets and poetry with his aunt and uncle. She was such a passionate creature under all that cautious coolness she used on the outside world and the sad thing was she didn't even realise it. How would she fare with the polite and careful husband she thought she needed? He shuddered at the thought of her trapped in the safe little world she thought she wanted to find and wondered if he was such a bad bargain after all.

She would be miserable with that paragon, he concluded gloomily. He frowned at his half-empty plate and felt what he had already eaten threaten to curdle in his gut at the very idea of her half living her life because of a pair of long-dead strangers. That was all they were, those dead lovers; strangers who once faced a choice between their children and their own wants and needs and took the easy one. Neither had a right to shape their children's lives or who they loved and how much, yet somehow they still did.

Colm felt the injustice of it bite deeper than ever as he slid another glance at Eve Winterley and almost wished he'd never set eyes on her. The desolation she would leave in his life threatened, but how could she be happy married to him if her money paid for everything? Sitting at my lord's breakfast table, Colm let himself know that he loved Miss Evelina Winterley. He sighed and thought how joyful most men could be about such a realisation, but they had the means to keep a wife, or knew that there was nothing between them but love and hope for a better future. Either a man and his wife had nothing or everything together. In his mind that was the equality of marriage and loving Eve made him even more ready to walk away from her.

'Well, I'll be...' Lord Farenze suddenly exclaimed, then stopped just in time and looked about him as if he had forgotten exactly where he was for a moment. 'My apologies,' he said abruptly.

'You didn't actually get as far as saying anything awful, Papa, but whatever is the matter?' Eve said anxiously.

'I have some surprising news from Sir Gideon,' her father said absently, as if that news and whatever he felt he must do about it lay heavy on his mind.

'Is Lady Laughraine unwell, or my dear little godson? Or is there something wrong with the new baby, or Lord Laughraine perhaps?'

'What? No, no, of course not. Sorry to alarm you, love, and they are all well. There is nothing like that for you to worry about.'

'Then what is it, Papa?'

'Nothing bad, or at least I don't think so, but it's not my news to tell. I think some of you may need to hear about it in time all the same,' he muttered as if conducting a debate with himself. Eve couldn't recall seeing her father this torn and uncertain about anything since shortly before Chloe agreed to marry him. 'Yes, there's been too much concealment and lying already. If you would join me in my book room as soon as you are done here I shall be obliged to you, Mr Hancourt, at least then the rest of it will be up to you.'

'I can eat no more, my lord, so I am ready now. We must be away by mid-morning if we are to stand any chance of reaching Durham before dark,' Colm said warily, as if he was uneasy about anything her father had to say to him at Sir Gideon Laughraine's prompting.

Feeling as if all the certainties of life were shifting

around her, Eve watched in silence as her father and Colm left the room together. Colm was nearly as tall as her powerful father and, despite the halt in his step, looked almost as dangerous as he loped at the side of the mature man of power her papa had only truly become when he wed Chloe and learnt to be happy at long last. Despite all the differences in age, wealth and status between them, Colm wasn't diminished by Viscount Farenze as so many *ton*nish gentlemen were in comparison. His lithe strength and leaner build hinted at potential not yet fully explored and picked him out as younger and less certain of his own worth than the Lord of Darkmere Castle, but Colm was very much a man for all that.

Chapter Nineteen

After a few minutes passed rather flatly in the breakfast room a footman came in and muttered something to the Duchess, then the Duke of Linaire and they left the room as well. Now only Eve and Verity were left sitting in ignorance of what was going on and Verity was too preoccupied with her crossed and recrossed letter to notice the strangeness of it all. All this mystery must have something to do with the past if Uncle Gideon had got involved. Eve felt panic rise at the thought of what he might have uncovered and Colm was finding out at this very moment. Her fingers tightened involuntarily on the remnants of a piece of toast she was still holding for some odd reason and turned it to a handful of dry crumbs before she could order them to stop.

'If I did that I would be told to go to my room and not to come back to the breakfast table until I learnt manners,' Verity told her as she eyed the pile of breadcrumbs Eve let fall to her plate as if she had no idea where they came from.

'Why would you do anything of the kind?' Eve said hollowly, trying to cope with the awful suspicion Colm meant far more to her than he should.

'Because I was upset that a handsome and heroic gentleman whom I liked and admired a great deal more than I was willing to admit was about to ride off as if he meant nothing to me, perhaps? Or maybe I might wish I was going with him, but lacked the courage to say so?'

'Stop! You have no idea what you are talking about,' Eve said, on the verge of tears as she heard all Verity was saying and nobody else had the gall to say out loud. Not that it made any difference. She couldn't go after Colm and tell him her life would feel bleak from the moment he left Darkmere.

'You think not? I was old enough at the time to know Aunt Chloe and your father nearly turned their backs on love because of things their families did or didn't do years before. You were as keen as I was back then to see them united and happy together as they have been these last five years. What happened to you, Eve? Did you listen to the scandal when the world found out who my aunt truly is and what my mother and father went through at the hands of her family? All the head shaking and tut-tutting in the world can't change a thing. It's just words and those who matter don't take any notice of them; I should have thought you were clever enough to work that out for yourself by now. I know your mother left you with your father so she could dance off and do whatever she wanted, but that wasn't your fault and it isn't Mr Hancourt's either.'

'I know that.'

'Then why are you punishing him for something he had no say in? Your mother didn't desert you for his sake. Mr Hancourt was just a boy at the time and he certainly had no say in any of it.'

'That's absurd and unfair; I'm surprised you can even think such things about me, let alone say them out loud.'

'Maybe I don't want to see you grow sad and a bit too brave for the lack of your love in your life as my aunt did for your father? Ten years is a terribly long time to waste pining for a man for the want of a little truth-telling. Then there's my own father wasting his life longing for a lady he thinks too young for him as well, even though he hasn't bothered to ask if she agrees with him. I don't intend to be such an idiot with so many examples of what not to do in front of me. I love you like a sister, Eve, so how can I *not* say you are being a fool? And please don't pretend you have no idea what I'm talking about.'

'Well, that certainly told me, didn't it? But don't forget you're the one who ended up having to be rescued from Warlington House dressed in a pair of breeches, Verity Revereux, and not me.'

'Nobody will be able to accuse me of being faint-hearted though, will they?'

'I don't think any of us will ever be that foolish.'

'A blind trust, you say?' The Duke of Linaire said with a dazed look on his face.

Perhaps realising shock had stopped Colm's tongue, Lord Farenze nodded for him. 'A very well hidden one, your Grace,' he said. 'Sir Gideon Laughraine seems to

think he would have had an even harder time finding
out the details if the trustees were not in such a puzzle as to how they were going to discharge their final
duties on the day your nephew turns five and twenty
when nobody else seems to know it exists.'

'And Christopher truly set it all up and managed to
keep the woman he was so besotted with from finding
out, all to make sure my late brother-in-law couldn't
get hold of Colm's inheritance if anything happened to
him in France?' the Duchess said as Colm tried to take
in this astonishing turnabout in his life and fortune.

'Yes, because apparently the last Duke was the one
with debts and an expensive mistress to keep. He used
Lord Christopher's personal fortune to pay his creditors off, then told the world how feckless and extravagant his little brother had been before he died. Although
the Lambury Jewels are still missing, I'm afraid, so
Lord Christopher still gave them to my late wife when
they were not his to give. Gideon says that when the
late Duke found he couldn't break the trust he put the
tale about that everything was gone and refused to do
anything for you or your sister. I can't pretend my first
wife wouldn't have done her best to spend everything
Lord Christopher had and your fortune as well if she
could have got her hands on it and lived long enough
to spend it, Hancourt, but she didn't and the rest of it
is still intact.'

'The rest of it?' Colm said in a voice he hardly recognised as his own. 'So my Grandfather Lambury's
entire fortune will truly come to me in a few weeks?'

'Apart from the not insignificant loss of the Lambury Jewels. Even the diamonds have disappeared, despite the fact my first wife doesn't seem to have lived long enough to wheedle them out of your father from her complaints in her diaries.'

'I think Derneley had the rest cut up and my late uncle probably did the same with the diamonds, since he must have found them after my father died,' Colm said, still struggling with the idea he was going to inherit a huge fortune in six weeks and, somehow more important, his father might have loved him after all. 'Derneley should have gone under years ago and he's stayed afloat far too long, you see? Apparently he set off to France on the excuse of finding out how his sister-in-law really died when the Treaty of Amiens was signed.'

'You think he took the jewellery my wife cozened out of your father with him and sold it piecemeal to the highest bidder?' Lord Farenze asked.

'Probably,' Colm agreed with a shrug.

'Then I should recompense you. My wife stole it and her sister's husband has lived off it all these years.'

'No, a gift is just that, so I will not take your money if you try, my lord.'

'Don't look at me, Farenze, it's no business of mine,' Colm's uncle said with a shrug. 'Colm is a gentleman of fortune now; he can do whatever he wants.'

'Except I own nothing much for another six weeks, Uncle Horace,' Colm reminded the Duke with a wry smile. 'Lord Derneley is no relative of yours, my lord, so you have no right to his debts. A legal document shall be drawn up renouncing any claim on you and your heirs for the Lambury Jewels, or their value. I'm not a greedy man, Lord Farenze; one vast fortune is quite enough for me.'

'At least you and your sister can take your place in society and your pick of several estates to make your home,' the Viscount said uneasily.

'If I can persuade her to do any of that I shall think myself lucky,' Colm said ruefully. It would be an uphill struggle to persuade Nell to leave her four noble waifs, but at least she could never be cast out penniless now. Convincing her it was downright peculiar for the sister of a rich man to earn her bread might take him some time, but the urgency to protect his little sister from the harshest aspects of poverty was fading for the first time since their father had died. He had no idea how tightly that need had wound him up until it was gone.

'And Sir Gideon believes my late uncle knew that this trust existed?' he asked.

Silence. He looked up and saw something uncomfortably like pity in the eyes of all three.

'I conclude everything I will inherit in six weeks reverts to the dukedom if I die before I'm five and twenty?'

Odd how painful it felt to find out his late uncle and guardian bought him a commission in the most dangerous regiment he could think of in a time of war and blithely sent him off to die, so he could get his hands on the Lambury fortune he had always begrudged his nephew.

'I do hope he is rotting in hell,' his aunt said so softly her words seemed all the more potent. 'I have to trust God to judge him, because if he was in front of me now

I wouldn't hesitate to put a bullet in Augustus's black heart,' she concluded with a defiant glare at her husband and her host to tell them she meant every word.

'You'd have to find it first,' Uncle Horace said darkly, then the hint of a smile lit up his gloomy countenance, 'and you couldn't hit a haystack at ten yards, my love.'

'True, and after you tried so hard to teach me when we decided to cross the Atlantic as well. It's just as well I never did get pursued by a bear, isn't it?'

Colm laughed and love for these two extraordinary people lifted him out of the dark place his other uncle's villainy had threatened to push him into. He was truly blessed in the family he had now and the past was dead and done with, wasn't it?

'Gus had a mean soul, for all he grew up as heir to our father's honours and the fortune they both spent so lavishly,' Uncle Horace went on. 'I didn't realise how mean it was until I got back to England and found out what he had been up to while we were away. Poor Chris was the youngest of us and always did as Gus and my father bid, so it must have come as a shock to them when Chris fell in love with such an unsuitable female, begging your pardon, Farenze, and she taught him to rebel. He would have handed the bulk of your maternal grandfather's fortune over until then for the sake of a quiet life. That must be why Sir Joseph Lambury made sure Chris couldn't inherit it through your mother, Colm, and why he didn't leave much to your sister for fear she'd be sold off for a share of her marriage portion. So you see, Lord Chris Hancourt was a better man than any of us thought him and I owe him an apology for believing he could behave so carelessly he'd risk leaving his own children with nothing a year to live on.'

'He wasn't a saint though; he still died with another man's wife at his side, but are you really trying to say loving the first Lady Farenze put courage into him?' Colm asked his uncle with an apologetic glance at her one-time husband.

'He learnt guile from somewhere, since he made such clever arrangements for your future before he went on that mad journey. I expect he wanted everything neatly wrapped up before he embarked on a life of wild adventure,' the Duke said as if he'd been given his little brother back this morning as he really was as well.

'True, and it's a shame your father underestimated Augustus's malice and cunning, Colm, but he outwitted him in the end,' Aunt Barbara said pensively. 'The last Duke was cruel and selfish and the world is a better place without him,' she added and nobody argued. Colm thought it a sad memorial, but after such a betrayal of the man's own brother and two vulnerable children the man deserved no better.

The Hancourts departure was delayed by the momentous news from Sir Gideon. Eve's father mumbled some nonsense about apologies to be made and accepted when he lured her into his book room after dinner that night, then he left her alone with Colm. She sighed and shot a longing look at the door he had left open a bare inch as a sop to propriety. It was obvious what this was by now and it wasn't an apology for that heart-stopping kiss. Or at least she hoped not, because that would be an insult to something that had been impulsive and true and deeply passionate and she didn't want a mumbled *sorry* spoiling it.

'You don't have to ask me again,' she told Colm flatly.

'I don't have to ask you what?'

'To marry you.'

'I believe it's usual for a young lady to wait to be asked before she turns a gentleman down.'

'Well, now we don't have to endure the embarrassment of you asking me, since I won't marry you however often you ask.'

'I might be convincing,' he said ruefully and there he was again, the man she could so easily love if she let herself—or if he let her. 'This time I might have a poetic speech ready to dazzle you into accepting me and making my life worth living.'

'You might have,' she replied and how hard it was to resist him when he was almost the light-hearted, teasing beau he could have been if he'd never had to be Mr Carter first.

'I could be about to sweep you off your feet,' he continued the farce of being a willing suitor, then seemed to realise he had already done that by kissing her until there wasn't a single coherent thought in her head but Colm Hancourt the other day. 'Or plead with you to excuse my fumbled attempts to show you how much I adore you last week and let me try again with a little more restraint and refinement. So you are wrong, you see, Miss Winterley. I am here to apologise, even if I hope you will accept me as well as my very sincere sorrow for losing my head and kissing you as I have longed to from the first moment I laid eyes on you in Derneley's library.'

'You hid it remarkably well, then,' she said sceptically. 'I quite thought you despised me on sight.'

'I regret giving you such an untrue idea of how I felt about you then. I am not very good with words and have too much experience at hiding my feelings from the world. Indeed, I am not very good at knowing what I feel myself at times, let alone showing it to those I care about.'

Eve decided he was a lot better at it than he thought, then reminded herself most men had urges and passions she still didn't fully understand and she had yet to see any sign he felt anything more for her. 'You had last night and all day today to propose to me, yet you waited until you found out that you truly are a man of fortune before you tried again,' she accused him.

'I did,' he admitted, tight-lipped and unreadable as ever again.

'No doubt my father informed you he knows that you kissed me and you told him you had no desire to wed me. Since you two did not sneak off to fight some silly duel at dawn you must have agreed that you were unsuitable and I suppose you undertook to remove yourself from the Castle forthwith. Am I right so far?'

'You are; how did you know?'

He looked so pained and betrayed by the idea she and Papa might have been talking about him behind his back that Eve felt her hand get ready to touch his tense jaw and remind him how human they both were.

She put it behind her back and gripped it with the other one because she really didn't want to marry a man who didn't want to marry her.

'I know my father. I thought I was beginning to know you, Mr Hancourt, but you put a full stop on that when Chloe came upon us kissing in the rain, didn't you? How fortunate that I said no to your grudging offer the first time,' she added as she saw what almost looked like hope in his eyes before she said she was glad she had said no when the blood was still hot in their veins and his kisses a wonder on her lips. No, he didn't want to marry her and she wasn't going to be talked into it now that he was rich enough to afford any wife he chose.

'I was too poor to afford a wife until today,' he confirmed her worst fears so coolly she was tempted to shout, *no, you weren't, you just didn't love me.* Luckily she bit back her fury and faced him with nearly as closed an expression as his own.

'You don't trust any woman enough to want the sort of marriage I do and I refuse to be a burden you shouldered, a duty your conscience won't let you escape.'

He looked as if she had stuck a knife in him for a moment. There was a flare of powerful emotion in his eyes before he shook his head and argued, 'I shall be deeply honoured if you will agree to be my wife, Miss Winterley, and can promise never to see you as a duty or a burden, because nothing could be further from my true feelings towards you than that.'

She almost softened, almost took the spark of hot gold in his eyes at face value, but she had been deceived like that before, only last week in fact. How could she share the rest of her life with a man who could shut her out the moment he thought she was getting too close to the real Colm Hancourt?

'If you had said so the night after you stood and raged at the storm for trapping you in the summerhouse with me and leaving you time and chance to want me for a while I might have believed you, sir. This far on from that day I do not.'

'I could not support you then,' he protested as if that was an excuse for refusing to make a life with her and to hell with hows and whys.

'I have a good dowry and a manor of my own, it would have sufficed for me, but I suppose a duke's grandson thought it contemptible.'

'No, what I thought contemptible was the idea of me living off my wife. What sort of a man would it make me if I had to ask you to make me an allowance? How do you suppose a husband lives with himself if he has to ask his wife if she would prefer to be a secretary's lady, or try to find out if he will be accepted as a nobody in her home instead and batten on her for the rest of their days?'

'I don't know; how do you suppose a wife could live well in such a marriage when she knew her husband resented every penny of hers that stood between them? So you are quite right, you see, Mr Hancourt, we want different things from marriage and simply would not suit. Thank you for your dutiful proposal and I think I will pass on it once again. A very good night to you, sir.'

'Eve, don't,' he burst out almost as if it hurt to see

her go with so much hurt and misunderstanding between them.

'Don't what? Don't feel hurt or let myself feel battered by your insistence on still being Captain Carter,
even if you call yourself by another name? Don't want
more from a man who belongs to nobody and wants
nobody to belong to him? Don't imagine there is a real
person under the stiffness and resentment you have built
over the years against your hard lot in life? Very well,
I won't. Goodnight, and I hope you find some joy in
your new life, because there seems precious little in
the old one to me.'

Deciding she had endured enough of being asked to
marry a man who looked as if he would rather be having his teeth pulled, Eve finally brought this painful in-
terlude to an end by leaving him standing there like an
austere and rather well-dressed statue, since he didn't
have the grace to leave her in possession of the field
with an insincere smile and a relieved sigh because she
said had no to him yet again.

'Don't ask,' she told her father, who was hovering as
if he might be getting ready to send for his best wine to
celebrate her nuptials with a man he would have ordered
her not to marry only yesterday. 'I can't believe you
just did that. How could you change your mind about
him because he's rich today and was poor yesterday?'

'You truly think so little of me, Eve?'

'Yes…no—oh, I don't know,' she said unsteadily,
suddenly on the edge of a storm of tears nearly as cata-
strophic as the one outside on the night she last kissed
Colm Hancourt.

'Chloe informed me I was wrong to try to stand between you and a man who might love you, and never mind how much or how little you had to live on. I stamped about a bit and argued a lot, then finally had to admit she's right. You must make your own decisions about who you marry, love, and I am sorry I ever tried to keep that stiff-necked young Galahad of yours away from you.'

'He's not mine, Papa, and *you* didn't keep us apart, he did. Now I'm going to bed,' Eve said so she didn't have to burst into overwrought tears with Colm silently listening from inside her father's book room where she'd left him. 'We can talk about it in the morning when I might be able to tell wood from trees,' she said, gave him a quick peck on the cheek to say she almost understood, then ran upstairs to her room without sending for Bran to help her undress. 'I never, ever want to see that idiotic man again,' she informed her reflection in her dressing mirror, then went and locked her bedchamber door before anyone could come in and tell her this would pass and her heart wasn't breaking and how the devil did they know?

Colm stood as if he'd been frozen to the spot and listened as the sound of Eve's light steps faded away down the ancient stone corridor not even the wealth of the Winterleys could make other than stark and echoing. There was no point wondering if the constriction in his chest was brought on by hearing her words to her father or too much rich food on a tense stomach at dinner because he knew it was far worse than that.

'You made a right mull of that, Carter,' he whispered into the chilling air of his lordship's book room and hoped the man had gone away and wasn't standing outside nodding his agreement.

Colm almost smiled as he imagined the colourful language of some of his former commanding officers if he failed in a mission for them as spectacularly as he had at this one. For all the lives that depended on him getting it right back then, this felt like a worse disaster somehow. He had wrecked his chances of a better future *and* made her despise the passion that had torn at him heart and soul from the first moment he set eyes on her. Why the devil couldn't that letter of Sir Gideon Laughraine's have come either a few days before it had or a few days after? If he had only known he was about to be rich, he would have begged her to marry him with every word and action he could come up with the instant Lady Chloe found them together in the summerhouse. At least Eve couldn't have said he was cold then. Even the memory of how she felt in his arms, what it felt like to feel her lips soften under his, then kiss him back made his heartbeat thunder and that tightness seem more like a great hand squeezing his heart now, when he let himself know it would never happen again; not now he'd made her think proposing to her again was only an untidy end her father would insist on being stitched back into place before he could leave here unencumbered by a wife.

Did the ridiculous female think he was about to go off to London this spring and find a substitute because she wouldn't wed him? If so she was deluded and didn't understand him at all. So why did she matter so much, then? It should be a relief that she'd turned him down again, but instead it felt as if a bullet had slammed into him and was lodged somewhere a lot more crucial than the last one had been. Not that it made any difference, since she said she never wanted to see him again and sounded as if she meant it. He'd better oblige her and leave before she could glare daggers at him across the breakfast table tomorrow. He didn't think he could look back at her as if it didn't hurt any more, so persuading his aunt and uncle he must leave early to smooth out the kinks in their ducal progress would occupy some of the hours that must creep by before he could set out on that self-appointed task with the dawn. Since he wasn't going to sleep he had to find a way to occupy the rest of his last hours at Darkmere. Fantasising about how it would feel to be Miss Winterley's husband and polish every hour of the night with the joy of loving her and doing his best to persuade her to love him back would get him nowhere except shut up in the nearest madhouse.

'Your Mr Hancourt has gone ahead of his uncle and aunt to arrange for changes of horses and beds for the night, Eve,' Verity said next morning as if nothing very momentous had happened.

Eve knew her too well and saw the sly glance at her face to see how that news affected her and somehow managed to blank her shock and surprise. 'He's not my Mr Hancourt and must have gone very early, for I heard nothing,' she managed coolly enough as she helped herself to food more or less at random and wondered how she could not have known he wasn't here any more by instinct alone. Suddenly her home felt vast and lonely without him and that was absurd; she loved Darkmere and her family was here, so what more could she want from life?

'I suppose your room is on the wrong side of the castle for you to hear anyone ride out from the stables,' Verity went on with a cheerful relentlessness Eve found almost unforgivable right now.

He was gone though. She could plan the rest of her life without him and he would be fully occupied with putting his huge assets into stern military order and reviewing his assorted properties. She wouldn't put it past him to take on the task of dragging the ducal lands and grand houses into the nineteenth century at the same time. By the time he finished all that *and* bullied his sister into living the life of a lady of birth and fortune at his side, Eve would have time to find a true gentleman, marry him and get on with making a family of her own. Colm Hancourt wouldn't matter a jot by then, so why did it feel as if more of her was being torn apart with every mile he rode from Darkmere?

'Your Mr Hancourt seems a very proud man. It will be a challenge to get him to come back now you have made him go away,' Verity said as she eyed Eve's odd mix of breakfast food as if she knew how bereft she was feeling because the wretch wasn't even under the same roof as her to quarrel with.

'He's not my Mr Hancourt and you're the last person

in the world who should urge me to think twice about a fine masculine figure and a handsome face.'

'Ah, so you're ready to admit he's handsome at last, are you?'

'Of course he is, if you like austere gentlemen and not human ones.'

'And you do, Eve Winterley, or you wouldn't be pretending to eat that mess.'

Eve wanted to shout, *Stop, he's gone and he won't be coming back and I might have made a terrible mistake, but he's still gone and he still won't be coming back*, but she frowned at her plate instead.

'I don't love him and he doesn't love me,' she told it dolefully, refusing to meet Verity's gaze and let her see how much it hurt to admit she had killed off any chance Colm would love her back last night, even if she was silly enough to have let herself fall in love with the blundering great idiot in the first place.

'So why do you look as if the sky has just fallen on your head then?'

'Maybe I have the headache after facing your impertinent questions over the breakfast table every morning?'

'Or you have the heartache and won't admit it,' Verity said. 'Oh, well, if you truly don't want Mr Hancourt maybe he'll wait until I'm old enough to marry him. I won't worry about ancient history when I look for a husband and he is very handsome.'

'By the time you're out he'll be in hiding from the husband hunters or already married to one,' Eve said gloomily and went off the idea of breakfast altogether.

Chapter Twenty

For weeks Eve felt as if part of her was standing aloof and glowering while she tried to go about her daily business as though nothing had happened. The Eve who went wild in Colm's arms, the one who yearned for him so passionately butted in every now and again to remind her how empty her life and her bed felt without him. So she did her best to get lost in the solemnity of Christmas, then the headlong delights of Twelfth Night and the celebrations of a day when life turned upside down and lords and ladies waited on maids and boot boys.

On the other side of all that merriment she sat in her sitting room in one of the towers and stared down at the sea where waves roared and rain dashed against the glass as nature lost her temper again. It reminded her so vividly of that afternoon Colm kissed her passionately, then stamped off and risked everything he was to rail about who they were against the raging sea, that she could almost feel his arms around her again as she snuggled deeper into the cushioned chair and yearned for comfort that wouldn't come.

Mr I-Don't-Need-Anyone Hancourt once wanted
her so urgently she cursed him now for not taking the
final step and making them lovers that stormy day. If
he had been as lost in need and passion as she was that
afternoon, he couldn't have helped himself and Chloe's
coming on that particular scene would have made it
impossible for her to refuse to marry him. He could
have got her with child and they would have been wed
by now. He would be here with her, lounging on the
bed next door with a stray cat smile on his face and
remembering heat in his gold-shot eyes. They would
flare into a blaze of need if she turned her head and
gave him a siren smile as she rather thought she would,
if he was here.

She wondered how many society beauties had beat a
path to his door since they found out he was about to become very rich indeed. Her fingers curled into claws as
she thought of their insincere simpering and greedy eyes
on the man who ought to be her lover right now, if only
she had the sense to let him seduce her. The Colm Hancourt about to celebrate his true coming of age would
make a fine catch for any eager husband hunter and
how dare they lay hungry eyes on him when he was…

No, he *wasn't* hers, was he? She had no right to be-
grudge them a single look or smile from her Mr Carter.
She might be the one who wanted him when he had
nothing and did his best to pretend to be nobody, but
she was also the idiot who let him go. Now he was rich
and a superb catch on the marriage mart, she finally
let herself realise Captain Carter had been her passion
and her true love. So why was she staying here and

letting the darling brusque idiot be lost in the indecently rich grandson of a duke. Gruff and defended Mr Carter would fade more and more every day as Mr Hancourt gained assurance and learned his way round a new world without her around to remind him of the wounded soldier she first met at Derneley House that eventful night she'd thought so disastrous at the time. It had turned out to be the most important night of her life, but did she love a man who no longer existed?

Coward, she accused that attempt to get herself off the hook. Either she loved him or she didn't and never mind what he called himself. As the gap between them stretched out more painfully every day she was more certain she loved him and less hopeful he loved her back. It was mawkish to sit here and mourn a future they might have had, so she took a deep breath and went downstairs to take up smiling and laughing and pretending to be delighted with her life once again.

And it was truly wonderful that her best friend after Verity had just agreed to marry Captain Revereux and he and Alice seemed so determined to be happy together at long last. So perhaps throwing yourself at the man you loved and making sure he had no excuses left about being too old, or too cynical, or too long at war was the way to win your way to a happy ending after all. Eve wondered if her friend had been as shameless with her lover as she wished she had been on that early December afternoon she remembered with such doting fondness with hindsight. She hoped so, because they deserved their chance at happiness and Alice would make the slightly melancholy captain happy at long last, but he had better reciprocate and forget all that nonsense about being too old and jaded for such a young and vivacious lady.

What idiots men were, Eve decided, as she pictured the scene when Alice told her over-gallant beau exactly what she thought of his gentlemanly scruples and grinned. She could just imagine him open-mouthed and dumbstruck as the usually self-contained and rather flippant Miss Clempson told him exactly what she wanted from him and why and refused to be dismissed as too young to throw herself away on the likes of him.

So Papa had done everything he could to avoid loving Chloe for ten years, Alice took far too long to rebuke Captain Revereux for making her decision for her. Was she really going to sit and stare at the sea until Colm came to his senses and finally admitted they might have been made for one another? They might both be old and grey before then, so could she seek out *her* love and never mind the risk of a rebuff that would sting until her dying day? Seeing where patience and resignation got a woman, she began to think she might have to, before one of them went mad with longing for the other.

'Happy birthday, my boy,' the Duke of Linaire toasted his nephew with an exquisite Sèvres coffee can the morning of Colm's twenty-fifth birthday.

'Indeed, and I wish you many happy returns as well, Colm, dear,' his aunt said with a sly, questioning look that asked if he was quite as happy as he ought to be the day he became one of the richest men in England.

'Thank you,' he said with a guarded smile as he gathered his own breakfast, then hid behind his own cup of coffee as best he could.

'It's a shame young Eleanor is so determined not to leave her post and run one of the houses your trustees invested in,' the Duke said with a sad shake of his grey head.

'And that Miss Winterley was so steadfast in refusing your offer of marriage.' The Duchess walked in blithely where angels feared to tread. 'You will be driven half mad by fortune-hunting young ladies and their mamas from this moment on, I'm afraid, Colm. It would be so much better if you were engaged to marry a lady who has no need of your fortune before you brave the *ton*,' she finished innocently.

'I am not about to do the Season like a giggling debutante, Aunt Barbara,' he replied rather shortly.

'Then there is sure to be a plague of carriage accidents, lost puppies and badly twisted feminine ankles near any house you decide to live in if you don't settle on a wife soon,' his uncle warned happily, as if it was not a worry to him that Colm might end up wed to a designing female when all he wanted was the one who wouldn't marry him if he came wrapped in gold.

'I still won't marry them, so they might as well save themselves the trouble.'

'Might have to,' his uncle said with an uneasy glance at his Duchess this time, as if the joke had gone too far. 'A man needs contact with his neighbours if he's to make any sort of life for himself, be he rich or poor.'

'I shall have to put the tale about that I wed a ravishing Spanish lady and have carelessly lost her somewhere along the way then. That should hold them off; not even a husband-hunter would try to wed a bigamist.'

'I think you may be underestimating some of them,' his aunt said gloomily.

'Give up whatever scheme you're hatching, love,' Colm begged her wearily. 'Miss Winterley would rather marry the stable boy than tie herself to me. Please face that fact and let me get on with living my life without her. There's a good duchess.'

'I hear that Revereux is getting married again,' the Duke said with a shifty glance at Colm. He might have looked a little harder at his not-that-vague scholarly uncle if the wild notion that Revereux was about to marry Eve hadn't stormed into his head and made him feel as if he'd been shot again.

'Yes, and whatever is that deluded girl thinking of?' the Duchess put in. 'He is over a decade older than she is and even more stiff-necked and battle-hardened than you, Colm.'

'I'm only five and twenty,' he snapped back and wondered what difference that made when he felt nearer to a hundred right now.

Revereux was rich from the prizes he and his crew had captured during his career as a dashing frigate captain, then commodore in charge of his own fleet. A tried-and-tested hero whose golden looks had been refined by war and hardship *and* he trailed a tragically romantic past behind him, so, little wonder if he was irresistible to a much younger lady. Oh, and his daughter was Eve's best friend. What more could a sensible, well-born and unforgettably attractive female want in a husband? Nothing, he decided gloomily, put down his coffee and frowned at his breakfast as if it had been made from husks.

'Her family are unsure about the match apparently, but I dare say they can be persuaded to announce the engagement before everyone goes to town this spring,' his aunt reflected as if she hadn't noticed his revolted expression and sudden loss of appetite.

'He's too old for her. How the devil does she think he will make her happy?'

His uncle shrugged and looked uncomfortable. Colm wondered if he had shouted in his fury that Eve Winterley should give herself to a man who would never treasure her unique qualities as he would. She was too unique to play second fiddle to a long-lost love, too vulnerable under that careful guard she kept on her heart. How could she accept anything less than complete love and commitment from the man she intended to spend a lifetime walking next to? The very idea of such a marriage for her made him shudder and wish the bullet that left its mark on him had been an inch or two lower after all, so he need never have met her and lost her to another man.

'It is a good enough match on both sides and solves a great many dilemmas for both families, although I can't say I envy any girl of her age for having to bring out the man's daughter one day. That child may look like an angel without wings, but Verity Revereux will be a handful for any chaperon, let alone one barely half a dozen years older than she is herself.'

'Why the devil does it matter to me who she marries?' Colm muttered under his breath. They must have heard him since they both seemed uneasy as they eyed him with what looked horribly like compassion.

'It is not a sin to fall in love, Colm,' his aunt told him gently.

'That depends who you fall in love with,' he replied dourly.

'And you have control over that, do you?' his uncle put in, as if he heartily disliked of the notion such a mighty emotion could be turned on and off like a tap.

'No,' he admitted wearily. 'I have no hold on it at all. I may be new made, but Miss Winterley still doesn't want Lord Christopher Hancourt's son and I still don't blame her.'

'Then I shall do so on your behalf,' Aunt Barbara told him with a fierce glare to say she wasn't done yet, so he had better not interrupt. 'I hope you don't really intend to stand by while she promises herself to another man. The girl might be almost as stubborn and hot tempered as you are, but she loves you, Colm.'

'Then why would she marry another man?'

'Perhaps you ought to ask her that question yourself before it's too late? How terrible if she wed another man before you two realised you might have been put on this earth to love one another. She is not like her mother, who seems to have been able to transfer her passions from one man to another with hardly a pause, but only imagine how you will both feel if she marries another man and you two find out too late that you love each other. If you don't think that was a hair shirt to your father now you know he was not the hard-hearted monster his eldest brother painted him, you are not the man I think you are either, Mr Carter.'

'Oh, him,' Colm said, all the years that humble fool spent soldiering fading to nothing as he recalled standing staring at Miss Winterley like a mooncalf that first night. That idiot could afford to love a lady he would never aspire to marry; it was being Colm Hancourt again that had wakened impossible needs and feelings in him and set them both on a path to potential disaster. 'At least that looby is properly dead and done with this time.'

'Is he, my boy? I truly hope not,' his uncle said and had the last word because Colm gave up pretending to eat his breakfast, threw his snowy napkin down on the table in disgust, then stormed out of the room to brood in peace. His aunt and uncle were so intent on telling him things he didn't want to hear that they could hardly blame him if he couldn't sit and listen to any more of them on his birthday.

Chapter Twenty-One

'I can't give you the best bedchamber, sir, as it's already been took. Nor the second-best neither, nor even one of the rooms over the tap. It's all this snow, d'you see? It come in like the lion it did, just when we all thought the worst of the winter was over with. There *is* our Joe's room, I suppose. He can turn in with the lads over the stables if you want it.' The landlord looked doubtfully at the tall figure who had tramped in from the stable yard looking more like a snowman than a benighted traveller.

'I don't mind the loft if your son is averse to it; I've slept in far worse places in Spain. All I need is shelter and a good billet for my horse until this infernal storm has abated and then I can go on my way again,' Colm said absently.

'You was an officer, once upon a time then, sir?' the man asked, looking a little less uneasy about his latest visitor now he'd heard him speak.

'Yes, now can I come in and rid myself of this snow and some of my wrappings?'

'Right you are then, sir,' the innkeeper said and stood aside at last.

'Out of the way, Fletcher,' a large woman demanded when the landlord stood and gaped while Colm shook the worst of the snow off his shoulders, then stepped into the taproom. Sizing up her latest guest with shrewd eyes, she made a silent gesture at his snow-encrusted hat. Colm obediently shook off what snow he could outside and was finally allowed in to take his boots off under her stern gaze.

'Fine workmanship,' she told him. 'Shame to risk ruining them by being out on a day like this one.'

'Indeed,' he said, amused by this mismatched couple now he was out of the driving snow and bitter wind and his horse was safe, warm and fed.

'That's a good hat as well.'

'One of the best.'

'So if your purse isn't heavy enough to pay your shot, we'll keep both until it is,' she said as if it was natural for a landlady to ask for proof he could pay before he took another step inside her pristine inn.

'I would have my work cut out walking away and earning more barefoot in all this, but I have means enough for my needs,' he said and dug in his pocket for a guinea. 'This for a seat by the fire and a down payment on the room your husband says I can have at your son's expense,' he added, because he wasn't fool enough to let her know he could buy and sell her inn so many times over it would make her head spin.

'He'll bide with the lads and be glad of it.'

'Good, now I would dearly like to feel the heat of that fire.'

'Take your coat off then, I'll not have all that wetness messing up my fireside, guinea or not.'

Colm did as he was bid and felt the woman's assessing gaze on the well-cut coat and modest waistcoat underneath and was glad he'd insisted on Scott as his new tailor, since the quiet elegance of his work seemed to impress her. At least one woman was taken in by his fine new feathers. He fought his frustration at not getting closer to the one he wished to impress before all others. No point trying to outface his horse and forge on against the odds, but he'd hoped to reach Northampton today and he was still twenty miles away. Revereux wasn't an impulsive youth though, they wouldn't marry in indecent haste, or so he told himself as the drive to go on even in the teeth of the weather plagued him once again. He had to be patient and not stump back out into a blizzard to hire the first horse anyone was fool enough to lend him. Hadn't he learnt anything from Wellington? Patience, steady resolution and the long game often won in the face of very stiff odds, but now he was fighting time itself.

'Oh, my,' a diminutive woman who looked vaguely familiar gasped at the sight of him dishevelled and weary from the road, but she left the room in a hurry with her head down before he could take a proper look at her.

'It don't look that bad to me,' the landlord muttered as he gazed at the scar on Colm's forehead as if it was a disappointment to him.

The cold had made his leg ache like the devil so at least his limp passed muster. A gruff coachman made room for him on the bench beside the fire and the landlady became almost maternal as she insisted rum punch would do more to keep out the cold than French brandy, even if they were at peace now and she supposed folk could drink the stuff if they really had to.

Sipping the spicy mixture gratefully, Colm stretched his bad leg to the warmth and almost managed to relax at last. He had nearly nodded off when the landlady began to berate her husband and the inn staff so loudly in the kitchens that they could hear her through the walls. Apparently some fine lady had changed her mind about dining in her room and wanted to come down to the coffee room after all.

'And we're neck deep in folk now and most of them must eat dinner in the tap if the gentry want my coffee room. Give me a nice quiet lawyer's clerk or a farmer or two any day, for at least they can't afford to keep changing their minds.'

She emerged to harry the pot boy and innkeeper as they moved most of the tables out of her best room and chivvied her guests to fetch their own chairs and benches if they wanted to sit down to eat their dinner. Colm sat and watched while the cramp gradually eased out of his misused leg and he resigned himself to yet another day on the road after this delay to try it even further.

'You can take yourself off in there out of the way and wait for the young lady and the reverend gentleman and his wife, since you're quality make as well and I can't keep the place empty just for her highness to dine in state,' the landlady told him once he'd thawed out enough to offer his help.

He limped off to do as he was bid so they could all eat before midnight. No doubt there was another fire in the coffee room and he didn't care where he ate. A rustle of movement from within told him the lady was a lot less tardy than her hostess thought she was and had probably heard all the fuss and carry-on as the public rooms of the inn were rearranged at her whim. He prepared himself to be polite to some spoilt young woman who changed her mind at the drop of a hat and then stopped in his tracks when he realised exactly who she actually was.

'Eve, but how…I mean why? I don't quite know what I do mean any more,' he greeted her clumsily as the shock of seeing her when he'd longed for her so desperately for so many miles took his breath away. Fatigue and hope made him stumble and hastily right himself after her gasp of horror when she saw him looking so travel stained and weary. 'That is, Miss Win—' Fingers he had so longed to kiss all that way pressed his lips together and silenced the rest of whatever it was he'd been going to say. So he simply stood and breathed in the fact of her, the closeness and the wonder of her; here, when he thought he had a hundred more miles to go before he was anywhere near her, and a tough naval commander to fight before he could make a last desperate bid to walk with that hand in his whenever they could get it there for the rest of his life.

'I told them my name is Winter,' she whispered as

if everyone else in the building was listening to what they had to say to each other, when the old oak door had closed itself behind him and they were alone here in the low-ceilinged room and the premature dusk of a snowbound afternoon with only firelight to guide them.

'I can't let you do it,' he burst out as soon as she took her hand away. Shock at the unexpected sight of her, his weariness and the longing he'd fought for so long finally loosened his tongue. 'He doesn't love you like I do. He can't love you even half as much, or he would have offered for you long ago and even if he does, he's not the right man for you and you can't marry him.'

'Colm, I really have no idea who you're talking about, but you're quite right,' she said on a soft laugh that sounded not very far from tears. 'Nobody loves me like you do and I shall never love anyone else as deeply as I love you.'

'Eve, oh, my darling, I love you so much I can't even think straight,' he whispered and sank his fore-head down to meet hers, stared into her eyes since he would never get enough of the sight of her and kissed her ravenously.

Or at least he would have done if he wasn't dizzy with cold and the delicious shock and relief of finding her here and still his Eve and not Captain Revereux's. Lack of breath nearly made him swoon even as her mouth moved under his in a tender kiss, then her lips kicked up in a glorious smile he could feel rather than see as she made a tiny distance between them to whisper, 'Idiot, you're nearly frozen to death and exhausted into the bargain. Did you ride here from Linaire Park

ventre à terre to prevent me marrying this gentleman
I didn't even know I was engaged to?

'Do you know I rather think I did,' he managed to
murmur as the fact of her truly began to sink in at last
and joy fought a battle with his wobbly leg and won
long enough to get them to the ancient sofa by the fire
without him dragging them both down on to the floor
because he couldn't bear to let her go.

'I used to picture the wild young lover I was going to
have one day doing that when I was a girl,' she said as
she settled against his shoulder with a very contented-
sounding sigh and Colm grimaced at the difference
between that image and his own unheroic almost col-
lapse. 'He was nowhere near as handsome and dashing
as you are, though,' she said with a beaming smile as if
she truly believed it and who was he to disillusion her?

'And I used to dream of you to distract me from battles to come and cold nights on bare mountains with no
rations or baggage.'

'Hmm, I suspect you dreamt of lovely Spanish
señoritas, but we'll pretend you didn't as long as you
stop doing it from now on.'

'No, truly I dreamt of marrying the love of my life
and loving our children together while I waited to find
out if I was to live or die that day. It was that or run
away, so you see, you have kept me from disgracing
myself all these years.'

'Did I indeed? Well, I shall choose to believe you,
even if Pamela Verdoyne's daughter as a wife would be
your worst nightmare.'

'Not once I'd actually met you it wasn't,' he said

with a stage leer that made her chuckle deliciously and wasn't it a delight to laugh with this woman who had turned his life inside out and upside down and made him like it that way?

'I love you, Eve,' he said seriously as soon as he could wipe the foolish grin off his face because she was here with him and all that cold and loneliness had been worthwhile, and his journey through a snowstorm to find her before she wed Revereux had been as well, which reminded him, but first he had to convince her he really did love her after all that shilly-shallying. 'Not Pamela's daughter or Lord Farenze's beloved eldest child, but you, my darling, you're my one and only love.'

'You do say the nicest things, Mr Carter,' she told him solemnly.

'And how you did dislike that plodding fool that first night.'

'No, I didn't, I was just better at pretending than you were. I love him as well as Colm Hancourt. You won't forget to be him as well now you have a new life, will you?'

'I can't cut myself up into neat pieces and be one man here and another there. If you really do intend to marry me, you might regret I was Carter once upon a time. I have nightmares and a few memories I find hard to forget even now I'm home and Colm Hancourt again.'

'From now on you will have me to wake you and talk to until the dreams fade, Colm, and of course you remember that other life, why should you forget it?'

'Ah, love, you take my breath away,' he managed to murmur shakily, because how could he be suave and collected when she was here, now, with him and loving him right back?

'And there I was hoping you had recovered enough to kiss me again,' she told him with the most inviting pout he'd ever seen and what else could a gentleman do but oblige a lady?

'Well, I don't know where we're supposed to put a real live lord,' the landlady informed them as she bustled into the room without seeming to notice her most inconvenient guest until now had just been kissed breathless by the limping gentleman she shooed in here to get him out of her way. 'Everyone will just have to move round and your coachman and groom will have to sleep in the stables, Miss Winter. For all this one here said he'd be content there if he had to, we can't have that, what with him being a gentleman and that leg of his giving him gyp and all.'

'I'm sure they will make the best of it,' Eve said as soon as she could get a word in, but the landlady had whisked herself away without waiting for an answer.

'Of all the places we could choose to seduce each other this is possibly the worst, love. Before she comes back and tells us royalty has rolled up and we all have to sleep in the barn, will you promise to marry me?' Colm asked urgently, his dear face so painfully anxious and eyes every bit as intense and intriguing as she dreamt of them night after night as he made love to her in her wildest fantasies that she almost forgot to answer.

'Yes, of course I will, Colm—you and no other. Now do you promise never to leave me alone for so long again? Then you can hurry up and kiss me again before Papa comes in and starts acting like a bear with a sore paw because I put him to the trouble of chasing after me in weather not fit for man nor beast.'

'What a happy reunion this promises to be, but I promise. And you can come with me even if I decide to search for the source of the Nile or the tears of the last dragon. I will be such an overly attentive husband you will soon be wishing...'

'Never say I shall want a lover, Colm. I would rather stay single all my life than marry even you and expect to do that,' she said very seriously.

'I was going to say you would be wishing me at Jericho. And don't you think I know that about you, love? I will do my best all our lives to make sure we never stop loving one another, but you will be as true as steel even if we do. Hush,' he said when she drew breath to argue that was impossible. 'Before your father gets here to breathe fire at me again for wanting his daughter immoderately, can we vow to take time to fall in love with each other all over again at this time every year? Being besotted as husband and wife in a nice little snowstorm like this one is a much better idea than our parents' peculiar way of going about things, don't you think?'

'Oh, Colm, I do,' she replied with a smile that felt blissful and smitten and amused all at the same time. 'It sounds wonderful,' she said and kissed him this time because he was far too gallant to risk it when her father was in the same inn and about to glower at them until he had properly thawed out.

'Good evening.' A plump lady dressed in a dark blue

wool gown with a snow-white collar interrupted that
kiss from the doorway just as it was about to get very
interesting indeed. 'I see that you two already know
each other, or at least I hope so. In my younger days a
lady never kissed a gentleman so enthusiastically unless they were very well acquainted indeed.'

'We are going to be married,' Eve said with a misty
smile.

'Are you now? In my younger days a *gentleman*
asked a lady's father for his permission before they
announced their engagement to the first person who
happened along,' Viscount Farenze commented over
the lady's shoulder.

'Papa, you're cold and cross and you know perfectly
well Colm asked to marry me weeks ago,' Eve said, not
sure if she was glad to see her father or not for once.
His presence meant there was no chance Colm would
find his way to her bedchamber tonight and she badly
wanted to be his lover, now they had got all that nonsense about the past sorted out. *Ah, well*, her wild inner
Eve sighed. *It won't take for ever to marry him if we get
on with it before Lent. Then we can be improper every
night for the rest of our lives if we choose.*

'That was when I knew you would say no,' her father said glumly.

'Well, I changed my mind,' she announced, hearing such joy and happiness and surprise in her own
voice that she nearly laughed for sheer delight and relief. She was going to be so happy with Colm. After all
they put one another through since that night they met
in Lord Derneley's library it seemed such a wonderful

surprise it was a shame her father wasn't delighted for her as well.

'Be very sure of it this time,' her papa urged her, with a challenging glare at Colm and a worried frown for her that almost made her forgive him.

'We have to be, sir,' Colm argued so she wouldn't have to, 'we love one another and there would be no point enduring all the gossip and speculation our marriage will cause if we did not mean it.'

'Aye, well, I might remember I like you when I can feel my toes again and have found out if all my fingers are still in place. Right now I need a good fire, something warm to drink and a good dinner before I feel well disposed towards you or anyone else, Hancourt. I apologise for entertaining you with our family arguments, madam, but I expect you understand how these things will fall out willy-nilly, even in the best regulated families and mine has never been one of those.'

'I have four grown-up daughters of my own, sir,' the lady admitted with a placid smile. They exchanged names, were joined by the lady's unworldly husband and fell into a discussion of the most unlikely weddings the Reverend Stow had presided over during his thirty years as a parish priest.

Eve wondered how her grand dash south, Colm's knightly quest north to rescue her from some marriage that never existed except in his head met in the middle and turned from high romance into this. She didn't care what it could be classed as, she decided, as she slipped her hand in his under the table. The delightful feeling of being able to share such contact with her lover for the first time in her life felt huge and generous and very much like the beginning of a totally new life. Here was her mate; she had found him, the one man in the world exclusively right for her. Her silly, selfish mother spent her life looking for love, then didn't even recognise it when Colm's father fell at her feet. At least Pamela's daughter had enough sense to learn from her example.

'I love you so much, Colm,' she whispered when Mrs Stow diverted her father's attention long enough to slip a murmur past his sharp ears.

'I love you too, Eve,' he replied softly, 'but if you don't eat your dinner your father will probably call me out and the landlady will never speak to either of us again,' he added with a nod at her almost full plate.

'That's so unromantic,' she accused and wondered how she could have been so hungry when she got here after that interminable journey in the teeth of the snowstorm still raging outside.

'I know, but eat your food, love, we'll feast on one another when we're wed.'

Chapter Twenty-Two

'I thought they'd never go,' Colm told his wife grumpily when he opened the door between their grand bedrooms. Eve stopped gazing anxiously at herself in the peer glass and scuttled into bed, pulling the covers over her scandalously exposed body. 'Even now we're wed at last I was almost expecting to find your father in here waiting to make sure we only intend to read sermons to each other all night long if he finally leaves us alone. I swear there was never a stricter chaperon to an engaged couple than he has been this last fortnight and your stepmother and my aunt were nearly as bad.'

'They love us and want us to be happy,' she said with a shrug that agreed they had endured a long and aching wait to be man and wife at last, or at least it had seemed like it at the time.

The trouble was all the hope and love and confidence that got her through the wedding ceremony so blithely was beginning to wilt. There had been a wedding breakfast, a family dinner and a wedding ball to get through since then and Colm was right, her father had been so strict with them since they agreed to love each other for life that they hardly dared steal a kiss from each other during the weeks of their engagement. She knew Papa was determined to show the world how different this was from the last Winterley and Hancourt left-handed connection, but it had made her nervous about tonight. By now she suspected most affianced couples who loved each other would have found a way to prove that love to each other somehow and never mind the conventions. Not so for her and Colm though; they had been as closely guarded as if they were the only heirs to their respective kingdoms.

'Lady Chloe is the best of mothers-in-law, Verity is a scamp and I'm glad her father's new wife will stay in the area once they marry because she will need all the help she can get with the minx. Your Bran is a treasure and loves you like a mother, but please, love, can we lock them all out now? If one more person recalls a last piece of advice they simply must give you on your wedding night I shall very likely break down and cry.'

'I can't quite imagine stern Mr Carter in floods of tears somehow,' she replied, relaxing a little as she recalled that stiff-necked, intriguing gentleman and realised how much Colm had changed since they first met, even if she loved Mr Carter as well as her official husband.

Knowing his father had loved him and been almost as badly treated by the last Duke as Colm, he had lost that fearsome self-sufficiency he used to convince her he didn't need her for far too long. Thank heaven she

had seen through it to the real man and now he was letting the deep feelings and heady passion underneath
it show. The fire in his brown and gold eyes was un-
masked as he met hers now and even his limp seemed
better. Her Colm was younger somehow, less burdened.
So how could she be scared of her wedding night with
this lithe and handsome man who loved her so much
he had learnt to defy the past and seize a bright future
with her? Any other man and this would be terrifying,
but he was Colm: her love and her lawfully wedded
husband. She watched him prowl towards the bed with
hardly a trace of a limp and was awed by the fact they
had made it to being man and wife against all the odds.

'What if I snore, Colm?' she asked suddenly, the
appalling idea springing into her mind from nowhere
in particular.

He laughed joyously and how good that sounded.
There had been so little for him to be light-hearted
about until so recently it almost made her cry to think
of him being so self-contained and alone for so long.
They must laugh a lot in future to make up for the past
and love enough to chase the last shadows from his eyes.

'I suppose I shall learn to endure it,' he said solemnly
as he came closer and looked at her with a heat in his
eyes that said he was wondering how to get those covers
off her with the least possible delay. 'I had to when we
were in winter billets or camping in the field. Can you
imagine how much noise an army full of ruffians makes
in its sleep? No? Just as well, but my first sergeant could
outdo the artillery, so I don't think you could ever come
close to his nightly performances even if you do.'

'His poor wife,' she said as she gazed at her husband and recalled how lucky she was he had survived so much to tease her like this tonight.

'Yes, she would have been, if he had had one,' he murmured with a sadness that told her the man did not survive.

'Poor man,' she said, refusing to look away and pretend she had no idea war killed good men and bad indiscriminately. Theirs wasn't that sort of marriage; she wouldn't allow it to be.

'Yes,' he replied quietly.

'I want to be your everyday lover, Colm, not some fragile lady you put in a box marked wife and feed sweetmeats and pretty words,' she told him seriously.

'As if I would dare,' he said with that old wry smile she realised was put on to defend his tender feelings. 'We make each other real, Evelina Hancourt,' he added with a more piratical version of it and how had he pushed back the covers without her even noticing? Now he would see the almost-not-there nightgown and peignoir the Duchess gave her in such plain wrapping paper Eve was surprised the stuff didn't combust with embarrassment.

'Could we work on being more so right now, do you think?' she whispered as his eyes dwelt longingly on her outrageously outlined body and the hot gold sparks in them enchanted her so much she forgot to blush.

'Do you know, I think we could,' he replied and traced the folds that filmy fabric had fallen into first with his eyes, then a whisper of his index finger that sent shudders of longing through her and never mind how this would go. He was sure and intent on her pleasure more than his own, so it would be wonderful whatever happened.

'More,' she invited with a long sigh that stuttered as he deepened that feather touch and played with warm, eager curves under thin silk. She pushed away the last of the bedclothes to kneel up and meet him kiss for kiss, exploring touch for touch. 'My Colm,' she muttered into his mouth as she sat back on her heels to look up at him and wonder. 'My husband,' she added with another butterfly kiss on his waiting lips. 'My lover.'

'Love,' he said as if more words were beyond him.

So he took over that kiss instead of her and it became deep and hungry. She met him with everything she had to give back and found more when he cupped her needy breasts and her nipples peaked to hard nubs that he greeted with exploring fingers and an approving hum. She arched backwards and thrust up against his touch, eyes heavy and lips open on a moan of sensual approval. Heat shot through her as his hot gaze met hers and promised riches she hadn't dared dream of until this moment. He bent to take one of those begging nipples in his mouth and play with it. All the bones in her body seemed to turn to honey when heat blazed through her as if it might burn them both up and still never be satisfied. Something close to pain ground inside her and she moaned softly to tell him that she didn't know how she could feel so much and not break.

If it wasn't for the fact that he was shaking with need and nerves she might feel exposed and vulnerable when he slid the last whisper of soft silk off her and she was

naked. It only took a reproachful look at his fine waistcoat and breeches for him to get out of them so fast she
wondered if officers practised dressing and undressing
in record time before they went to war. That fast idea
faded away as she saw the marks of war on his body
even as she wondered at the intriguing differences between satiny male skin over taut muscle and bone. He
was lean and toned as a greyhound, and every nerve and
sinew of him was eager for her as that hound would be
for the chase. Even so, her loving eyes lingered on his
poor damaged knee, up to a healed slash on his upper
arm, then, worst of all, a wide graze that came so close
to his heart it made her own thump in dread of what had
almost happened to him on some faraway battlefield.

'Oh, love, look what your evil uncle nearly did to
you,' she gasped and traced the path of that old wound
across his chest.

'Nothing,' he said with a smile that wanted to reassure her, but went a little awry, as if he was wondering
about a hard world where he died of it and neither of
them would ever know how it felt to love another this
deeply as well. 'He meant to do me ill, but made a man
of me instead. Can you imagine how soft and despicable
you would find me if I had grown up as the pampered
heir to a vast fortune? Yes,' he said with a sly grin Mr
Carter would be proud of, 'so can I.'

'Don't you try to divert me, Husband. Doing good
by accident will not help your eldest uncle at the Day
of Judgement,' she said with a severe nod to say Colm
might forgive that wicked aristocrat his sins but she
never would.

'I am who I am, Eve. That was little enough as far as you were concerned the night we first laid eyes on each other,' he teased her.

'If not for Mr Carter, I might never have let myself love you, I will have you know, Colm Hancourt,' she informed him as militantly as a woman could when she was stark naked with the new husband she loved desperately and wanted even more. 'You would have had to work far harder to charm me if you had lived as your true self all those years. Money doesn't buy everything, you know.'

'It bought me a marriage licence. I'm very fond of that piece of paper and my new wife, but if she doesn't stop her tongue and let me love her I might have to ask the Bishop for my money back tomorrow. I am very careful with my investments now I actually have some at long last, you know.'

'An investment, am I?' she demanded, running a finger softly down his throat and feeling his Adam's apple work as she slid further down and settled at the bottom to count his pulse. Then she explored the supple flex of his muscular torso and the tight masculine nipples that made a tiny echo of her own still-aching ones. He jerked as if she had burned him, so she repeated the caress he had tortured her with just now. 'Is that value for money?' she said with a sly look sideways at his flushed face and hot, unfocused gaze.

'Do that again and you'll have been robbed,' he said huskily and broke his leash, at last, passionately kissing and caressing her until she moaned for more.

There, his sensitive touch on places she hadn't known

she had until tonight tipped her over a dizzying edge. She shouted for him as she went, protesting at the loneliness of being love shot and at the end of the world without all of him. Then he was there, riding the breathless joy of it with her, both within and without her, all around and as gentle as such a desperate lover could be when he finally took her. Another landscape she had never expected to see spread in front of her as she reached it with him hard and rampant inside her and the fleeting pain and strangeness of that invasion a pause on the way. He held himself at bay for her sake, waited to tip her into delirium where all she wanted was for him to go with her. How had he known it was easier for her to take him as she fell into that new world of sensual pleasure? She stuttered a delirious sigh into his heaving chest as he bowed almost upright in the extremes of it all as they soared together into a final climax.

'I think I love you even more now than I thought I could, Colm,' she gasped as he let himself rest for a moment against her softer curves and slender limbs, feeling her with every inch of his body against hers like a full body kiss.

'And I love you, Mrs Hancourt, so very much. I never thought I would have one of those, by the way—a wife. I was certain I wouldn't the day I rode away from Darkmere and you didn't even get up early to stop me.'

'It took me far too long to find out that love matters far more than what people think or say about us, didn't it? There's no need for you to look so smug either, since you thought money mattered more than love to me for far too long. I can't believe you left me alone so long after that obstacle was out of the way either.'

'I thought you might decide that I only asked you to marry me because I can now afford a wife and we were caught kissing each other by your stepmother.'

'I almost understand that, so I must be in love with you.'

'I hope so, considering how thoroughly we just made love to one another.'

'We did, didn't we?' she said with a reminiscent sigh. 'Have you ever felt like that with another woman, or am I a fool to ask?'

'It's your wedding night, woman, you have the right to ask any question you feel you need answering. That one will be, no; not even a shadow of it. We kicked up almost as great a storm in here as Mother Nature is working on out there.'

She listened to the wind lashing rain against the windows and dreamt of summer anywhere with him, maybe even with the promise of their child growing in her belly as they strolled along the avenue here at Darkmere to the first place they nearly made love. This time they might dare even further in the warmth as they nearly did in the full fury of an even wilder storm on that December day.

'Soft southerner,' she murmured as he pushed himself up, rolled over to pull her into his arms and twitched the covers back into place over them now that the blazing fire had died to a glow and neither of them wanted to be parted long enough to make it up again.

'Guilty,' he said and wrapped his arms closer, so this

time she was the one body on body, learning him avidly as she wriggled herself as close to him as she could get.

'That's not all you are guilty of,' she murmured as she felt his sex wake again beneath her.

'Ignore me; we have all the time we need to learn about each other now, love.'

'We have and isn't that a luxury?' she said sleepily as she thought about that day she sat and truly thought about the years stacking up wearily on each other until she met her maker, if she let this one chance of love pass her by. 'You are my best minutes and hours and days on this earth, love. Without you I would have existed until I didn't; with you I love and am loved and I know we are far more together than we ever were apart.'

'And you only have to be in a room to stretch my senses and lift my heart, my darling Evelina. Whenever we argue, we will have to take out the wild promises we made tonight and make them true again, for we will argue, my love. Sometimes you will ask yourself why you ever put yourself through the ordeal of loving a stubborn idiot like me.'

'What will my answer be?'

'That you couldn't help yourself, any more than I could. We might as well tell the sea outside this window to stop thundering and the wind not to throw rain at us as if it wants to get through glass and stone to us as not admit we loved each other almost from the first moment we met.'

'You were such a gruff bear of a Mr Carter as well, were you not?'

'And you such a proud and defiant Miss Winterley

you dared a Hancourt to want you from the moment he laid eyes on you.'

'I thought you despised me, especially after reading my mother's diaries. Your Uncle Augustus would have been a better match for her, don't you think?' she said idly as she realised they had both been as stony hearted as each other. 'Your father sounds as if he had a generous heart after all.'

'The last Duke and your mother would have driven each other mad with greed and selfishness. Now let's forget about them both and live, my love, for I've had enough of my life being governed from the past, even if you have not.'

'I have, but what about your sister, Colm? Wasn't she the reason you felt you had to stay unwed and save up for her dowry? Now you have settled enough money on her to satisfy the greediest of suitors and she still intends to be a governess. No fine gentleman will be able to meet her and realise what a very fine wife she could make him.'

'I'm sure Nell has told you she can look after herself by now, if she had time before she insisted on returning to her charges when the ink was barely dry on our marriage entry, of course. She certainly told me so when I offered to hire a whole school full of mistresses and the finest chaperon I could find for the infernal brats if only she would come home and live with us.'

'Mr Hancourt hates not to be in charge of his troops, doesn't he?'

'Never having been in control of his sister or his

wife to start with, he will have to get used to not being anything of the kind.'

'Sometimes he worries too much about control and refuses to let go of his at the most frustrating times,' she informed him with a provocative wriggle.

'No, go to sleep. There will be time for us to love each other senseless again when I get over the strain of having a wild ex-virgin in my bed.'

'There will never be enough time for that,' she chided even as she felt her eyelids grow heavy and the exquisite novelty of sleeping in her lover's arms call to her for the first time. 'But I do love you, Colm.'

'And I love you more than I ever dreamt I could love,' he whispered and kissed the top of her disarranged hair, since she was still on top of him and it would be a shame not to. 'If ever a man found treasure beyond price when he wasn't even looking for it, I did the night I met you in Derneley's dusty library, my lovely, lovely Eve.'

'True,' she told him and twisted to look up at him with a smug smile. 'I met you and dreamt of gruff and limping heroes all night long. Now I don't have to dream, because I've got you in my bed,' she said with a contented sigh.

'And I've got you in my heart,' he whispered and how could she cap that? She couldn't, so she went to sleep to the steady beat of her lover's heart and she didn't even have to dream of him any more, because he was here.

* * * * *

If you enjoyed this story,
you won't want to miss Elizabeth Beacon's
A YEAR OF SCANDAL *miniseries*

THE VISCOUNT'S FROZEN HEART
THE MARQUIS'S AWAKENING
LORD LAUGHRAINE'S SUMMER PROMISE
REDEMPTION OF THE RAKE